MY IMPENDING DEATH

MY IMPENDING DEATH

—or—

The Fool's Soliloquy

a novel by

MICHAEL LASER

THE PERMANENT PRESS
Sag Harbor, NY 11963

For information, address:
The Permanent Press
4170 Noyac Road
Sag Harbor, NY 11963
www.thepermanentpress.com

Library of Congress Cataloging-in-Publication Data

Laser, Michael—
    My impending death : a novel / by Michael Laser.
        pages ; cm
    ISBN 978-1-57962-400-2
        1. Recluses—Fiction. 2. Suicide—Fiction. 3. Self-realization—
    Fiction. I. Title.

PS3562.A752484M9 2015
813'.54—dc23   2015013674

Printed in the United States of America

To Jack and Maggy,
With gratitude

Self-pity is our worst enemy and if we yield to it, we can never do anything good in the world . . .

No pessimist ever discovered the secret of the stars, or sailed to an uncharted land, or opened a new doorway for the human spirit.

—Helen Keller

I guess that's how it looked to her.

—Angus Truax

30.

Because I can barely persuade myself to climb the stairs each day—

Because, if I have to tell one more heart-tugging tale of misfortune, I will go on a rampage with a machete—

Because the prospect of escaping the pain in my ankles and osteoarthritic knees arouses something close to joy—

Because it's impossible to accomplish anything worth doing—

Because I'm weary, stale, fat, and unprofitable—

Because I don't really give a shit about anyone, and that's no way to live, or so I hear—

Because my own glib wit has grown tiresome to me—

Because no one will miss me—

Because I'd rather choose the date and manner of my departure than be found by EMTs, naked on the bathroom floor—

I choose to be done.

It was Dr. Bronner who inspired me. Unable to summon the will to leave the shower, I read the entire loony label on his liquid soap, and found this amid the prophetic babble:

Face the world with a smile, life is always worthwhile!

The optimism drove me like a golf ball to the opposite edge of the universe. While hot droplets pelted my back, I saw that nothing obligates me to keep going. I'm free to open the door and let myself out at any time.

If a book gives you no pleasure, you can stick with it till the unsatisfying end, or you can put it back on the shelf. Chances are my life story isn't going to turn into a white-knuckle thriller two-thirds of the way through.

There's no unbearable misery here, no howling despair. That's what makes the idea original.

Note to self: eschew melodrama, and don't leave a mess. Just step quietly off the night ferry when no one's looking. A splash in the dark, covered by engine noise. (Not literally, of course. No way will I go by drowning. My last words will not be *blub blub*.)

Brother Bob, I'll address these notes to you. Though you're far away and my opposite—you don't mind that I find your monkhood ridiculous, do you?—you're the closest thing I have to a friend, and the only one who might wonder what I was thinking at the end. When you read this, take me at my word: to escape is, for me, the best possible ending.

'Twas work that murdered my soul, BB. To show you what I mean, here's yesterday's column.

Raising His Children Alone, An Immigrant Gives Thanks

By Angus Truax

All was confusion in the Adesina household. Little Patrick—his family calls him Tiny—had lost his prosthetic foot under a mountain of laundry. Jonathan was arguing with Jacob over a battery-powered dinosaur while Eliza interviewed her father for a homework assignment. "What do you give thanks for, Baba?"

Mr. Adesina, a 34-year-old bookkeeper who lost his wife to pancreatic cancer a year ago and is raising his four children in a two-bedroom apartment in East Orange, nodded and smiled as he considered the question. Addressing a visitor, he said, "I like this American holiday. We have nothing like it in Nigeria. It's good to forget your problems sometimes and remember the good that you have."

Eliza's refractive amblyopia required special glasses that depleted her father's savings. Innocent of his troubles, she prodded him. "Baba, what should I write?"

"Tell your teacher I thank America for the chance it gives to my children, to learn and work and someday become rich. Then you can support your father in style."

Mr. Adesina laughed heartily at his own joke, displaying strong, straight teeth. A weary sigh followed close behind, however, because the rent is due next week and his children have all outgrown last year's winter coats.

So poignant. So worthy. Well, curse them, I say! Curse all the wretched refuse who have trapped me in their web of need. I refuse to go on spewing compassion so that gullible hearts will weep dollars.

These people are strange to me, Bob. Their endless troubles bore and annoy me—to death, I almost said.

Have you read my profiles? If not, here's the gist: my subjects have lost spouses, jobs, limbs. They live with vermin and unending pain. Their maladies, or their children's, include spastic quadriplegia, spina bifida, Guillain-Barré syndrome, kidney failure, Crohn's disease, mitral valve stenosis, paranoid schizophrenia, and undiagnosed seizures. Heavy responsibilities fall on their heads like anvils on Wile E. Coyote: a wife with diabetes and a fear of needles, an autistic, hearing-impaired brother, a child who wakes up one morning needing stomach surgery. They work as security guards, gypsy cab drivers, Laundromat attendants—or else they're too depressed to work. They support family here and in Ecuador, or Slovenia. Incredibly, despite their epic woes, all they need is enough money to cover a missed mortgage payment, chemotherapy pills, the fee for a chauffeur's license, or a new mattress.

Because of me, they all get what they need.

But I lie, Brother Bob. That's the secret of my success: I leave out key details. In the Adesina family's case, I omitted the fact that Jonathan threw his brother against the wall so hard that the carved Festac mask crashed to the floor. And that Mr. Adesina's gaudy new fiancée, overflowing from a lime-green minidress, slapped Jonathan and cursed him for behaving like a thug in front of a guest. Nor did I mention the noxious, mingled odors of catfish stew, ginger, and Pine-Sol. Or Mr. Adesina himself complaining that our government lets too much riffraff in, and they give skilled immigrants a bad name.

I've done this work for too long, Bobby. Turning the needy into machines for extracting donations. Making their eyes look big, dark and imploring, while veiling their less attractive features.

Mr. Misery, our automotive writer calls me. The name fits better than he knows.

I'll give myself thirty days. Just enough time to dispose of the accumulated paraphernalia and look back with pangs. For thirty days, I'll observe the world through the prism of my secret. I'm almost looking forward to it.

30, the reporter pecked with two fingers, ending the piece.

(I'll be gone before another Christmas darkens my sight. Hallelujah!)

Let the countdown begin.

Dry leaves are crunching outside my kitchen window. It's Mrs. Nieminen, the landlady, back from Thanksgiving dinner at Ahvo's house, or else Kai's. She scolds her son in impatient Finnish as he helps her up the steps. Boards creak; the storm door whomps shut; her cane's rubber shoe thumps above my head. Eka thanks her employer's son, *Have good holiday*—that grating voice. Now she'll help Mrs. N out of her clothes, into her housecoat, and take her to the toilet, and the stoic Mrs. N will moan, because whatever she does in there hurts like hell. Eventually, she'll snap at Eka, who will absorb the insult patiently.

Mrs. N used to be strong as a mule. A week after her husband died, she toted a sack of Portland cement on her shoulder, mixed up a batch of concrete, and repaired the patio by herself. She hates her weakened state. Who can blame her?

Once we achieve an insight, the world supplies plentiful evidence to support it. Mrs. N's living death screams, *Don't let this happen to you!*

You may see it differently, Brother Bob—decline and decay as a stage in the process, an integral part of the grand design, not proof of nature's cruelty—but then, your mystical optimism always struck me as a load of crap.

29.

I stopped noticing most of this junk years ago. Each item has its little story. The ukulele, a garage sale whim, which my sausage fingers could never play. (Did I buy it to compete with your *charango*, Bob?) The mannequin arms arranged on my wall *a la* God and Adam, retrieved from a neighbor's bulky waste at the insistence of a girlfriend whose name I can't remember.

The stories no longer touch me. Everything must go!

So much dust: slowly floating, coating my underground world like snow. When they find me, they'll judge me a pig. Ah, well.

In the medicine cabinet, just now, I found Lotrimin, Clobetasol, Afrin, Compound W, Elidel, Robitussin. Let me dump it all before they discover that I was just a clump of fungus, dandruff, snot, warts, eczema, and phlegm.

Shoe box overflowing with credit card slips. Folders of tax returns. Manuals for appliances set out by the curb years ago.

Here's a folder of fortunes saved from Chinese takeout dinners over the decades. Let's see, randomly, before all of it goes in the Hefty bag:

Show your love and your love will be returned.

How apt. And even truer in the negative.

The old notebooks, though.

Their varied covers, yellow, red, and mustard-brown. The spiral wire, still shining like new. The brands, Mead, Pen-Tab, University. The evolution of my handwriting from jagged disorder to jagged regularity.

Once, Bob, I hoped that these rancorous seeds would magically grow into a book of allegories, aphorisms, and acid observations—an acknowledged masterpiece that would earn me universal admiration. Deluded as I may have been, I'm still fond of the notebooks. I touch the paper tenderly and feel the faint engraving of the ballpoint from the other side; it's as if I were stroking my child's hair.

> *Thinking you've finally understood something is a sure sign that you've got far to go.*
>
> *Lunatic on subway bench, feverishly scribbling a deranged dissertation on a thrown-out newspaper. Notes from Underground.*
>
> *The Big Vote. Americans are given the choice: eliminate world hunger or reduce the price of gas by 20¢ a gallon. No contest!*
>
> *There are too many people for the planet to support. Humankind has made the Earth sick. The world has a fever, its temperature is rising—a self-regulatory mechanism like our own, the fever that burns out infection. Melting ice caps will submerge densely populated coastal areas. The flooding will continue until sufficient millions drown and balance is restored.*

Look at that, I beat Al Gore by two decades.

Letting go of my life is no problem, but consigning these spiral-bound pages to the trash—that I cannot do.

So I won't. I'll leave them for you. If what you read strikes you as mediocre and unimpressive . . . that was me, all right.

One thinks, I'll do that eventually. Scuba dive in Micronesia. Pilot a small plane. Learn to bake pastries. Become happy. It seems I won't be achieving my old goals after all: one more thing to let go of.

Many lasts lie ahead. Last beer. Last piss. Last sight of another person. Last syllable spoken. Last thought. Last breath.

I admit to a flinch of hesitation. Despite appearances, I'm human, and subject to the survival instinct. This intention is stronger than instinct, though.

The question is, how?

Not by grisly gore, no sirree. No gun barrel in the mouth, no leap onto the train tracks, not even if I could still leap. Self-centered I may be, but I don't want my remains to give strangers nightmares.

Nay to the noose—involuntary flailing lacks dignity, and anyway, my ceiling is too low.

I don't seek violent self-destruction, just a painless exit. Pills are the obvious choice. Or else carbon monoxide.

If one lies in a waterless bathtub, any involuntary mess will be contained. The thoughtful suicide must consider such things.

Here's something: Thatgoodnight.com recommends a sedative, and then a plastic bag over the head, taped snugly at the neck. The danger is being found too soon, and forced to live out your remaining years as a blob. Not much chance of that, though—no one but the meter reader has rung my buzzer in years.

What to wear? The brown summer suit: I've been mistaken for a professor in that. A tragic tableau, the great man in his final repose, with his head in a trash bag.

A month from now, I won't exist. My grasp of this fact comes and goes. One moment I have it, then it turns to air between my fingers. I'll follow through when the time comes, no doubt about that, but we can expect vacillation in the meantime.

If you're reading this, Bob, then you know I meant every word.

Cast down by all this dreary biz—and what's the point of setting yourself free if you're going to mope about it?—I hauled myself upstairs and went to explore the Death section at Barnes & Noble. An unseasonably warm November afternoon awaited me, full of neighbors I usually avoid. The brilliant, blue-bottomed clouds, the laughter of unseen children—all of it seemed to sing, *There's beauty right outside your door/You just need to get out more.*

A girl went skipping by in the street, twirling a glittery ball around one ankle. Two boys practiced jumping and catching their spinning skateboards. A cracked voice called to me from behind, "Angus, this is you in the paper? Writing about poor people?"

I don't think you've ever met my landlady, or the others who live in the house. I'll introduce you—because, after all, summing people up is what I do.

Mrs. Nieminen spends many of her waking hours at the redwood table behind the house. She waved her folded newspaper at me—battleship gray hair wrapped around green mesh rollers, yellow daisies on her housecoat psychedelically vivid—and said, "I never knew you did that."

Actually, she has known since my first week on the job, but her stroke zapped certain neurons, with interesting effects. She doesn't talk much, but when she does, it's often to tell the same story, about her husband getting shot down behind enemy lines and parachuting into a swamp. She drops plates and utensils so frequently that the clatter overhead no longer alarms me, and sneaks licorice cats and gummi worms whenever Eka isn't looking. When I moved in, she was a young woman of sixty, who unloaded her own groceries and baked barley bread every Sunday. Now she needs help to put her shoes on.

The local landscape struck me as blighted and sad today. Dents in the old white aluminum siding, weeds sprouting through cracked concrete, overhead wires everywhere you looked. Admittedly, though, I was in a cranky mood.

Eka gave me her usual wan smile and kept typing on her laptop, presumably chatting online with her family. This is how she spends her days: leaving her employer to her lonely newspaper and magnifying bar while she loses herself in her computer, humming contentedly, or else chatters away on a cell phone in her native Georgian, an octave higher than when she speaks English. *Shishkolish kavadjsky dadiskotish*, or something like that. Six years of American servitude have wilted her Snow White beauty. The milky skin now looks pallid, the striking eyes have sunk deeper into their sockets. (I used to wonder. *She's young, pretty, and imprisoned. Does she lust? Might she ring my buzzer in desperation one night? . . . Nahhhh.*)

Mrs. N, meanwhile, rolls her eyes at the Georgian gibberish, and wishes (aloud, sometimes) that she could have her house to herself again. It's as if each of them were the other one's punishment for crimes unknown.

Garrett and his mother were lugging a model of a brown castle on a masonite base. They'd just shown it off to Don Quinones across the low hedge, and now it was my turn to encourage the lad, who turned twenty-one recently. "You recognize it?" Garrett demanded.

It takes so little to mark a person as different. A minor intellectual deficit, a subtle obtuseness about when and how to address others. Everyone knows within seconds.

The castle had tubby turrets and crooked crenellations. "Not a clue," I said.

"It's Hogwarts! We built it from sugar cubes."

"It took two months," his mother added.

"Pretty impressive," Don called over the hedge.

What could I say? "You were born too late. You should have been a medieval stonemason."

Garrett frowned, as usual. It's not that my responses confuse him, but that dealing with people takes so much out of him.

I remember the day perky Cindy Olekas moved in upstairs. She shook my hand: her skin satin against mine, softer than any before or since. I don't remember what I said to her, but her laugh made me think of sleigh bells. And then little Garrett tugged on her shirt and said he'd made in his pants. Endlessly sweet, she never loses patience. She had a boyfriend for a while, a swarthy contractor with slicked-back hair and a Porsche Carrera, but it didn't last. And now, incredibly, Cindy must be close to fifty, still alone with her son, building sugar castles.

You can see her fine features on him, if you stare, but his sour expression obscures the resemblance. "She should put him in a home and give herself a chance," Mrs. N told me once. But Cindy knows how the world sees her son. She'll shield him as long as she can.

I could tell you all about neighbor Don, too, but I'm tired of talking about other people.

A question arose as I made my way around the corner to the garage. Why am I the one planning suicide, when each of them has more reason than I to despair?

Answer: because they're blinkered horses, who will turn their respective millstones until they drop.

Or so I thought as I drove off in the Shitmobile. Looking back, I see it differently. They don't *need* to escape I'm the one with the defective soul, not Mrs. N, or Eka, or Garrett, or Cindy.

A surprise awaited me at the shopping plaza. I'd forgotten what day this was. Enraged, thwarted drivers prowled the lot, seeking spaces that didn't exist. My handicapped placard never came in handier. (You didn't hear about my knee surgery, did you? Well, a kindly coworker took the original and photoshopped a few fakes for me. I've been punching new expiration dates in them ever since.)

A small whirlwind stirred the dead leaves in circles—so symbolic that I laughed.

The bookstore on Black Friday was festive, bustling, a coffee-scented bazaar. Gazing down from the escalator at the shuffling throng, I saw the book shoppers babbling with their friends, choosing among cutesy calendars, and moving about as randomly as ants in a glass-sandwiched colony. What, I wondered, are they so happy about?

The shelf of books on death turned out to be pitifully small. Most had to do with surviving grief—not a single How-To manual in the bunch.

While browsing titles, I noticed a man in the next aisle who was even fatter than I am: a gabby, grinning buffoon, who practically begged the young salesgirl not to despise him. My contempt knew no limits. Then his wife and children came to fetch him.

On the way out of the store, I spotted a consolation prize: *1,000 Places to See Before You Die.* A tailor-made invitation, and one that I gladly accepted.

Before returning to my hole, I had one more trial to endure.

At the Chevys near the bookstore, sipping a mango margarita while waiting for my Grande Chimichanga, I watched a cowboy-hatted jackass make a play for the tanned young queen of the hostesses, who wore a red napkin tucked into the rear of her waistband. As she whisked back and forth, ignoring him, the red tail bobbed provocatively. Once he gave up and left, she punched an order into a nearby computer, and I commiserated with her back. "Must be tough. You bait your hook, but you never know what fish will bite."

She whirled around and cauterized me with an indignant glare. *Know your place, slug!*

Beauties don't scare me, Brother Bob. I asked innocently, "What?"

I understood her point of view, though. Just so you know, I've put on weight since you saw me. Last time I visited a doctor, my BMI was 42, if that means anything to you. (It's about twice yours, I'm guessing.) The playboy cowpoke was just an everyday annoyance, an occupational hazard. For someone like me to address her—no goddess should have to endure such a thing.

Ah, well. Soon I'll trouble no one with my unsolicited comments.

If I visit 34.5 places daily, I'll reach number 1,000 on the last day.

Maestro—traveling music, *per favore!*

Cliveden (Taplow, Berkshire), *overwhelmingly grand, this National Trust property is England's most majestic country-house hotel*—in the photo, it looks massively overbuilt; might be fun to ride a big tricycle up and down the halls, though— *dinner in the excellent Restaurant Waldo's is reason enough to drive from London* . . . (better than this chimichanga, no doubt) . . . *fifteen-foot-high window . . . antique boats*—oh, here's something, *Nancy Astor's silent electric canoe.*

Okay, one down, 999 to go.

Windsor Castle. The walled city of Closter. Penzance and Land's End. The artists' colony of St. Ives.

Flip faster.

Biarritz. The Dordogne and the Cave of Lascaux. The Walls of Carcassonne. ("What are you doing with that carcass, son?") Sans Souci . . .

My amusing plan is turning sour already. I have a reverse Midas touch. Always did.

Keep on.

Mount Etna. The Anne Frank House.

Marvão, U Fleků: meaningless syllables.

Sidi Bou Said, Ngorongoro Crater.

Why am I doing this?

The Heart of Bali.

Cape May and its charming B&Bs, just a two-hour drive on the Garden State. Victorian gingerbread, sea breezes, a lovely setting in which to stop breathing.

Good night, Brother Bob. Another delightful day is done.

28.

THE SLOUGH OF DESPOND, November 24—Until today, I've managed to miss every birthday party Greer has made for the beastly little nephews. But a last-minute inspiration told me to show up and say good-bye to Sis. As a result, I'm wasted and dejected, and my shin is throbbing, possibly fractured. This is what comes of good intentions.

Toys R Us, a hopeless task. What would the birthday boy enjoy most? A radio-controlled Lego Star Wars All-Terrain Battle Station? Spotting some olive-skinned lads swarming around a shelf of dolls, I pushed my way through and grabbed the box on which their longing converged. I find it hard to imagine that the yellow robot man with wheeled feet will thrill young Zachary, but that ranks low on my list of current concerns.

To imagine Greer's new home—her fourth since she married Craig—just picture a normal house inflated to thrice its size. Multipaned windows everywhere . . . rhombi of sunlight falling on glossy hardwood floors . . . ceilings lofty enough to accommodate a sailboat. This is how she has solved the problem of living: marry a screaming Hawaiian construction executive, double your living space every few years, fill your days with PTA work and gardening, leave your dissertation unfinished. She herself says she took a wrong turn, but doubts she could have done better. It's an open question.

While the boys chased each other through the house, shooting Nerf balls at each other with a phallic cannon, she took a moment to stand by her brother. "The carnival guy is late," she sighed. A boy slid in his socks, crashed into a brass door handle, and cried. "See what you missed?" she said, and went to comfort the guest.

We do share certain genes and memories, beneath the differences. We survived the same parents, endured the same schools. I wondered how I might phrase my farewell without provoking a panicked intervention.

The party guests' clamor made it impossible to think. Was I ever like these boys? Shouting, boasting, doggishly following leaders, taunting their more peculiar peers, frantically manipulating joysticks. When you and I were boys, we built model airplanes and set stuff on fire to see what would happen. These inattentive creatures can't breathe for five minutes on end without returning to a computer for recharging. But then, every generation is a falling-off. I can't pitch a tent, which Dad could. He couldn't cut a dovetail joint, which *his* father could. And so on, back to George Washington.

A young mother with Jennifer Aniston's hair (stop! thief!) documented the boyish mayhem with a long-lensed camera, the internal mirror flapping loudly, over and over again. Another mom nursed a newborn on the leather couch in the den while chatting with a friend. Greer was the oldest of these women, by far. I can't imagine she feels like one of the gang. But there's so much I can't imagine.

One thing I'll say for Craig Pookalani, he keeps a well-stocked bar. Evading the boys and women, I helped myself to a tall party cup of Dewar's. The lovely amber liquid put me in a contemplative state. What will my obituary say, I wondered. *Portly, irreverent, diligent in his personal hygiene, Angus Truax endured ten years in journalism's subbasement and never complained aloud. He enjoyed solitude, foreign travel (in former years) and frozen desserts.*

Among the drifting thoughts, only one merits recording. Looking back on childhood, I could remember only one birthday present, a xylophone with colorful keys. (Olive green, taxicab yellow, faded grape.) The mallets were thin rods with wooden balls at the tips, and one of the notes rang dull due to defective mounting. Nevertheless, I loved that toy more than I ever loved any human being.

Is that really true?

Maybe.

Zachary's older brother found me in the den with my cup and bottle, munching pretzels shaped like tennis racquets. His hair, above the round, semi-Hawaiian face, reminded me of Moe, the dominant Stooge. "Hello, boy," I greeted him. "Have a drink?"

He's a hulking kid, prematurely cursed with facial hair that seems to grow out of his pimples. He snorted to show that he got the joke, then wandered off before his perverted uncle could molest him.

By then, the backyard carnival man had arrived. I watched the party games (wheelbarrow race, tail tag, egg and spoon race) through the sliding french doors, while trying half-assedly to construct a coded farewell, something Greer can look back on a month from now and belatedly understand.

"I see you found the good stuff," said a pale woman in black slacks, skulking in the doorway. Despite the jesting tone, she seemed droopy and without energy. Her mouth formed a crooked crack; the scarlet smear of lipstick contrasted unflatteringly with her sallow skin. She gave off unhappiness like body odor.

Always a friend to the despairing, I invited her to join me for a drink. "It's on Herr Pookalani."

Her sardonic, embittered flirting reminded me of at least three ex-girlfriends. We exchanged words fluently, without engagement. Soon enough, she interpreted my neutral friendliness as rejection, and started emitting little *hm*s. It's amazing how much a few curt noises can convey: resentment, anger at the futility of her efforts, and simple defeat. (*If even* he *doesn't want me . . .*)

When the doorbell rang, I seized the chance to escape—partly because she had just said, "You remind me of someone." I preferred not to be there when she realized whom.

"Don't answer the door," Greer called from the kitchen, "it's Jehovah's Witnesses."

Sorry, Greer, I make my own rules.

Greeting the missionaries cordially, I accepted their literature. "You'll find this family open-minded," I told the leader of the pair, a wrinkled gentleman of color, wearing a somber gray suit with a green shirt and plum tie. "I'm just a visitor, but you should come back another time and share your message."

He shook my hand, only partially skeptical. I believe his was the most prune-like face I've ever seen. "We'll come again."

His nostrils narrowed when he picked up the Dewar's on my breath. I figured he would leave that alone, but he leaned in close to warn me privately, "Alcohol is a dead-end street. I know whereof I speak."

Though it came from a man who had dedicated his life to a bizarre cult, I appreciated his counsel. "You're right," I said. "I vow that, starting one month from now, I will never take another drink."

"I hope you're serious."

"I hope so, too."

My depressive drinking buddy had eavesdropped. "That was interesting," she said.

I fled again, this time to the backyard, where I enlisted in the sack race.

My difficulties climbing into the pillowcase provoked snickers among my puny rivals, which woke in me a determination to crush them. Defying Greer's "Please be careful," I willed a longer hop than was wise. Landing reminded me that my suffering ankles can barely support my weight when standing still; momentum made it impossible to stop, however, and my second hop ended with the sound of bones cracking, or so I thought. The distraction cost me my balance. Down I went; the earth shook.

Noticing the rock beneath my shin, and the pain that went with it, I howled. There was nothing to do but roll over on the new sod, watch the clouds travel past, and contemplate my suffering. In a way, the agony was interesting: something new. The grass smelled thickly sweet, with undertones of dirt. It made me think of horses grazing. If I were one, they would have shot me then. I had no idea how I'd make it inside the house, let alone back to Belleville. Choosing not to worry about that, I turned my attention to the father in the next yard. This dad was throwing his son grounders, then holding out his gloved hand for the peg to first. His contentment was absolute—leading to the conclusion that getting what you've always wanted actually does yield happiness.

Greer and her pale friend lent me their shoulders. They escorted me inside and dumped me on the leather couch in the den. The friend sat with me, sideways in the corner of the couch, one knee pointed my way. Responding to this legible sign, I told her, "You're thirty years too late."

Her smile looked inexplicably fond, not bitter. "Can I just sit here for a while, so I don't have to go back out there?"

Her hair was scrizzly, limp, uncooperative. She had deep striae in her forehead. I decided I liked her.

"You're an outcast among the mothers? Divorced?"

"Obviously."

"Puzzled to find yourself living this peculiar life?"

"Not puzzled. Outraged one day, grief-stricken the next."

Suddenly, she remembered the celebrity I reminded her of: "Orson Welles, on those old wine commercials!"

My first impulse was to strike back—*And you look like Morticia Addams, many years later*—but you'll be proud of me. I mastered my inner child, and instead delighted her with a Wellesian, "Indeed."

Craig Pookalani's scotch caught up with me around then. I hope she didn't take my falling asleep personally. It really had nothing to do with her.

The guests had all gone. Greer was collecting Nerf balls and empty cups. From another room, John Madden called football plays. "Look," a nephew laughed, "my guy ran right through your guy. Replay!"

"Did you know about Dad's heart attack?" Greer asked. "I should have called you—it happened a few weeks ago. Apparently it was a bad one, but he's fine now."

"Whew," I replied. "Close call. We almost had to fly down there."

She squatted, knees far apart, and sponged a puddle of cola from the floor. This is how I'll remember her. For twenty-eight days, anyway.

"Ironic, isn't it," I said, "that the daily exerciser has a heart attack while I'm the picture of health."

She knocked on the wooden coffee table, a little joke that also expressed a certain solicitude for her elder brother, which I didn't know what to do with.

From the other room, the boy who had laughed a moment before shouted, "You stupid idiot!" A younger voice shrieked, "I hate you even more than you hate me!" Reverberations ricocheted from the bare white walls and stone-tile floors. Greer went gloomy.

A memory: she was in trouble in the schoolyard, a kindergartner with dandelions in her hand, dragged by the arm because she'd ignored the signal ending recess. Eyes wide, alarmed, not really comprehending, while I stayed on line, afraid that, if I went to comfort her, I'd be—what? Shot?

It was too awful to dwell on. "I remember when you used to worry that you'd never meet someone and have children. Things worked out in the end. In the larger sense."

Rumple-faced, with jowls beginning, she pulled back the corner of her mouth skeptically. The leaning stack of multicolored cups in her hand made her look like a sad-sack clown who might surprise me with a feat of juggling.

I wonder if this face is why Craig works on weekends. If that's really what he's doing.

"But on a lighter note . . ." *I'm not planning to stay alive much longer.*

Something plastic broke against stone nearby. The younger boy screamed, a wordless eruption of rage and grief.

"I'd better clean that up before their father comes home."

"Will he abuse you if he spots a stray shard?"

"Only verbally. I probably deserve it."

While I digested this disturbing new information, she offered to let me sleep over. The implication was that I shouldn't drive just yet.

The prospect of dining with her and her husband, the burly Hawaiian bully, was unbearable. This would probably be the last time we ever saw each other. I wished she could have left room for a good-bye, but she was too deep in her own woe to notice anyone else's.

It's pointless to complain, though. What is she to me? We grew up in the same house, but that ended almost forty years ago.

I tottered out of the house, having failed in my mission. Mainly, I was glad to be alone.

My last words to my sister, fraught with hidden meaning: "Toodle-oo."

Cold rain fell on a dark planet. The Van Ryper Funeral Home caught my eye.

Entering the narrow driveway, I imagined the funeral director recording my information on a printed form, his pen's tip pausing when I explained that I would like to set a date.

Green grass, red mulch, baby shrubs lined up like cabbages. Something about the place wilted my audacity. I only got one foot out of the car before I changed my mind and drove home.

By comparison with Greer's grandiose subdivision, Belleville looked positively slummy. The houses on my street are so meager and shoved-together, there isn't even room for a driveway between them.

Coming home to all this tarnished aluminum siding for twenty years may have stained my spirit a bit. What might I have become, somewhere else?

Brave, handsome, and thin: yes, Angus, whatever you say.

How does a man end up in a hole like this?

Simple. Just keep doing exactly what you're doing, and let the years pass. Eventually, you dig your own grave without even noticing.

Last chance I'll ever get to go wild, and what do I do? Drudgingly account for my days, hour by hour, and moan miserably. This needs fixing.

Possessed by an impulse to wreck something, I visited the Hendricks House website just now. The ladies were chirping over the latest doings of Dr. Gerard Jones, chairman of the board. It seems the good doctor paid a visit yesterday and harmonized with the ElderSingers, helped the Safe Harbor kids with their homework, and donned a smock to finger paint with the tots from Tanya's Room, where battered moms can rest in peace, or something like that.

Let me explain, Bobby. I wouldn't have a job if not for Dr. Jones. My column was his idea, and he recommended me for it; therefore, I hate him. He's exactly my age, but his résumé makes mine look like a hobo's. Chief of Neurosurgery at St. Dominic's; inventor of the Jones collar, a helmet attachment that protects motorcyclists from head trauma; accomplished violist and watercolorist; faithful husband for thirty years, father of three Ivy League graduates, major donor, and tireless volunteer. He won't be satisfied until they call him Mahatma.

The comments read like fan club minutes. *He painted Georgia O'Keeffe flowers with our special needs kids last month. What a gracious, attentive man . . . I've served on several boards with him. You'd never know he's done all he's done, he's so unassuming . . . If we could just clone him . . .* One Tami D. (whose profile picture showed a leaping terrier) wrote, *It's such a pleasure to talk with him. He makes you feel more interesting and intelligent than you really are. A rare gift!*

Like a dog in a chicken coop, I enjoy rousing these females into a flap with my noisy barking. It's my sole remaining entertainment. Signing in as *Masked Marauder,* I posted this tale:

Dr. Jones treated my wife for her incapacitating headaches two years ago. In the course of examining her, he fondled her nipples and delivered a lewd lecture on the penises of the animal kingdom, from the two-inch nub of the gorilla to the corkscrew-tipped pig's member to the eight-foot bazooka of the blue whale. She kept the incident secret from me until just before she died, five months later—with an undiagnosed glioblastoma the size of a clementine. I hope the doctor's admirers will take this story to heart. In fact, I hope you'll ask him about it the next time he visits. "What do you have to say about poor Ilse von Hochschmeck?" See how gracious and attentive he is then!

You disapprove, Bob. I can feel it from here. I won't try to defend my behavior. I'm just a bloated jerk, pocked with failings. No argument there.

For a few minutes, though, I enjoyed myself.

Not sure what to do now, however.

27.

Twenty-seven days may be too long to wait.

Today, then? And let others sort out the mess.

My kitchen, my world:

On the counter, toast crumbs, empty Pepsi cans, ant traps. Vials of Prilosec, Lopressor and Naprosyn on the table beside the laptop. Overhead, dead bugs in the concentric grooves of the glass shade covering the light. A *whunk*, as the Nixon-era refrigerator cycles on. Up above, a football game on Mrs. N's TV. Does any of this entice me to go on living? Guess.

What a relief it will be not to have to fill up weekend days like this one. (How long can you read the newspaper while lingering over your Frosted Flakes? How long can you outrun the question, Why am I bothering? Isn't it obvious, when I find myself searching for chores to do— what do I need at CVS? Is it time for an oil change, or new underwear?—that this show should have been cancelled long ago?)

Five Benadryls would knock me out. A Hefty bag sealed with duct tape would finish me off. Let's see if I have the supplies on hand.

Nope, all out of trash bags. Off to the supermarket I go. On my merry way.

The flesh is weak in so many ways, Bob. Though I went for suicide gear, I also came home with a tub of orange sherbet, Little Debbie Swiss Rolls, sour cream and onion chips, and a six-pack of Yuengling. One last binge.

While I enjoy the sherbet, I think I'll cast one last glance back across time. I wonder whether H. G. Wells kept note-books too, and visited them later in life. *Bing!* Inspiration!

She got me again.

I thought the wound had closed, but I was wrong.

For the last hour, I've been staring helplessly into the darkness of What If, and No, It Couldn't Have Been, and If Only I'd.

This makes no sense to you, Bob. I'll clarify (and hope that telling the tale will cure the fever).

In a notebook from 1987, I found something that stopped me. A short story, supposedly, but the only fiction was that I made it up.

Years have passed since I shut this out. I'd forgotten her, after believing for half my life that I never would.

What am I supposed to do with this?

Long ago, before I became me, I met Lena Sjöman while traveling on a train from Munich to Garmisch-Partenkirchen. She had a round bowl of brown hair, red canvas sneakers, and a red sweatshirt that matched her high-boned cheeks; she was studying a German phrase book. She concealed her beauty behind the plainest of trappings—a virgin princess, striving to escape notice—but the simple clothes and the blushing cheeks worked on me like a potion. Ravenously lonely, I asked if I could look at the map she had open on her lap.

We ended up touring Garmisch for two days together. All I remember is walking uphill to the Café Panorama in a thick fog, passing the twelve Stations of the Cross on the way, and seeing nothing but Lena.

She ditched me fairly abruptly, deciding she needed to head south to Florence. I understood that I wasn't invited.

This was long before I put on weight—it wasn't that. No, she ran away because I'd fallen in love with her. According to Lena, this habit of falling instantly in love is a particular folly of Americans. I patriotically resisted the slander, though later—after much pain—I did accept the part about falling in love being a mistake. You yearn to meet the one who'll complete you, but at best, you get a few weeks of mutual self-deception, all the while hiding from the suspicion that This Isn't Really It.

Anyhoo . . .

I should give myself a bit of a break here. It was impossible *not* to fall in love with her. To cite just one reason, the way she pronounced *Tycho Brahe* stirred my brain like a swizzle stick: a murmur, lips pursed, and then the quiet tick of the k sound, like a marble tapping glass.

She was always analyzing my errors, psychotherapizing, political-theorizing. I suppose it was her way of holding me off, keeping the adoring puppy at arm's length. Back then, though, I couldn't understand why anyone would want to argue so much.

For a year, I wrote her letters, transmuting my longing into multipage outpourings of playful wit. She wrote back terse, impersonal nullities on weightless blue tissue paper.

Nevertheless, I studied Swedish and allowed my fantasies to bloom and proliferate. The following summer, I visited her. She hugged me at the train station, a friendly, floppy hug, and I told myself this was everything I'd hoped for. It was all downhill from there. She already had a boyfriend—a fact she'd mentioned in Garmisch, which I had stubbornly ignored. He was an aged American expat professor whose English had deformed over time. The agonies climaxed my first night there, in a room with a cold stone floor and tall, open windows. Sheer curtains billowed in the breeze like grieving ghosts. She assaulted me for selfishly trying to make myself the center of her life. She also critiqued the personality I'd sculpted for myself—the pose of urbane disdain—as a suit of armor that I hid inside, fearfully. What could I say to that? *Same to you, Bud.* No, I couldn't reply at all. I simply sat with my lips slightly apart, conveying innocence and injury.

That should have been the end of the story, but I'd flown across an ocean to see her, and had nowhere else to go. Six days of torment followed. We visited the rocky shore where *The Seventh Seal* was filmed; attended a Communist party (birthday of a leftist friend); and took the hydrofoil across the channel to Copenhagen, where we strolled in the Tivoli Gardens and gawked at the Little Mermaid in the harbor. In spite of her outbursts of exasperation, I couldn't believe that she felt nothing for me. It didn't seem possible, given my admiration and yearning, my *devotion* to her. Always, I hoped she would finally give in and snuggle against me.

It didn't happen. By the time I flew home, getting away was a relief. I doubted life would bring me any happiness from then on, and it seems I was right.

Oddly, however, she came to stay with me for a week the next summer, at my old apartment in Jersey City. (If she couldn't stand me, then why did she come? I've always clung to this as proof that I wasn't crazy to hope—but it may be that she couldn't pass up the chance for free lodging ten minutes from New York City.) By this time, I had changed. She'd succeeded in burning away my belief in love. She slept on a foam mattress on my floor—I bought it just for her—and I never touched her. She appreciated my restraint so much that she commented cheerfully on how well we were getting along. I bore my burden stoically, and took her all over Manhattan, from the Battery to the George Washington Bridge. (We walked across in a heavy wind. The bridge swayed under our feet; her T-shirt blew up above her shoulders, exposing her breasts, which were no more than pale swellings. This registered as nothing but a neutral fact.)

On our last night together, after steak and wine in my apartment, she confessed that she'd never been able to show affection straightforwardly. Instead, any time she liked a boy, she would hit him. Later in the evening, demonstrating how old-time tennis players planted their feet solidly on the ground (did I mention that she had been a champion in her teens?), she took my old wooden Slazenger racquet and hit me with it—playful taps on the back of the thigh, on the arm, on the hip.

That's what skewered me, Bob. That's what left me haunted and obsessed, like an Edgar Allan Poe madman, seeking his beloved beyond the grave. Lena sent me a message in the code she had taught me, and the message said, *What you've wanted for two years, more than you've ever wanted anything in your life, more than you'll ever want anything again, I offer to you now.* And I let the offer pass.

It wasn't that I missed the signal. I just couldn't believe it. She had trained me to understand that I was foolish, self-centered and wrong to want her. Like a dog shocked repeatedly by an invisible fence, I dared not put a paw over the line. Unlike Charlie Brown, I refused to believe that, this time, Lucy would let me kick the football. Rather than make that mistake, I chose to forgo happiness for all time.

Now, though—

I can't make my mind sit still. Any man with a beating heart would have held her, stroked her red cheeks. If I'd kissed her, the last thirty years might have been unrecognizable, the opposite of what was.

Or, maybe nothing would have changed.

I'll never know.

I shouldn't accuse myself this way. I couldn't have behaved differently, any more than I can will myself, right now, to do a thousand push-ups. Someone else might have—not me.

Even if we had kissed, etc., she still would have climbed into her cab in the morning and gone back to Sweden.

I hear her saying her nonsense word, *Shingaling*. I see her walking beside a golden field, telling me that this crop is called *raps* (which isn't in my Swedish-English dictionary), and that the pure blue sky above us, together with the yellow raps, gives her country's flag its colors. I ask if I'll ever see her again after I return home, and she says, "Mebbe."

It's not fair to blame her for the souring that followed. Everyone rejects somebody sometime. I've left my share of disappointed women behind—all because they couldn't compare with Lena. (Hillary comes to mind, with her obsessive collection of Disney figurines.)

I can't wriggle free of this hook, though. *Somehow, somewhere,* we could have been together.

Sleeping. Waking. And back to sleep again. If only I could drift off forever.

If I'd changed careers and gone to work as a kindergarten teacher, a job Lena respected, and then I'd flown to see her one more time . . .

Impossible to sustain the fantasy. It's like a computer game, when you stray past the borders of the programmed world, into the gray zone where nothing is. Us, Together: two words that, side by side, make no sense.

I found her, Bob.

Four other *Lena Sjömans* appeared, but only one in her old town, offering *Psykologi & Psykoterapi*. (*Vad söker du?* the search menu asked: *What do you seek?*) I have her e-mail address, and her *telefon*. I could call her right now.

More terrifying than death, by far.

Hello, Lena. Do you recognize my voice?
Angus?

Good of you to remember me.

It has been so many years. Can you say so? (She asked that often. Using me to improve her English.)

I just wanted you to know . . . (What? That I'm about to kill myself and thought I'd say hi?) *. . . that you're still inside me.*

No, that makes me sound like a carnivorous whale.

I think, in your nun-like way, you were afraid to be with someone who passionately desired and admired you, as opposed to a peculiar old man. I assume he's dead now?

No, he is my husband. But he is sick. Really, it is sad. (Rilly, she used to say. My face tingles, remembering.) *He lives only a short time now.*

So you'll be available soon.

If I actually dialed her number, though, what would happen?

1) I wouldn't recognize her voice—changed, older, harsh—and I'd have to face the fact that my Lena no longer exists.

2) She would ask, *Why do you call me?* and I would have no answer.

3) Her pedantic lecturing would annoy me.

4) She would ask what I've been doing all this time, and my answer, no matter how I put it, would show both of us that I've done absolutely nothing with my life—a fact I accept, but hearing her say, *Mm-hm . . .*

If we arranged to meet, she would see what I became. Which must never happen.

I don't know what to do with myself, BB. I fled just now to a different notebook, desperate for distraction, and found on every page a strained pose of superiority and lame attempts at cleverness. Everything I wrote on those lined pages was a received idea. My time would have been better spent bowling.

My shin is throbbing again, a souvenir of the sack race. The painful pulse offers a sort of relief—something else to think about, for a few moments, at least.

Experimenting, I put the trash bag over my head just now. It's not opaque from the inside, in case you ever wondered. I could see everything, as if through brown smoke and a dirty windshield. Warmth quickly surrounded my head, the November chill disappeared. Not unpleasant at all.

Wonder of wonders, I just had a visitor, first in years. Panting up the stairs, bunched-up bag in hand, I found Jerri White at my door—my boss, a dark-brown beanpole with bug eyes and hoop earrings. She's been trying to reach me since Friday night, when I turned off the ringer on my phone and stopped checking e-mail. She knows I live alone, she said, and was afraid "something might have happened." Eyeing the black bag, she asked, "Are you in the middle of something?"

"No, I'm all done."

Neither she nor any of my coworkers has ever seen my apartment, and that's not an accident. She didn't ask to be let in, and I didn't invite her. We had our tête-à-tête at the top of my stairs.

"Is everything all right?" she asked, stuffy-nosed.

Most of the time, Jerri is all brusque business, but now and then a tender soul peeps forth. You can tell it's happening because she looks at you.

"I'm involved in a personal matter, Jerri. I can't accept an assignment right now, if that's why you're here."

She pinched her lips together, expressing pained indignation. "That's not why I came," i.e., *We've known each other for ten years. I thought you might have dropped dead.*

The truth didn't take long to come out, however: Hendricks House is holding its annual gala the Friday after this one. The theme is a celebration of the clients I've profiled, and they want me to speak. Dr. Jones himself called her to make the request.

"I'm sure you'd rather not," she said, "but that would be hard to explain. The publisher plays squash with Dr. Jones. I'm asking you to do what they want, as a favor to me."

A different editor might have put it more bluntly. *You'll do this and not fuck up, or I'll stab you in the eyeballs, and any other balls I find on you.* But Jerri never raises her voice, never indulges in flavorful language. Her M.O. is quiet black-mail. (Smart, self-conscious, unmarried and ill-suited to the supervisor's role, she has a master's from Columbia, yet here she is, trapped in the Tales of Our Towns department, with amber deodorant stains at the armpits of her white blouses and no idea how to escape. Poor soul!)

My sympathy for Jerri has a limit. I won't perform like a eunuch emcee for a ballroom full of self-satisfied oncologists and dentists—not for her sake or anyone else's.

The time had come to burn some bridges. If I really mean what I've been chattering about, then I had to give my notice. If not, then I had to stop playing make-believe and get back to work, because there are bills to pay.

Looking into my boss's froggish eyes, I said, "Sorry, Jerri. I've loathed this job since the first day. I can't write another sentence for you. And you'll have to find another after-dinner speaker."

Where was the exhilaration? You don't free yourself from indentured servitude every day—but there was Jerri, avoiding the sight of my face, embarrassed by my rudeness—a peculiar, nervous woman who now had to tell the saintly Dr. Jones that he couldn't have his way.

The sound of weeping came from behind my back. On the other side of the wall, in Mrs. N's kitchen, Eka struggled to speak. Gulps of Georgian tumbled out amid sobs. She rarely has visitors; she must have been on the phone.

In that narrow space, with unhappy women fore and aft, I tried to wrap things up and get back to business. "It shouldn't be hard to replace me. Any English-speaking primate will do."

"I'm sorry, Angus. I should have noticed you were unhappy. I could have found more interesting things for you to do. I still can. Would you let me try?"

I hope you'll forgive me, Bob, for jesting in the face of her earnestness. "As Descartes said just before he mysteriously vanished, 'I think not.'"

Time to say good night. My stomach is reproaching me for the Yuengling, the chips, the sherbet. With luck, I'll pass out quickly.

1:10 A.M.

Darkness beyond the windows. I'm an island of insomnia in a slumbering world.

Slow ticking from a hidden pipe. The radiator whistles a melancholy note.

Somewhere in Sweden, Lena is dreaming her early morning dreams. I send my soul to her across the sea. *Remember me?*

26.

Clippings, résumés, medical records, expired passport, trumpet sheet music from high school, beloved centerfolds of the seventies and eighties (so old, they have pubic hair)—into the black bag all of it went.

While dumping files, I happened upon Lena's letters, hidden behind the last folder. There were more than I remembered. A thick stack, all written in the same swift hand, all somber and distant. She never referred to my infatuation, not once. *It is a silent Saturday night. I feel like running away from the silence since it somehow makes me nervous. I am not quite satisfied with my situation.* Or, a few years later, *I think I am the loneliest person you know.* The thin blue paper, *Flygpost—Par Avion*, torn where it says ÖPPNAS HÄR. The unused space beneath her signoff, *Take care, Lena.* There is so little here, despite all the paper. The letters leave me suffocated, disappointed, resentful, just as they did long ago. Couldn't she give me *any*thing?

Let's get to it. Face the end, confront it for real.
(Waiting for insight.)
I hear myself breathe, and think, *That'll be over soon.*
Nodding out, I shake my head to wake up.
Does flesh dry out and wither on the bone, or does it fall away and damply decompose?
(Does this happen to you, too, Brother Bob? Do you fall asleep when you meditate?)

Not many people will notice I'm gone. Maybe one neighbor will say to himself, Whatever happened to that fat guy with the beard? Haven't seen him around for a while.

What if she changed her mind and tried to reach me, years ago, but couldn't find me? I've moved twice, and my number has been unlisted since I went to work for the *Register*. (What am I hiding from, you ask? From greedy unfortunates asking me to profile them. One offered to split the proceeds.)

I could go to Sweden. Search for her, find her, astonish her. Before leaving the stage, let me make one last scene— and perhaps, by sheer, crazy bravado, win the happiness I gave up on long ago.

But I'm afraid of seeing her, and being seen. Let her remember me, if she does, the way I was.

What would I say, if I were to send one last communiqué?
Kära Lena,

My, my, my, how the years fly.

It's impossible to find the correct tone. I give up.

I found your letters again today. The power of ink on paper, to conquer time! Every word reminded me of all that never happened between us, to my unending sorrow.

How strange for you, to find this strangled cry from so long ago washing up on your rocky shore.

How are you? What's new? I hope the decades have been good for you. For me, not so much.

I discovered today that you still have the power to rip my heart open. Is that satisfying to know, or horrifying?

I'll stop.

Kära flicka, you remain luminous inside me. I remember everything.

Forever devoted,
Angus

I just realized why she, alone among women, still haunts me. It's simple: we never slept together. All illusions intact!

What have I done?

Bob, oh, Bob—in a moment of madness, I hit Send. Never have I regretted a brash act more. I want to hide. I want to die, before she reads it.

Shit.

I've destroyed my own serenity. I've dropped a fork into the cosmic garbage disposal. Until now, if she ever thought of me, she may have assumed that I married, found satisfying work, made a life. Now she'll know the truth.

I would jump out the window right now, if I lived higher up.

In the space of that skipped line, a great deal changed. Has this ever happened to you? While obsessing about Problem A, you're run over by Truck B. (Not recently, you say? I suppose dramatic reversals are rare in a monastery.)

Remember Eka crying in Mrs. N's kitchen last night? Well, she just left. It seems I have one last task to finish before I make my exit.

The buzzer interrupted my hysteria over the e-mail to Lena. I assumed it was Jerri White, back for another try. Annoyed beyond endurance, panting from climbing the stairs, I threw the door open and found Eka. Oddly, her eyelid was twitching.

Buttoned to the throat in a tomato-red sweater, she asked timidly if she could talk, please, to me. My guess was that she'd dropped Mrs. N and didn't know what to do with the body.

As it turned out, I was right to suspect mortality, but I had the wrong victim.

She apologized and said she must sit. I sent her downstairs ahead of me. My descent afforded ample time to reflect on how little I wanted this visitor. I needed to concentrate on my panic over Lena, not listen to yet another immigrant's problems.

Here's what she told me:

She supports her mother and son back in Georgia. Ever since she arrived in America, she has been trying to bring them here.

Recently she started waking up with a *vibration* in her arms and legs. It's gotten worse and worse. Mrs. N finally ordered her to see a doctor, so she went to the emergency room. (At this point, I noticed a tremor in her hand, which persisted through the end of her visit.) They took x-rays, a CAT scan, and blood for testing. The tests showed elevated levels of methyl mercury in her blood. The doctor prescribed a pill and the mercury level came down, but the tremors haven't stopped.

Yesterday the doctor told her that the poisoning had gone too far to reverse. There's nothing anyone can do.

She grew up south of Rustavi, near the border of Azerbaijan, where she ate fish daily from the heavily polluted Mtkvari River. (Rustavi, an industrial center under the Soviets, was home to steel works and chemical factories, though most of these closed when communism collapsed.)

Along with the tremors, she has been suffering from pain in her legs and exhaustion.

Her son is supposed to come to the United States as soon as his visa is approved. She doesn't know what will happen to him now, or to her mother. She's afraid he'll end up living with her cousins in Brooklyn, who will put him to work in their floor-refinishing business and not let him go to school.

Her eyes filled with tears, her mouth took the shape of tragedy's mask. She's still an attractive woman, but it was not a pretty sight.

She gripped the threadbare armrest of my couch and went on.

Her mother has severe *bone thin disease* (osteoporosis, I assume) and can't work. Who will support them?

Her English is densely accented and grammatically fractured. She seems not to have learned much in her six years here.

And now we come to the punch line: "You are important man of newspaper. If you write this story, the people could help. For my family, to support . . . after."

Though her yammering on the phone annoys me, I'd had a favorable impression of her before this. The tale of woe raised red flags, however. It seemed quite possible that she'd made it all up, as a scam. That she could call me *important* while sitting on my shabby couch, in a living room that hasn't been painted in twenty years (the water-stains look like brown fingers pointing at hell), with one dungeon-like window just below the ceiling and nothing decorating the walls but a dusty ukulele, proved her insincerity. Also, as a person who intends to be dead in a few weeks, I found her claim of terminal illness offensive. One corpse at a time, please.

I told her bluntly that I'd quit my job. On the off chance that she really is dying of mercury poisoning, I suggested she contact Hendricks House. Whether she's here legally or not, a social worker may be able to wring some benefits out of the government.

She had the pallid, haunted look of someone about to vomit. Her eyes closed; she slumped forward, and then she was on the floor, forehead on the carpet, arms extended toward me as if praying to Allah. (Is Georgia a Muslim country? No, according to Wikipedia, though it borders Turkey, 82 percent of the population is Orthodox Christian.)

In response to her name and a gentle shoulder-poke, she groaned softly. I went to the kitchen, where I'd left the laptop, and looked into her story. It turns out there is a "metallurgical" factory in Rustavi, dating from the Soviet era and recently reopened, as well as some chemical plants. Yes, the Mtkvari River is badly polluted: "the dumping ground of the Caucasus," one article called it. Yes, mercury poisoning produces tremors, and can be fatal.

I don't think this home health aide could have concocted all of these supporting details. Do you?

Her hair, I noticed on my return, is Japanese black. She may dye it, I have no idea. Dark strands, crooked as mountain roads, clung to her damp white neck. There she lay, half-conscious on my floor, a victim of industrial pollution. The human sacrifice exacted by our chemical dependency.

What a neat allegorical tale. The hopeful immigrant crosses an ocean in search of a better life, and slaves to bring her family here. Unbeknownst to her, however, the toxins she absorbed in childhood are nibbling away at her central nervous system, and they'll kill her before her son steps off the plane. The story of our poisoned Earth, embodied in one person.

A book: *Eka's Story*. A slim volume, in the first person, from taped interviews.

But I wanted to be done. A project like this would screw up my deadline.

Nevertheless.

It wouldn't be a petty story of misfortune, like my profiles. Her suffering has a larger meaning.

Kneeling beside her, I revived her with soft pats and hoped my knees wouldn't break under the pressure. She didn't know me at first. Finding herself on the floor, she sat back on her heels and closed her eyes to recover her balance. "I am sorry I bother you," she said.

The carpet had printed a grid of red stipples on her forehead. No longer hopeful, she grimly studied a nearby electrical outlet. The outlet stared back at her, a startled, appalled little face.

I told her I had an idea. Possibly, my idea might generate money for her family. Would she be willing to tell me about her life? *Everything* about her life?

Yes, she said solemnly. All questions I ask, she will answer.

Do I have the stamina to finish this? We'll see.

25.

It's been a peculiar afternoon. A tall glass of vodka and OJ will settle the nerves, I hope, before Eka comes down. In her honor, I'm drinking Georgi.

I'll tell you the story. You may think it's funny.

I spent the morning regretting the e-mail I sent Lena, to put it mildly. In fear and dread, I kept a safe distance from my computer, lest I rashly check for a response.

Around noon, while vacuuming the clots of hair and dust from the corners of the living room for my visitor's sake, I heard ringing. A hallucination, I assumed—but no, the call was real.

It's her.

If anyone could have seen the size of my terror, I would have been humiliated.

The caller wasn't Lena, but the voice was just as soft. Dr. Gerard Jones invited me to his home in Summit for lunch.

Stopped Heart: the Sequel. *He Knows It's Me.*

"Any particular reason?" I asked.

"Let's wait and talk face to face."

He's a small man—on a seesaw, two of him in wet clothes wouldn't lift me off the ground—yet there I stood, immobilized. The elephant challenged by the mouse.

I could have dodged the invitation, but this close to the end, I'd rather not sully my self-image with acts of cowardice.

Truax's Paradox: You can never get where you want to go. Resolve to smother yourself, and the Girl in Red returns to torment you. Send her a pathetic message, and a dying immigrant faints on your floor. Agree to write the immigrant's biography, and your despised benefactor invites you to lunch. One could say, *I can't wait to see where this will end,* but I just find it irritating.

The winding streets of Summit are full of imposing brick homes, many of them mottled with faux-antique whitewash. The biggest manse, the king of the hill, flew the rippling Stars and Stripes; I assumed I'd arrived, but no, my host lives down the slope, in a modest ranch house with a wood shingle roof. His lawn and shrubs are neatly barbered but without the deep mulch and undulating acreage of the larger homes. Doubtful that the eminent Dr. Jones could live in this *Leave It To Beaver* house, I double-checked the address. Yup. He can and he does.

On his doorpost, he has one of those slanted ceramic tubules with a Hebrew inscription. How's that for unexpected?

A possibly Vietnamese girl in a pink tracksuit led me to a den furnished with pieces from other worlds: a dark armoire with bas-relief dragons carved into the doors, a striped kilim on the floor, a Hindu-ish mantelpiece with mother-of-pearl inlay. I heard my host in the next room, consulting with a colleague by phone. *Vision loss, angiogram, aneurysm, scar tissue, clips*—these were the only terms I understood.

The room smelled like my Aunt Gerda's house, long ago: classic Jersey mildew. A photo showed a less bald Dr. Jones with his teenage children on a long-ago safari. A framed letter from the king of Thailand thanked him for saving the prince's life, on royal letterhead.

Dr. Jones appeared in clean jeans, moccasins, and a zippered cardigan. Our handshake was comical. The tiny fellow!

The maid, Sue—or maybe Thu—served us oranges, scones, and triangles of BLT on white toast. The doctor drank Sam Adams; I opted for cranberry juice and seltzer, having already dosed myself with mezcal in preparation for this meeting.

A new odor had entered the room with him. I remembered it from our long-ago interview. The smell suggested cleanliness, with a tinge of hospital. Disinfectant? Could be.

Breezily postponing whatever lay in store for me, I asked, "Why the Judaica at the front door, Dr. Jones?"

He said his father was born Jacoby and changed his name as a young man, "for business reasons."

His manner was subdued, calmly cordial, distracted, elusive. It seemed possible that he planned to blow me out of the water with a direct question, *Why do you write these ugly libels about me?*—or else that he only wanted to talk me into speaking at his gala.

Rather than confronting me, he asked if I'd seen today's paper. "Despite my profession," I admitted, "I haven't read a newspaper in years." His point: an earthquake in Guangdong province had destroyed most of a small city where he once taught a seminar on dural repair techniques. "The mayor was so proud of the new construction in his city. Now it no longer exists. I wonder if he survived."

"Senseless deaths, distant multitudes. The eternal headline."

"You're right. The farther away the suffering is, the less real it feels." He ate an orange segment with small, unassuming jaw movements. "You have a skill I admire," he added, an apparent non sequitur.

"You know about my years as a jockey?"

With an aloof quarter-smile, he let the quip pass.

"You show your readers the humanity in your subjects. And you do it with such a light touch. The tragedy shows through, but it's never a heavy syrup. I don't know how you pull it off."

His use of the present tense bothered me. "I assume you know I've retired."

He sought my eyes, but I wasn't lending them out.

In general, I'll say anything to anyone, as you know, Brother Bob. With this petite physician, however, I found myself silenced. Muzzled.

"I wanted to discuss that with you," he said. "Was there a specific dissatisfaction we could address?"

"Yes. I hated everything about the job."

Have I mentioned that Dr. Jones is the one who got me this job? I profiled him once, when I used to write features about Jersey bigwigs; after I fell into disgrace, he resuscitated my career by recommending me for the Neighbors in Need column. In other words, I had just spat in his face.

Rather than take offense, he studied me with seeming sympathy. "Usually, what we do well gives us pleasure and pride. Why didn't you enjoy the work?"

I began to writhe internally. I had no desire to undergo therapy with this minuscule overachiever. There seemed something wrong with his paying this much attention to me. Aha, I thought. This is his revenge.

I said, "It offends me to lie every day."

"How were you lying?"

"By portraying these people as colorful Dickensian unfortunates. They're not nearly that lovable."

He has a nervous tic, an involuntary blink. Knowing his résumé, one expects arrogance, but he gives the impression of perfect humility. If you saw him in a restaurant, you might guess he taught bookkeeping at a community college.

A phone call interrupted us. He took it in the next room something about the dedication of a hospital in Botswana. They wanted him to cut the ribbon but he preferred to leave the spotlight to other donors. Apparently, however, Dr. Nkate was counting on him to be there, which swayed him.

On his return, he peeled a second orange. A rime of white pith coated his fingers. "I'm sorry you've spent so long doing something you considered dishonest. I can see why you'd want to escape. Have you thought about a career you'd prefer?"

It was a fair question. If I'm so unhappy as Mr. Misery, why not just change jobs? Must one really kill oneself?

"I have no idea," I said, quite sincerely.

From the little secretary behind him, he took a silver and gold fountain pen, and began to scribble on a pad of graph paper. He wasn't solving my problem; he was drawing rhombi and trapezoids, each contained within its own blue square, each made of wet black ink that dried almost instantly. My irresponsibility had so dismayed him that all he could do was doodle.

The danger of a confrontation appeared to have blown over. There seemed no point in my being there, but no way to escape. Contrasting thoughts wafted through my mind:

- He must have a shameful secret. Boy prostitutes? Shaved pubes?
- Despite his achievements, our sizes put us on a near-equal footing—a vestige of caveman times.

"Why," I asked, because the silence had grown difficult, "are you so unassuming?"

While weighing the question, he drew three circles of increasing size that shared a bottom point. "The people who come to me expect me to reverse the effects of degenerative diseases or head trauma. Sometimes I can help them, sometimes I can't. There isn't much chance I'll mistake myself for God."

I had the sense that, for whatever misguided reasons, he saw me as someone with whom he could speak openly.

Sue or Thu announced another call. I twiddled my thumbs—literally, to see why others have resorted to this inane pastime (no insights to report)—and found myself so exasperated by his sympathy that, eventually, I got up and slipped out the front door.

And now I'm back in my dungeon, waiting for Eka's visit and feeling a bit of remorse over my recent online aggression against the good doctor—while wondering if he arranged our meeting for exactly that purpose.

The contrast between his home and mine doesn't cheer me. After cleaning for an hour, the place still looks shabby and disreputable, though less foul. If I had a can of paint, I'd cover the water stains on the wall. Too late now, though.

I'm afraid, Brother Bob. I've been afraid all day. It's time to check my e-mail, but I can't make myself. Nothing good can be waiting for me.

Imagine the impossible. *From: Lena Sjöman. You were right, long ago. There was a special connection. But that frightened me. We have lost these many years but maybe it's not too late?*

What if she actually wants to see me? What then?

Calm yourself, man. There's no chance.

Drum roll . . .

All that agitation for nothing. No new messages, except a coupon for Payless.

Holy Shevardnadze, Batman. There's so much to tell. Where to begin?

I'll have to transcribe the tape—but not yet.

She arrived shyly, wouldn't accept sherbet or a Swiss roll, only water. She had dressed up for our interview, in a nicer outfit than I've seen her wear before, a black dress with red flowers, which looked out of place on my couch with the water stain behind her. The hand tremor seemed worse, though that may be because I watched for it.

Knees together, straight-backed, girlish, she watched the little geared hubs turn behind the window of the cassette recorder.

As a warm-up, I asked what living in the United States is like for her. She said, "I love this country. So much everything, all kind of food—Mexican, Chinese, hamburgers. I love hamburgers. But living here, I think so much, What do

· 53 ·

I do here? I want to see my family. We do Skype, but this is not satisfying me. My brother's babies grow, grow, two nieces. I don't meet them yet, never. And my mother grows old. What kind daughter I am, so far away?"

The tears were flowing already, and we hadn't even begun. Tissueless, I brought her a roll of paper towels and changed direction. "Tell me about your earliest memories."

In nursery school, which she called *baby children school*, "everyone must to take nap but I don't want nap, I look in dark at the dolls, which are for display only. But when commissar comes to inspect, they hurry, hurry, bring toys to show us happy playing." She owned a Vankastanka, a wobbly toy with a round bottom—her father managed a factory that made them. This versatile factory also printed books and magazines, and manufactured ladies' shoes. The managers would go traveling in Russia, selling their products.

She had a baby brother who died. "Too soon he is born, at six month. They give milk in hospital, but he got sick from hole in intestine."

Her accent goes beyond the standard Eastern European caricature. She pronounces *work* "vork." (Rhymes with *fork*.) *Regular* becomes "regoolar." Then there's the foorniture, and the things she like-èd, and the tasks that come easy-ly to her. Every syllable brings a new surprise.

Under the Soviets, she said, life was secure, if limited. The government provided for people. "The house is warm, we have clothes." But ten people shared their two-bedroom apartment, and they couldn't afford to go on a vacation, and when her father bought her a bicycle, he had to report how he got the money and they kept watch over him for months afterward. "My father never finds job again after Georgia independence, but still he like the new government better. 'Better to be free and hungry.' He says this."

I found her stories moderately interesting, but unusable. Granted, we'd only been together for ten minutes, but I had a bad feeling that we wouldn't arrive at the heart of the matter anytime soon. And neither of us has unlimited time.

I asked her to tell me about the river.

"Everyone knows, polluted. But my father say, 'Always I fish on this river.' So—he goes every day. Too many people fish there, not him only. They stand on road by the side. They swim also. Water is brown like chocolate, but they swim. So he brings home fish, silver fish, long like hand. My mother cleans carefully. We think this is safe because she cleans."

Her father died just before she emigrated. The many stories she told about him show a poignant devotion to his memory. She seems not to have realized that she wouldn't be dying if not for his stubbornness.

"Have other people who lived near the river been getting sick?"

"I don't know this. I will ask mother."

She studied to become a nurse at the university. Her husband went to Tbilisi after their son was born, to work as a meteorologist, and met someone else there. He never came back.

"I work in hospital, in cardiology. Too many people have heart attacks. Day and night we make EKG, we make reanimation. It was too hard job, long, long nights, but I keep working to support mother, son, and grandparents."

She stopped, eyes brimming. You must assume I have experience with crying people, but it's not so: my profilees generally hold it together in interviews. The point is, I don't know what to do with weeping women.

"Let's go back to childhood," I said. "Tell me more of your early memories."

Her mouth went small and pouty. I think she took offense at my impatience.

"We had on the wall nice Oriental rug. Too good for floor. And always, my father got big Christmas tree. One year, my baby sister, Maka, got doll. And she cut out mother's best dress to sew for her doll, a little dress like mother's. My mother screamed when she saw, 'What do you did?'"

Eka laughed, not at that memory, but the next one. "How we played! She was geese, I was wolf, other sister was other wolf. We called, 'Geese, geese, where you are?' In Georgian, this is rhyme. And she runs, and we catch, but she screams, afraid really of the wolfs."

What else? She skipped ahead twenty years or so. Her son was ten when she left; she talks to him two or three times a week, the calls are affordable with a special phone card (five dollars buys two and a half hours), but she longs to hold him the way she did when he was a baby. That will be difficult, since he's sixteen now and plays basketball in a youth league. He's very good, she says. He dreams of playing in the NBA, like Zaza Pachulia. But she missed his childhood: more tears.

If I'd let her go on, she would have told me a dozen more unrelated tales. I don't know how I'm going to manage this, Bob. I'm drowning in unusable tidbits. I could bang out a column on her in twenty minutes. But a book?

There was a moment when I thought I saw her peering at my gut, as if noticing my size for the first time. For all my experience with stares, I became self-conscious. My forearms, I saw, were thicker than her calves. Ordinarily, my size seems more or less normal to me, but for one hallucinatory moment, I saw myself as thin people must: inflated, grotesque. This did not endear her to me.

At my door, as I huffed and puffed and said good night, she asked hopefully, "You think book will earn much money?"

Her frankness chilled me. Even if she's dying, I don't like the idea of serving as a causeway to her pot of gold. Still, I swallowed my dismay and left her dreams intact. "I hope so. Yes."

She urged me to be tough with her. "If I don't answer good, you must say."

"I will."

As she turned to go, her cheek twitched. "You help me so much."

"It's what I do."

She was careful, however, not to say, *How can I ever thank you?*

So much glop. How to organize it all?

Begin with the river. Its path, its history, its defilement. The specific toxins poured into it, the names of the factories along its banks.

Next, Eka's earliest memories of the river. Swimming, if possible.

Eka in the river, the river in Eka.

Begin this way. The rest will come.

24.

In the past, hearing Eka upstairs on her cell phone, I've inwardly compared her voice to a blue jay's squawk and an electric knife. Many times, I've wished she would shut up.

Transcribing our interview, though, I find her accent almost charming. She speaks slowly in English, without that chattering bird quality. She struggles to find the right word, or something close. It's touching.

I used to fall hard for women with accents. The Irish girl at the dry cleaner's, she of the profuse freckles and sky-blue irises, would murmur, "Wednesday," and I'd be transported to a misty, verdant realm of fairy magic. And Marcella from Rotterdam, who sometimes tagged along to photograph my profilees—every time she told me the next turn to take, I wished I could kiss her delicate shoulder. And then there was Lena. American English is dull and familiar, but add the rhythm and melody of a distant land, and the music intoxicates.

Or, it used to. Thankfully, I've aged out of that particular folly.

No reply from Lena. I can calm down now.

I typed *obesity* into the Google box just now, for no rational reason, and tumbled down a rabbit hole, the cries of tormented strangers echoing around me. There was the guy who can't go anywhere without an oxygen mask and motorized scooter . . . the woman who can't laugh or sneeze without letting loose a gusher of pee, because of the weight pressing on her bladder . . . the mother who gets yeast infections between her layers of excess skin . . . the man who had to go to the grain co-op to get weighed on the truck scales . . . the wife whose husband won't appear with her in public, who has lost her joy, who can no longer look other people in the eye, who avoids the mirrors in her own home.

In the face of such anguish, I can only say, Shut up! Don't whimper and plead for understanding—tell the world to go fuck itself! Or, if you don't have the courage, at least preserve the last crumbs of dignity with silence.

Since Eka seemed to have forgotten our appointment, I climbed upstairs to ring Mrs. N's bell, and found the lights of a silent ambulance blinking out front.

First thought: She didn't realize how little time she had left.

I had it wrong again, though. The lights were flashing for Mrs. N, not Eka. Two EMTs wheeled her out on a gurney; her sons and Eka followed. Holding a tissue to her bloody nose, Mrs. N seemed irritated by all the fuss. She'd blacked out and fallen on the way from the kitchen to the bedroom, Kai or Ahvo explained. They were taking her to the hospital to see why she passed out, and to x-ray her wrist, which had already turned green and purple.

"So much trouble for nothing," the patient said, adjusting her hair curlers.

Was it Eka's fault that her employer had fallen?

"I was in bathroom," she told me. "I told her please you don't move."

The twitching of her cheek said, *I'm sicker than she is*— but I don't think her boss's sons have any idea. Here she is, wrestling with the angel of death, and she has to put their mother's hair in curlers until she drops.

"Angus, come here," Mrs. N said.

Her voice had more scratch in it than usual. When I came close enough for her to poke my wrist, she whispered, "She's too young for you!"

I couldn't tell if she was joking or delirious. Either way, some region of her brain must have bled, numbing her normal reserve.

I tried to fire back a blithe retort, but found the chamber empty. Click!

(Her moles and blotches, her magenta ankle veins, her soft wrinkles—all of it reminded me of how horrifying old people looked to me when I was small. Now that I'm nearly there myself, the signs of age seem more familiar and forgivable. But I assume I look just as hideous to the young as my grandparents looked to me.)

I asked Eka if she would come see me once the ambulance left. She said she had to go to the hospital with Kai and Ahvo, but promised to visit tomorrow.

Cindy from upstairs appeared at the curb, wearing a black satin Mets jacket over pajama pants. Don from next door wandered over, too. When she heard what had happened, Cindy scrunched her brow in sympathetic concern and said, "Ohhhhh," high then low then rising again, as if some local puppy had hurt its paw.

This becomes significant, Bob. Trust me.

One of the twins followed the ambulance with Eka, the other stayed behind to lock up the house. I couldn't tell which one had left and which one stayed; they have no distinguishing marks and they both sport blond mustaches. (Always a mistake.) When speaking to either of them, I float in an odd state of uncertainty.

The bland twin came over to shoot the breeze with his mother's tenants and neighbor. "She may need to go into assisted living at some point soon," he informed us.

Don tsked. "She won't like that."

"You're right. She'd rather stay where she is. But she's fallen twice. I think the time is coming."

I heard the implication. They'll be selling the house, and I'll have to leave. Or—cheering thought!—their plans won't affect me whatsoever, because I'll be gone by then.

Cindy and Garrett, though . . .

"Looks like we'll need to go apartment-hunting," I told her.

"That wouldn't happen for a while," the pudgy Finn said, "not with this housing market. But, eventually, yes."

"You have to do whatever's best for your mom," Cindy told him. "We understand."

Chubby-cheeked, inscrutable, he nodded like a lightly tapped bobblehead, and left.

"Do you know which one that was?" I asked as he waved to us solemnly from behind his windshield.

She waved back until she was waving at his taillights. "I can never tell except by their cars. That's Kai's."

"That's a shame, about having to move," Don said.

"It really is. I hate to disturb Garrett's routine. He's not great with change."

Having little interest in neighborly chitchat, I wished them both a good night. Don ignored my farewell, however.

"If either of you can't find a new place in time, we've got a couple of empty bedrooms. My girls are both gone now. Officially out of the nest."

Cindy, almost tearful in appreciation of his goodness, couldn't find words.

In the grand tradition of shy and honorable cowpokes, Don evaded her gratitude. "I've got to mail out some bills. Good night, Cindy. Good night, Angus."

My thoughts had already moved on—to indignation on Eka's behalf, *They'd dump her without thinking twice, those Finnish fucks*—so Cindy's next words caught me by surprise.

"He is just so . . ."

Don vanished behind his chest-high cube of yew and then reappeared briefly, entering his side door. Cindy hugged herself against the chill; pink bunnies capered on her pajama pants. I'm not the shrewdest observer of other people's secret longings, Brother Bob, but this was on the order of a floodlit billboard, with red letters twice her height: SHE LOVES HIM.

What do I know about Cindy Olekas? A hygienist for a periodontist in Nutley, crowned with finer blond hair than I've seen on any other adult. A non-complainer. The good girl, frozen in childhood innocence, though her son just turned twenty-one. Still beautiful, still sweet as pie, despite the hardest of knocks.

(The range of human attractiveness is remarkably broad. You don't see gorgeous and repulsive horses, or flounders. It can't be just a matter of perspective, *If you were a flounder, you'd see things differently.* I believe this is quantifiable. Measure facial proportions and you can demonstrate that some upper lips are just wide enough to produce the duck-bill effect, while others approach a Platonic ideal. Which raises the question: what is the evolutionary purpose of ugliness? But I digress.)

For all my rudeness, I have never spoken obnoxiously in Cindy's presence. Her beauty and sweetness constrain me. Knowing I'd never have another chance to utter these words, however, I mumbled like a fedora'ed newshound in grainy black-and-white, "You've got it pretty bad, huh, kid?"

The carriage light on Mrs. N's patch of lawn revealed the arrival of the color red on Cindy's cheeks and ears.

"Sorry, didn't mean to embarrass you."

"He's so good with Garrett. He reminds me of my dad."

I'd never given Don much thought before. Now I saw (the straight-up brush of hair emblematic of the Straight-Up Guy) that someone like Cindy would think him everything a man should be. And maybe he is.

"You'd make a good couple."

She let herself live in that impossible dream for a moment, then shook it off. I could have pointed out that people get unmarried all the time—especially when their wives are sour and demanding, and there's a lovely lass next door—but my code of ethics forbids raising unlikely hopes.

Another bolt of insight: his offer of temporary shelter wasn't aimed at me. The feeling may be mutual. If so, she doesn't know it. She wouldn't allow herself to know it.

"I'd better go up and see what Garrett's doing. You wouldn't . . ."

"Say anything about this? Of course not."

With a nervous smile, she zipped her jacket higher and slunk away, around the house, to the back door.

Here's what I think, Bob: the two of them have barely been living. For as long as I've known them, they've plodded along like cart horses, side by side but separated by a sturdy yoke. No frolicking in the meadow for them. No joyous sprints. No copulation.

If I could get them together before I go, that would be as grand an accomplishment as telling Eka's life story. Conjuring bliss from ashes!

Imagine them together. After a long day at their respective jobs, they converge on their happy cottage. (Let's ignore, for now, the eventual disillusionment.) Imagine her angelic, appreciative smile. *My Donny.*

Who'd have guessed that beneath my flab beat the heart of a Jane Austen heroine?

23.

Fearful. Chilled. Running from an invisible demon.

But what *is* the demon? I don't know, Bob. I can't confront it, can't look it in the face.

I'm on the PATH as I type this. Ass vibrating, plastic seat rumbling against my spine. The shuttling sound helps, like a mother rocking her children—in a jerking, lurching cradle. The sickly light makes the other passengers look greenish, cancerous. That's okay, though. I feel almost at home here.

Outside, the cold has sharp teeth, but in here, it's warm and smelly. You could blindfold me, fly me around the world, and set me down in these tubes; I'd know this stale, sooty tunnel odor in an instant.

The train speeds up, then relaxes, speeds up, relaxes again. I find this soothing. It reminds me of me: panicking then calming, despairing then accepting.

The Hudson is a heavy blanket, insulating us from the world above. A peculiar refuge, this, but I'm glad to have found a place where I can bear to sit still.

I interviewed Eka on Mrs. N's couch—first time I'd ever seen the Nieminens' living room. Kai and Ahvo and their sister, Pilvi, watched us from the wall, tow-headed, chubby-cheeked children growing up American despite their names. A blue glass dove sat plumply on the coffee table. The predominant impression was the smell of their meaty dinners, forty years' worth, baked into the paint.

Highlights of the interview:

Eka never learned to swim.

She doesn't remember any more about the river than she already told me. My questions—were there factories on the shore? could you see industrial waste pouring into the water?—brought forth no clear memories.

Thwarted, I moved on to other topics. "Tell me about your parents."

"Mother, age fifty-eight. Father, died in nineteen ninety-six. Very good parents."

"What is your mother like? Does she work?"

"She was accountant. After independence, the factory is privatized and goes bankrupt. They make over to apartments."

She talks to her mother three times a week. And she sends money via the Western Union at Kmart. (MoneyGram costs less, but the shop is too far away to walk.)

I asked for childhood memories of her parents. She remembered her mother dripping something called *mastica* on the floor and polishing it with a cloth. "It smells too much!" Her mother used to clean the windows with vodka and a crumpled sheet of newspaper. "We make our own vodka and wine, is not expensive like here. Windex cost more."

She frowned. Was she, like me, beginning to fear that this will never add up to a book?

"What are you thinking?"

"I miss mother. It's hard, to be here."

I realized something important. She can't see it herself, she has latched on so tightly to her role as provider, but she needs to go home. No matter how desperate her family's finances may be, she shouldn't die here, alone.

I delayed bringing this up, however, until I could find a way that didn't include the words *die alone*.

Since she'd mentioned Georgian independence, and since she couldn't tell me anything about the river, I asked what it was like for her and her family when the Soviet

Union disintegrated. It has nothing to do with her poisoning, but I was curious.

"Terrible, terrible time. Civil war, crime in streets, dangerous to go out. My cousins got robbed—coat, wallets. No food in stores. For one loaf of bread, we stand in line one full night. I bring book to read. Sometimes we have no electricity for three days. I make homework next to kerosene lamp. People is burning wood in apartment for heat, cutting trees. We do everything to survive."

"Go on. Tell me more."

"We drove to grandparents and loaded car with fruits and vegetables from their farm. Apricot, peach, grape. We pickle tomatoes and peppers, green and red."

"You're saying your grandparents in Georgia grew peaches?"

"Yes, is common."

I didn't explain why that amused me. "How did your family feel about the end of Soviet rule?"

"We was never Communist. But to me, life is good under Soviet Union. What we need, we have. But we don't know about everything in the world outside."

The more she talked, the more I doubted I'd be able to stitch a book together from these random anecdotes. She saw my gloom. "Is no good, what I tell?"

I said I needed more detail—how things looked, smelled, tasted. I asked her to tell me what she misses from home. This had nothing to do with the real problem, but I didn't want to shoot an arrow through her heart.

She did her best to satisfy me. "In Georgia we have flower like your violet. This flower have best smell, whole valleys have this good smell. I come here and see violets. I pick one, and find out, in America, violet don't have smell. So beautiful, and no smell! I eat an apple, same thing, no taste. I miss everything what Georgia got, too many delicious foods. Each kind apple got own special smell. And grapes. Everything, even vegetables got own special smell.

Our poets say, 'God gave us best place in the world.' It's different here."

I relished that polite understatement.

She thought of something she couldn't wait to share with me. Her hands flapped on the couch by her thighs. "You know this Jason and Argonauts? The story tells from Georgia! The Golden Fleece was in Colchis, on Black Sea— part of Georgia! Medea is Georgian too. The first woman who made medicines, from grass and wildflowers. *Medicine* is from her name, you can read this. But she fell in love with Jason, and love, for a Georgian woman, means too much."

Unspoken memories carried her off. I let her go and did some musing of my own. She had grown in my estimation. Eka the ox-like home health aide wouldn't have noticed or remembered the smell of violets and the taste of apples, or taken such pride in Medea, her countrywoman. She has a soul! Which makes her dying much, much worse.

She returned to our task before I did, and misread my sudden sorrow. "You can't use in book?" she asked.

I had something else on my mind, I told her. Since I couldn't say what, I went back to the other unspeakable truth. *Shouldn't you go home and be with your family?*

Her worried face stopped me. I think she feared I had changed my mind about helping her.

It was good to be able to reassure her. "I've been think- ing about your situation. Your illness. You're all alone here— wouldn't you be better off at home, with your family taking care of you?"

She nodded, frowning. "My son comes soon to America. He will have chance to make life here. I stay for him."

Wretch though I am, I respected her sacrifice. She'll never see home or her mother again—all so her son can escape poverty.

While I wondered whether her son's destiny would jus- tify her lonely death, she took over the role of questioner. "You make promise to me?"

Uneasily, "Hm?"

"Money from this book, you will give to my son and mother? Some people would keep money, but you I trust. You will give half of money to my family?"

I really hadn't planned to stay alive that long. Maybe, I thought, I can foist the responsibility off on someone else. Maybe you, Brother Bob.

"I'll make sure they get it."

With a probing stare, she assessed my sincerity. What she saw seemed not to satisfy her. "So much I depend on you," she said.

"I'll do my best not to disappoint you."

She has faint pockmarks on her cheeks, little white craters I'd never noticed before. She doesn't wear makeup. Her face is as plain as a nun's: pale skin, short dark eyelashes. And her mouth is small, cinched like the opening of a drawstring purse. I've never seen it open wide.

I'll do my best not to disappoint you. That means I'll have to keep interviewing her until the end, so she can go on believing I'll turn her stories into a best seller that will support her family for generations to come.

I'm too tired for this, Bob.

❋ ❋ ❋

I can't keep my promises. Anyone who deals with me will find out sooner or later that the best bet is to sever ties before I do too much damage.

My intention, as I descended Mrs. N's back steps, was to drink until Eka and her problems faded to a distant echo. Next door, Don Quinones was moving a carton of caulk cartridges from his car to his truck. The white nozzles pointed up like artillery shells, tightly packed in rows. Don called to me, "Hey, Angus, how's your landlady doing?"

I could have said *Dunno* and slipped through my door, but the devil whispered a mischievous idea in my ear.

Don and I conducted some small talk over the hedge. His younger daughter has gone off to Fairleigh Dickinson. What would he like to do, now that he's relatively free? Hike down into the Grand Canyon, he's wanted to do that ever since he was a kid—but it won't happen, because the cartilage in Denise's knees is shot, and besides, she has no interest.

Viewing him through Cindy's eyes, I saw a handsome face, in the rough, weary style of older contractors and firemen. That thick brush of vertical hair really does set him apart. Compared to the average blue-collar fellow, he's sincerely courteous—not to mention soft-spoken, honest, dutiful, patient, kind, and selfless. He's the Boy Scout ideal, grown up: a good man, in the traditional sense, i.e., my opposite. Works hard for his family, spends his free time doing whatever Denise or the girls want. I doubt there's anything she ever asked him to do that he hasn't done, pronto. How many times have I seen him maneuvering a new piece of furniture through their doorway?

You know what I had on my mind. But I didn't know myself whether I would actually speak—not until the words popped out.

"What do you think of Cindy?"

Like a shyer Gary Cooper, he gave the impression of shambling without moving from the spot. "She's a wonderful person. Why do you ask?"

We don't come to such forks in the road often. She had asked me to keep a secret, but I saw no kindness in that. It's years too late for me to find a happy ending, but they still have a chance.

"She's in love with you," I said. The words had a painfully insipid, early Beatles sound, but saying them aloud cleaved time into Before and After, as decisively as the whack of an axe.

You wouldn't have thought I'd said anything unusual. He'd been leaning one hand on his truck, and he didn't move it. The last knuckle of the ring finger was bent—broken, it seemed. Eventually, he said, "Gee." His sober gray eyes searched mine. "Why do you think that?"

"I saw the way she looked at you, and asked some questions. She didn't want me to say anything, but I thought you should know."

Unable to refrain, he peeked up at her window. So did I. The changing blue TV light represented the lighter-than-air spirit of our perky neighbor.

"She's really a special girl," he said. "She doesn't have it easy, but I've never seen her without a smile. I always admired that about her." A pause, while he absorbed the news more deeply. "Wow."

I had the pleasure of imagining them at the altar, all because of me. But he snuffed that candle out.

"I wish you could let her know that I think she's just . . . the best. But there's nothing I can do about it."

Like a crab in a seagull's beak, I'd enjoyed the panorama before being dropped on the rocks.

Denise's head appeared between the drapes in his living room window, searching impatiently. Finding us watching her, she pulled her head back in and straightened the drapes.

"On second thought, you'd better not say anything," Don said. "I'd hate for her to be embarrassed whenever she saw me."

I should have understood that a man like Don would cut off his hand before he'd abandon his miserable wife and run off with the girl of everyone's dreams. The more I think about it, the more my mistake bothers me. I'm losing my acuity. And what else do I have?

Ah, well. Soon I'll leave all of my failing faculties behind.

Halfway down the stairs, I couldn't bear to stay inside. My home spat me out like a watermelon pit.

For a while I drove without a destination. I tried taking only right turns, on a whim, but that kept leading me back to the same abandoned factory. Next I got on the highway, hoping to escape my invisible enemy by outrunning it. By the time I could see Manhattan, I'd lost the race. I had to get out of the car, into a public space—so I parked in Hoboken, sat in the rail terminal, and watched people hurry. I had more in common with the vagrants than with the commuters, i.e., lack of any place to go where someone might want to see me.

Hurtling through the Hudson tube offered some relief. I made it to Thirty-Third Street and almost back to the river again before the heavy-breathing demon found me and chased me off the train.

I've been sitting in the Ninth Street station for a while now, typing this and waiting to be rousted again by my nameless pursuer. The platform is long and mostly deserted. It's pleasantly warm, if malodorous, until a train pulls in (like the one arriving now) and pushes a frigid wind through the tube.

They don't put backs on these benches, so as not to invite bums, but there's a slumping guy (or possibly gal) in a long beige parka one bench down, face hidden in the hood, nodding off.

After a sigh of release from the brakes, the train pulls out again, dragging the cold wind behind it and leaving us to shiver.

Typing this has helped, Brother Bob. Not that I've solved any problems, but at least I managed to sit still.

22.

Searching for *Reasons not to kill myself,* I found a swarm of unctuous lifesavers spewing earnest, cloddish words.

Think of those you'll be hurting forever.

No need to hesitate on that score. My mother will shake her head and go back to her card game, my father will sneer and revise his low opinion of me downward. And the siblings? Let's be honest: the sadness will soon pass.

It's not as bad as it feels right now. It will get better.

O clairvoyant one, who sees everyone's future as if reading a map: your optimism is spread too thin to be convincing.

Medication can cure your depression.

Happy pills? Sorry, not for me. Treat the disease, not the symptom.

You have a purpose. You were put here for a reason. Don't waste your life!

I like this one. It's inspiring, in a make-believe sort of way. But it raises two questions. Who put me here, and what's my purpose?

You might botch it and end up as a vegetable.

Thanks for the tip. I'd better make sure I know what I'm doing.

You may meet someone who will change your life. Or, someone may need help that no one but you can give.

Sweet. I can imagine Cindy typing these words, alone in her bedroom at midnight, throbbing with compassion, offering hope to the hopeless. But the sentiment doesn't fit me. (No, Eka can't save me. Even if she could, it wouldn't be for long.)

I did manage to come up with one argument of my own. It's only temporary, but here it is: Finish the book. Overcome the obstacles, and produce something you're proud of, while providing for her family. Seize your last chance to play the hero.

A rotten plank bridging a chasm. I wonder how long it will support my weight.

Imbecile!

I've fallen into the world's oldest trap. Now what?

Like a bear with an arrow shallowly penetrating his hide, I examine the alien barb, curious and uncomprehending.

Some people only fall in love with those they can't have. Whether the object of desire is married or homosexual, they can only give their hearts when there's no danger of actually winning the prize. Well, I've got them all beat—except, I suppose, the detective who falls in love with the girl whose murder he's investigating.

I've got to shake this off. See clearly, man! Don't make yourself hopelessly ridiculous.

Kai and Ahvo gave Eka the day off. Today is their mother's last day in the hospital; they'll take turns at her bedside.

Eka buzzed after lunch and made a bizarre request. Could I take her for a walk in the woods? I stared at her blankly—she arrived just moments after I'd searched for a reason not to kill myself—and she explained that she wanted to see a forest again before she's too sick to walk.

I hadn't set foot on a wooded trail since the family visited Acadia a century or so ago. Locating the largest patch of green on my Essex County map, I drove her to a muddy reservation where we tromped among the bare trees, up more hills than I ever want to see again. How ironic it would be, I thought, if my heart failed: if her dying wish killed me. (As it turns out, my heart can withstand more stress than I thought. My knees and ankles, though . . . but let's not moan and groan.)

She stopped to listen to a swirling brook and said, "To me this sound is the most peaceful one"; I noted the PVC pipe pouring what I hope was water into the stream. She pointed out how the low afternoon sun turned the tree trunks yellow; I worried that one of the thorny, dangling vines would cut me across the cornea. A deer sprang up a hill, showing us a white rump. "So beautiful," Eka said. *So what*, I replied inwardly.

My back sweated under my jacket. She pointed out little nests in the twiggy trees. After ten minutes that felt like ten hours, she stopped us on a path of rust-colored pine needles, and said with satisfaction, "You hear? No cars. No planes."

I heard myself panting.

"Here I can imagine we are the first people in world, before all others."

I had to fart. The need was growing more and more insistent, a product of the falafel I'd eaten for lunch. I suppressed it resolutely.

"I wish there is snow," she said. "Too pretty it would be."

Those were the last words she spoke for a while—which I appreciated, having tired of her Druid ecstasy. Then I realized she was silently crying, because (I thought) she would never see snow in the woods again.

Having spent so many hours submerged in other people's woes, I've learned not to let their unhappiness in, not a whit, not a jot. I like Eka more than past profilees, but while she softly wept, I simply waited for her to be done.

She said she needed to rest, and found us a fallen trunk with not too many fungi sprouting from it. Sitting, we looked down on a hillside of tan grass; in the medium distance, bare branches clutched at the eye-level sun. I took the tape recorder from my pocket and asked her to tell me more about growing up.

She said that, during the years when the country was in chaos, just after independence, they lived for a while with her grandparents, the ones who grew peaches. "Beautiful gardens and vegetables they got. We helped to plant little tomato plants, and raise chickens and turkeys, and milk the cow. The village kids laugh at us, 'City girl, you don't know to milk a cow.' When comes time for pick strawberries and tomatoes, the work is hard, so I hide."

She seemed to enjoy telling these tales. I'm guessing she hasn't had anyone to talk to in years—not this way, sharing memories. I encouraged her with questions (though I doubt I'll be able to use much of this), and she told how her grandmother used to bake fresh shoti bread in a clay oven, but she, Eka, complained because she missed the factory bread from home. She told how they went to a neighbor's house to watch the first TV shows from America, and everyone went quiet because the house on *Dynasty* was "beautiful like dream," and the cars were so "big and shiny new," and from then on, she yearned to live in the United States.

Immersed in her beloved past, she forgot the terrible present. I, on the other hand, saw her jaw twitching, and couldn't forget.

"Look at the little clouds," she said, and made one with a puff. "When I was young girl, I pretend I am train." And she puffed a series of clouds above her head.

The pathos was up to my neck and rising. I held my breath so as not to drown in it.

"You always were writing for newspapers?" she asked.

To escape her tragedy, I recounted my own. You don't know this story, Brother Bob. No one does, except the editor who fired me, and now Eka. Actually, I'd like you to hear it. This way, if you think of me, you'll know me better than you ever have.

Soon after the *Dispatch* hired me, I landed the shameful duty of profiling our state's titans: the governor, the CEO of Prudential, the owner of the Devils, even Frankie Valli, born in my very own town of Belleville. (Eka didn't know his name, but she recognized the falsetto chorus of "Walk Like a Man.") "I think your job is excited," she said. "To write on big people."

Was it excited, to write on big people? No, Roberto, it galled me. I refused to believe that these muck-a-mucks and panjandrums were better than I, no matter what they'd accomplished. I spoke to them tersely, sometimes insolently. They must all be dead by now: the shrunken lawyer Benjamin Whiteman, whose loose false teeth clacked as he recounted the biggest real-estate deals of his career; retired CEO Jack Hundzinger, ticking off the names of the pro teams he owned; Luis German Luna, former general from Argentina, shuffling around his kitchen in slippers, refusing to speak of the Dirty War and instead boasting about his gardens back home. "We had melons like this," he told me, holding his hands a foot apart, and I couldn't resist playing with the presumed murderer. "What?" I asked. "Invisible?" (He was either too deaf or too oblivious to notice the mockery. Unless he did, and only pretended not to hear.)

Old age: it turns powerful men into shriveled fools, and beautiful women into hags. We're better off without it, Eka.

She asked why I had stopped writing about *important peoples*. I told how, sick of fawning over bigwigs, I'd begged for the chance to report on something that mattered, and was assigned to follow up on a whistleblower's phone call. Frank Dowdy, a retired operating engineer at LC Electric's coal-fired power plant near Weehawken, swore to me that, by failing to install required pollution controls and then falsifying records, the company had released 60,000 tons of air pollutants beyond legal limits over the previous decade, resulting in thousands of preventable cases of asthma and heart disease. "Smog, soot and acid rain—that's the cost of cutting corners," he told me in his immaculate kitchen. The company's threatening denial only stoked my lust for corporate blood. My editor demanded that I verify the story with at least one other source, and Dowdy put me in touch with a very nervous shift supervisor, two years from retirement, who gave me a matching story, off the record. The paper ran the story on page four—a huge disappointment—hoping a jury might take this into account if LC sued.

To my astonished horror, Dowdy had his numbers wrong. LC's legal department produced twenty-two binders of documentation showing that the plant had complied with every EPA regulation, statute, and order. They agreed not to sue, however, if the paper printed a retraction on page one and fired me.

Just so you don't think I'm a simpleton, Bob: I did try to confirm the LC story on my own, by reading Dowdy's print-outs for myself. But the first page so overwhelmed me that I decided to trust him and hope for the best.

I didn't expect Eka to follow these twists and turns, but she understood enough to reach the logical conclusion. "This man lies to you? The factory didn't broke laws?"

As a matter of fact, I explained, they were the worst polluter in the state. The Justice Department sued them a few years later; they had to spend eighty million dollars on new pollution controls. They'd meticulously falsified their spreadsheets—but the original data was still there in the recorders. Someone had neglected to erase it, and investigators found that Dowdy's numbers had been accurate.

I didn't tell Eka the next part, how Dr. Gerard Jones rescued me from disgrace (and a deadly job proofreading economics textbooks) by recommending me for the column at the *Register*. I suppose he thought a stint as Mr. Misery might redeem me.

Eka's take on my tale of woe recast me as a hero. "You try to do important thing. Maybe the government readed your article and so they make investigation."

In all these years, I'd never thought of that. Can't say I believe it, really, but the possibility consoles.

As we sat on our log in the fading light, white grains floated down around us. They weighed so little that, like scant bits of ash from a crematorium, they lurched this way and that, knocked off course by mere air. Eka, happy as a bird in flight, cried out, "*Tovs!*" and studied the specks on her black coat sleeve.

"Excuse me?"

"It snows! How we say in Georgian—*Tovs*."

She sighed: that's how fast melancholy overtakes her. Not wanting to hear her weep over the snows of yesteryear, I preempted her. "They say every snowflake is six-pointed but unique. I don't believe it. They're not even six-pointed, usually. They're just little clots of ice."

She raised her forearm toward me. "Look."

A tiny, tilted star lay on the black polyester sleeve, perfect as if machine-made, with six feathery points. Another landed soon after, with a leafy finial at each tip.

The obvious moral: if I was wrong about this, I may also be wrong about everything else. Perhaps all is for the best, and people are basically good.

(Clap if you believe it! Or else Eka and I will die! But we'll die no matter what you believe, so don't bother.)

The sun was nearly gone. Fear entered my heart. There are no wolves in Essex County, as far as I know, but I really didn't want to be there in the dark, stumbling along a trail I couldn't see.

I suggested we head back to the car. We come now to the crux. I'll re-create it as best I can, one startling step at a time.

• We stood to go. She bumped against me. I assumed she'd lost her balance.

• She gripped my wrist, as best she could through the coat sleeve.

• My insides turned to stone. The biggest dolt in the Garden State, I'd missed what anyone else would have seen: a walk in the woods, intimate revelations, teaching me to say, *It's snowing* in her language. *A dying woman clutches at the only man within reach, begging to be held, comforted, loved, saved. What do I do now?*

• "I feel bad," she said.

• A film of sweat covered her face. Not infatuated, just ill: false alarm. Whew!

• "Do you need to sit down again?" "I'm sorry, yes, please."

• She sat back down on the log. I sat beside her.

• A pawn of my deranged id, I put my arm around her. It happened swiftly, without my willing participation. I honestly can't say whether the gesture was fatherly or something else.

• She huddled, somber and cold, and gave no sign that my arm was welcome.

• Horrified to find myself thus situated, I removed my arm.

• She cried again, as discreetly as before.

• I wondered whether her grief had to do, in part, with me and my arm.

A white moon followed us down the mountain. Saying she felt weak, she held my elbow, which I took as her way of telling me that she didn't hold my impetuous gesture against me. The kindness of that seemed to me almost saintly.

My shoes slid in mud hidden by fallen leaves, but we didn't go sprawling, thank the Lord.

The need to fart returned with double the force. This outweighed all other concerns.

On the way home, she requested a rest stop. We found a Dunkin' Donuts in South Orange, and used both bathrooms at once (could she hear my fanfare through the wall?), then snacked on donuts, cinnamon for her, Boston Kreme for me.

An unusually happy Indian family ran the shop. All four of them served us—petite mother with long hair and glasses, cute teen daughter with identical features (minus thirty years), impish son, confident father—all in their neat blue uniform shirts and tan baseball caps, all as hospitable as if we were eagerly awaited VIP visitors.

"Did you see the snow?" the mother asked as I paid.

"Yes," Eka said, "it was so pretty in forest."

It seemed I'd wandered into the UN commissary.

Their close-to-bursting enthusiasm made me wonder at the cause. Had the son (beginning a mustache, just like dad's) just gotten accepted at an elite university? Was this their first day owning the franchise? I didn't ask, because one owes strangers their privacy, but I almost wish I'd broken the rules.

The bright sanctuary defied the darkness on the other side of the glass. For as long as we sat in that magical shop, we were contented and unself-conscious. True, I could barely fit my thighs under the table, but the generous heat and light, the other contented customers, and our industrious, welcoming hosts—all of this created a compact paradise, a world I much prefer to my own.

What did we talk about? Nothing transcendent. She asked if Dunkin' Donuts is good business to own. I don't know the average annual net for these stores, but I reported the traditional lore, "Yes, they do very well, but the hours are long."

I craved a second donut, but didn't want her to think, He can't control himself. For resolve, I pretended that forgoing donut #2 would save her life; but in reality it wouldn't, and in the end, I was unwilling to go without, even for the sake of her good opinion. As the grammarian said in a moment of frank self-appraisal, Whom am I kidding?

Somewhere in the middle of that lemon-filled donut, I noticed her. She had on a gold satin blouse—she may send money overseas, but she loves clothes—and a necklace of what looked like obsidian pebbles. Although she never wears makeup, although she still bore a sheen of sweat, and although I could see her cheek quivering ominously, I found her lovely. What's more, I *liked* her, and enjoyed explaining to her the American immigrant tradition of employing newly arrived relatives in donut shops, convenience stores, and produce markets, where they work grueling hours for low pay, but earn the chance for their children to get an education and make a successful career. She nodded attentively . . . and then I remembered who I was talking to. "But you know more about this than I do," I said.

"No, I don't know. I like it this, the family all helping each new one."

Like an elephant on a crumbling precipice, I fell hard. Though I understood that I was romanticizing the dying woman, I couldn't make myself un-romanticize her. Was it possible that, despite my gross tonnage, she was feeling something similar? Think about it: six years of lonely work, far from home. Who wouldn't latch on to a kindly member of the opposite sex? It's likely that she's grateful for my help. Maybe she even respects me.

Like a sport on a date, I had the urge to spend money, so I took a plump bag of hazelnut coffee from the neatly stocked shelf below the counter. "I hope you enjoy it," the mother said, smiling warmly, as if she'd seen the change in me and heartily approved.

We're quite a pair, aren't we? She's going to die and doesn't want to. I want to die, but must wait.

Snow is falling, yet my inner crocuses have rashly spread their petals. Bad timing, to say the least.

Out in the parking lot behind the shop, the Shitmobile refused to start. The engine cranked slowly but wouldn't turn over. I cursed—I'd have to call a tow truck and pay the fee, since I never got around to joining the AAA—but then I remembered that I won't need money where I'm headed, so who cares?

This consoling thought brought the engine back to life. A double joy: not only didn't we have to wait for a tow, but

I had dodged a lightning bolt from my persecutors above. The victory may have been temporary, but I savored it.

I can't give Eka much—only, perhaps, immortality.

Here's what I've been thinking:

Anne Frank in her attic hiding place, Solzhenitsyn in Siberia, Dith Pran in the Killing Fields—these are the monuments, the names that stand for millions of victims. Eka, on the other hand, remains anonymous, a small face among the hordes who crossed an ocean seeking a better life—a copper penny, indistinguishable from all the rest. That is, unless I can turn her, too, into a monument.

Sleep won't come. This unwise tenderness has snaked its way between my ribs and encircled my heart. She's dying, yet I'm nursing a crush—on the same woman whose voice used to remind me of a blue jay. It's not possible.

I'll get over it tomorrow. For tonight, though, the torment is sweet.

21.

I dreamed that my belly came off. No gore, it just detached itself, a flat-bottomed dome. I turned away from it deceitfully, as if I'd just happened upon this odd thing on the sidewalk, which had nothing to do with me. There was some guilt over treacherously abandoning my own belly, but the prevailing mood was liberation.

Imagine—free of the gut!

But there would still be the rest of me to lug around.

My suicide has been pushed aside, displaced by clutter—even, for minutes at a time, forgotten. One might doubt the seriousness of the intention. You assume I'll chicken out at the last minute, don't you, Brother Bob? Or, no, if this has reached your hands, you know how the story ends. Which I don't.

I find that galling: you know more about the end of my life than I do.

Ah, well, it can't be helped.

Lona chose not to reply. She diplomatically ignored the raving madman from the land of yesterday. And I hate her for it. All those years of adulation—for what? So she could dismiss me as a sad loser and delete me from her Inbox?

Compare her with Eka. The delicate Swedish psychotherapist vs. the husky, pragmatic home health aide from Georgia. Oh, what a falling off was there!

But then, I've fallen off, too. Plummeted, actually.

Face facts: romance doesn't suit me. Pitiful and repugnant is the man who doesn't know his place. I was never meant to play the lead, nor the tragic hero—I'm just a bloated, gabby fool. The best I can hope for is some prince handling my skull one day with an *Alas*, contemplating his own mortality while remembering me as an amusing clown.

It's Eka's officially scheduled day off—she gets one every two weeks. (Yesterday was a once-in-a-lifetime bonus.) She has a friend, it turns out, a young Georgian woman who's studying industrial engineering at Seton Hall. They drove away for the day, to a big mall somewhere north of here. Conveniently, Mrs. N won't come home from the hospital until late afternoon, so Eka didn't have to find a sub and train her.

I should be transcribing her tapes. The sooner I finish, the sooner I can—

❉   ❉   ❉

1:18 A.M. Can't sleep. You, Brother Bob, have complicated everything. You've thrown a colossal wrench into my plans. I had weighty things on my mind, matters of life and death. You have no idea how fervently I wish you hadn't shown up here.

Stop turning around! Every time the couch springs squeak, it's like a sharp fingernail scraping my eye. You used to do the same thing when we were kids—rolled around all night on the other side of the room, never settled down. It drove me crazy then, and it's worse now. Each metallic whine reminds me of our miserable adolescence.

You've lost weight since last time. Two years of eating nothing but miso soup and radishes will do that, I guess. You remind me of those famine photos from our youth: Brother Bob from Bangladesh, by way of Biafra. Your eyes are set in mournful, cavernous sockets. And let me tell you, the shaved head doesn't suit you. Your skull is far too lumpy, your scalp too pasty. I liked the ponytail better—and, as you may remember, I despised it.

When you were locked up in your Zen monastery, I felt abstractly fond of you. Now you've gone and wrecked that.

How does one get thrown out of a monastery, anyway? Isn't that like getting fired from the post office?

I don't like seeing you old, little brother. The rumpled skin, the pouches under your eyes, the protuberant knuckles—arthritis, Bobby? As a teenager, your gangly, clumsy innocence appealed to certain maternal types, who mistook you for a poet. Now you just look lost, possibly deranged.

You held on to your idealism long past its expiration date. You never learned from experience: once burned, twice burned. It's not admirable, just willful.

Here's the key to our conflict: according to my belief system, yours is a joke. You're closer to me than anyone on Earth, yet each time you open your mouth, I want to tape it shut.

(I apologize, though, for handling your bruised spirit so roughly. You came to me in tatters, and I went at you with a razor. Sorry about that.)

Now that you've tumbled from your Himalayan heights and landed on my lumpy couch, to whom shall I address these reflections?

Let's say *to you*. Maybe I can drill some sense into your skull posthumously, even if I couldn't in person.

Do you remember this day, or have you blotted it out? Let me re-create:

You came Bob-Bob-Bobbing along with all your worldly goods stuffed in a bulging red backpack that has seen cleaner days. You'd been traveling by bus all day, from the mountains of upstate New York to the Port Authority terminal, and thence to my little village in the lowlands. At the door, you looked like hell, despite the hopeful, pleading smile. (Your teeth have reverted to their pre-braces configuration, I see. Ah, the vain striving that is orthodontia!)

I'm sorry that my first words to you ("What the fuck are you doing here?") were less than welcoming. Chalk it up to shock, and an instinctive fear that your needs will hijack the last weeks of my life.

You explained that Roshi had sent you out into the world because he felt that you lack a true monastic vocation; that you couldn't let go of your worldly enthusiasms and your endless questions; that you never wholeheartedly accepted the monk's life; that you had too much nervous energy to be still. You said you saw the truth in his assessment, but leaving made you cry.

I didn't ask for this detailed explanation, certainly not in the first five minutes. You still talk too much.

A small groan escaped as you set down your backpack, making it impossible to turn you away. As soon as we were downstairs, though, I wished I'd sent you off to a YMCA with a wad of cash. Did you think I failed to notice the grief in your face as you surveyed my dark, disorderly digs?

Stretching your back ostentatiously, you went on with the story. Roshi advised you to return to the world and pursue your interests, while continuing to apply the insights you learned at the temple.

A few questions yielded a significant Aha. Recently, you asked to be accepted as a postulant, i.e., a nonpaying guest, rather than a lay resident, and that was when Roshi perceived that you lacked the true soul of a monk. Too bad he didn't see it two years sooner, before you spent all your savings on room and board.

How strange your body seemed to me. The curly hairs at the small of your knobby back, and the colorless skin there, might have belonged to a wax figure at Madame Tussauds. I never see any flesh but my own that close up.

As you'll remember, I asked if you might be more comfortable at Greer's, since she has more rooms than she knows what to do with. Diplomatically omitting the fact that you loathe her husband, you said, "Her houses are so alien to me."

Does that mean you feel at home here, sleeping on a couch that's too short to hold you, sharing a dungeon with your old tormentor?

I know, I know: you were always willing to give me another chance, always hopeful for brotherly affection, despite my repeated abuses. Even when we played kidnapper and hostage, and I tied you to a chair with an extension cord and gagged you with Greer's undershirt and shut you in the dark basement while Greer and I watched *The Dating Game* upstairs, you still wanted to shoot cap guns with me the next day.

And now you're back for more.

Still can't sleep. Goddamn.

I don't want to be imprisoned in my bedroom all night. I can't even go to the kitchen for a snack, for fear you'll wake, find me at the refrigerator, and think compassionate thoughts. This is unbearable.

Hear me in your dreams: *Away—away—give your brother back his home.*

You couldn't eat any of my food, so out we went, to the supermarket, where I told you to choose any Zen delicacies you wanted—pickled buttercups, whatever. You filled the cart with enough oatmeal, bananas, ramen noodles, and peanut butter to feed a banquet hall of self-deniers. And let's not forget the aptly named yucca, which resembled a long, filthy turd.

As we made our way through the aisles, you let slip your ulterior motive for invading my home. At first, you simply said you were hoping we could spend some time together, and repair our relationship. When I failed to praise you for taking the initiative, you added, "I also had a sense that you needed help."

"Based on . . . ?"

"So much time has gone by, and you never wrote or called. I perceived unhappiness in that."

Hmph! Came to heal your poor depressed brother, did you? Physician, go fuck thyself! You came because your revered Roshi kicked you out and you couldn't face Craig Pookalani's mockery. Can't you see that you're worse off than I am? Your life has come crashing down around your ankles like beltless pants on a POW, yet you think *I* need help?

(I checked out your temple's website just now, by the way, and was disappointed to find that your fearless leader isn't even Japanese. Are you sure you were studying real Zen, and not some fraudulent knockoff?)

Pushing the cart up and down the immigrant-crowded aisles, disputing as we passed the frozen bacalao, the cans of Pulpo al Ajillo, the tall candles with images of Santa Barbara and San José, the Inca Kola and Yerba Mate—it was more comical than dramatic, really. But I'll give you this much: you impressed me when you spoke Portuguese to the scoliotic woman searching for sardines. Still, the happiness you took from that brief encounter proved that Roshi was right. You're too enthralled by this world to happily remove yourself from it. That's one more difference between us.

When I mocked your diet—"It's a miracle you haven't shrunk to the size of a praying mantis"—you defended the ascetic life. "It's not about abnegation for its own sake. There's a purpose. If you can remove yourself from distractions, you can turn inward and see yourself clearly."

"Sounds narcissistic and masochistic at the same time."

You winced, for the first of many times.

We sparred a bit on the subject of your esteemed teacher, Mr. Clean. When I pointed out that he'd given you the boot as soon as you raised the idea of not paying, you said, "To respect and admire and even love a man who has understood so much, so deeply—if you could learn to do that, Angus, instead of shooting arrows at everything that looks bigger than you, you might be happier."

How gently and kindly you harpoon your prey. Actually, your voice is your best feature. You speak like a bow drawn slowly across the deepest string of a double bass. You should have gone into radio—hawking herbal supplements between études for string quartet.

"I'm glad you want to heal my wounds," I said. "If you'd come with a grudge, I'd be disemboweled by now."

That served as your cue to launch an all-out attack. According to you, the many ways in which my life is wrong include:

1) I don't believe in my work. 2) My talk is clever noise that only distracts me from what matters—glib cynicism is poisoning my life. 3) I find fault with everyone around me, a habit learned from our father, but one that I should have unlearned, as you have. 4) I desperately need to feel superior to others, yet I'm keenly aware of my own inadequacies: an excruciating paradox. 5) I give so little of myself to others. Where are my friends, my lovers? Nonexistent, because of this eternal *withholding*. 6) I've put on weight steadily since I turned forty, a clear symptom of depression since there's no obesity in our family. 7) I'm all Pose. Why not take a deep breath and give up the outrageous comments, the endless play-acting at negativity? 8) I refuse to let go of my irrational, unprovoked anger toward my only brother.

"I doubt anyone has told you these things before," you said, summing up. "I hope you can hear the message and not bat it away without considering any of it."

To all of which I say . . .

All right. Your critique may be accurate in places, I'll grant you that—even as I suppress the urge to bash your skull with a beer bottle while you sleep—but will *you* admit the truth about yourself? That your openness and sincerity are as much a pose as my audacity? That you flit from one interest to another, making each your way of life until you exhaust its novelty and find yourself back where you started, in a panic because you have no ground to stand on? (Examples: animal tracking, veganism, gum arabic printmaking, campaigning for the installation of composting toilets at campgrounds. Then there were the months when you played the *charango* with an Andean band from Hoboken. And those are just the fads I know about.) You'll pardon me if I take your current hobby with a pound of salt.

You went on (and on, and on). I don't care to transcribe any more of it—except the part about daydreaming. "How much of each day do you spend thinking about the things you wish were different? Did you ever notice how much of your life you've wasted that way? There's a simple cure: just let go of dissatisfaction and start enjoying the world as it is."

My response may have been excessive, but I couldn't believe a brother of mine would spout such bunk. "I'll tell you why I don't feel the need to take your opinions seriously. You're a belief junkie: you have this hunger for an organizing principle, this tendency to absorb any nearby system and make it your own. Remember your girlfriend in college—Elaine? Eileen? The devout Marxist? Remember how you decided to familiarize yourself with the theory, and by the time you finished slogging through three books of explication, you were converted? Five years from now, you may be a jihadi with explosives in your underwear. Or a neoconservative. You're the sucker who's born again every minute."

You tried to respond, but I wasn't through.

"You're pleased with your analysis of my faults. But *any* system will explain me just as well. Let's try Christianity: 'You'll never be truly happy until you accept Jesus as your personal savior and acknowledge that you're a miserable gob of spit without Him.' Or Freudianism: 'You never confronted your wish to sleep with your mother and kill your father. Inevitably, you're warped.' Or radical feminism: 'You have a penis—'nuff said.' So you see, your worldview is just one among many."

By then, we'd reached the checkout. You thought you might get a word in. Wrong! Taking a horoscope booklet in hand, I played the professor. "Let's see what the stars have to say. Cancer: 'Go ahead and share your insight with someone close to you. You'll be helping more than you know.' So true! Leo: 'By year's end, you will finally finish a personal project that means a lot to you.' True for me, I hope. Taurus: 'Romance important right now.' Well, two out of three ain't bad."

Maybe it's because I'm aching with the need to sleep, but, after all these rebuttals, I'm ready to concede most of your points. What you see as a disease, though, I accept as my character. I know you'd love to cure me of being me, but I feel otherwise.

Loading the groceries in the trunk, I thought I saw tears in your eyes. I've been wondering ever since: did my taunts wound you that badly? Did it hurt that your only brother can't stand you? Or were you thinking about your own life, in shambles again, and frightened of having to live in this world of supermarkets and assholes?

If you really were crying, I give you credit. At least you're facing reality.

Under interrogation, you confessed that you had missed certain things while at the temple, among them pepperoni pizza, bicycling, and playing music. I thought the least I could do was to reintroduce you to worldly pleasures. Back at the apartment, we ordered a pizza and went hunting on eBay for an instrument—but you wouldn't let me spend $149 on a *charango* (you'll have to run over an armadillo and make your own), and the pizza caused you severe gastric upheaval, as you no doubt remember.

Speaking of upheaval, I can't imagine a starker difference than the pizza we shared versus rice and vegetables eaten in silence amid shaved heads. My bowels would be in turmoil, too, if I were you.

As a way of life, your asceticism is as foreign to me as a spider's. Here's how I understand it: you renounce things, especially things that give you pleasure, not simply to escape distraction, but to cultivate purity, which you believe will open the door to enlightenment. But renunciation means turning your back on the world's infinite variety—which is really all we have. It looks to me like hiding—chickening out—in the guise of a spiritual quest. Simply put, it's a mistake. What's wrong with enjoying a hot dog? Or a wild night with a big-hearted gal?

As you recovered on the couch from a rough bout in the john, you quietly, belatedly, answered my assault. "It's true, what you said in the supermarket. I've gone from one interest to another. My enthusiasms don't last. You're right: I keep searching for a way to live that will satisfy me. You think I'm wrong to search, because there's nothing to find. But I disagree. I've found fulfillment and insight along the way. What I haven't found is permanent contentment. But I don't think that exists."

The words sounded calm and reasonable, but that's deceptive. Gray-faced and stubbly, you seemed on the verge of coming apart. If there's such a thing as a life force, yours was down to a drip. I couldn't keep arguing with you; I'd already slaughtered you.

Which wasn't my goal. Honestly—I just wanted to shake the baloney out of you and force you to face facts. I didn't mean to crush you, bro.

While I considered apologizing (seriously!), you took from your shirt pocket a small notebook with a soft leather cover, and wrote some lines in it with a red pencil the size of a lollipop stick.

You're a peculiar fellow, Bob. Did anyone ever tell you that?

It seems that I must now serve as your keeper. I'll have to coax you not to give up, because life is good and you never know, you may meet someone who'll change everything.

"You'll feel better after you sleep," I said, without believing it. "And no more pepperoni—what were you thinking?"

Off you went, into your personal museum of regrets, visiting the dismal dioramas without me.

If you leave me your corpse to dispose of, I'll never forgive you.

(My own planned suicide is an entirely different matter. I would never passive-aggressively leave my remains to be found by someone with cause to blame himself. But I have no confidence that you, the gentle, spiritual one, would take a moment to consider the impact of your suicide on me.)

I'd better hide the knives.

A philosophical question: If it would be wrong for you to kill yourself, why isn't it wrong for me?

Elementary, my dear Robert. Your problem is temporary, mine is permanent. Insufferable as I find you, others have felt differently. You've got a decent chance of meeting a mate and spending the next thirty years in relative contentment. You've been happy before, and will be again. Ending your life would be a mistake; ending mine would not.

You said something earlier: that, if I could let go of my anger toward you, I might find a heavy weight lifted from my spirit.

Let's experiment.

I have no good reason to hate my brother. He's irritating but means well. He came all this way to help me, sort of. (Does he really think he's on more solid ground than I am? The self-deluding jackass!) In his way, he cares. But that makes me a shit for not reciprocating. What tyranny! Remember, though: before he showed up at my door, I considered him my closest connection on Earth.

The strands are tightly tangled. I doubt I'll ever undo these knots.

20.

I've spewed far too many words, pointlessly. Be briefer.

I'll address this to myself from now on.

Spending every waking moment with anyone is difficult. With my brother, it's unendurable.

I found him this morning facing the wall in the ladder-back chair, where no rump has rested for twenty years. Back straight, knees almost touching the plaster, he looked like he'd been put there by a teacher as punishment. The bowed head suggested shame, not meditation. Come on, I thought. Must you self-flagellate at this early hour?

Rarely have I looked forward less to the day ahead.

He needed clothes, and I needed not to be alone with him. We drove to Kmart. Inside the entrance, he wanly surveyed the landscape. Nearby shelves teemed with polar bears and other stuffed cuddlies. Only three other shoppers drifted about. Generic rock music from three decades back served as easy listening.

The vast and soulless space seemed to overwhelm him, but I refused to indulge his hypersensitivity. Leading him forward, I found him a pair of dark green cargo pants, cheap Wrangler work boots, and white socks. I couldn't talk him into the rayon shirt with palm trees against a turquoise sky. Just a thought: change the surface, change the weather within.

Three Memories of Bob

#1: He used to be pudgy, eager to please, Mom's favorite, a mediocre student who played every kind of ball with his friends. I—taller and leaner—disdained his jiggling white belly. So did our father.

#2: I helped him with his math homework a couple times when he was in seventh grade. Mixture problems— *how much water must you add in order to yield a 15 percent solution*? The procedure was straightforward, not that hard, but he couldn't get it. "Are you an imbecile?" I finally exploded. He cried.

#3: He found me cutting a worm in two with a dull penknife, on the pebbly concrete of our front path. He looked stricken, as if he'd just discovered that his hero was really a depraved monster. "It doesn't hurt them," I explained, scoffing at his ignorance. "Each half turns into a new worm." He wanted to believe, but couldn't, not while the little creature wriggled and writhed in bloody agony. And what did I do then? The only thing I could: finished the job and dropped one of the halves onto his sneaker.

We tiptoed around each other all day. There's no one he'd like to see from his former life, he said. The idea of going back to any of his past jobs (county park ranger, art museum guard, macrobiotic chef) makes him shrink visibly, and he has no new ambitions.

I had to tell Eka that we wouldn't be able to talk tonight. Afraid to leave him alone, I took him upstairs with me. A golden Christmas tree stood on Mrs. Nieminen's kitchen counter, twelve inches tall, alongside a pastry that looked like a trilobite and a ceramic trivet featuring Santa in an embroidered Finnish vest. Mrs. N wore a quilted robe and had her arm in a canvas sling. She was brushing her hair with her good hand, using an old silver brush; the yellowed bristles matched her teeth.

"You look like each other," she told Bob and me. "I see it in your eyes."

Neither of us could produce a convincing smile.

Eka shook Bob's hand sweetly and said, "I am happy we meet." Then her head turned sharply to the side, as if she were saying a curt No: the worst tremor I've seen so far.

"Angus," Mrs. N said, "you should lose weight. You're letting yourself go."

Unable to come up with a suitable retort—you can't strike back at an old woman whose brain has melted—I shrugged oafishly.

Upstairs, Garrett whined that he wanted to learn how to drive. Cindy asked him to please lower his voice. He repeated the same words, more loudly. She said something about managing his outbursts. He screamed, "*NO!*"

So much woe in one house. If a jet from Newark crashed through the roof and erased all our lives at once, it would be a mercy.

Back downstairs, Bob asked if Eka had Parkinson's. When I explained her condition, he went still as a rock. I believe I saw tears. That annoyed me—*you never even met her before!*—but now I see it differently. I'm glad the story hit him hard. Maybe her problem will put his in perspective.

I took a break just now from transcribing one of Eka's interviews, and went to the kitchen doorway. There was Bob sitting upright on my couch, with my old *Bartlett's Familiar Quotations* open on his lap. Unable to detect any signs of life, I said, "Hey."

He mumbled, "Hm?"

I keep seeing Eka's head twitching to the side. Who'll be with her at the end? Her cousin from Brooklyn, I suppose. Her friend, the student. And me.

I can't imagine that day, not really.

If it were a simple matter of needing a new heart, I would crash the car and give her mine. But nothing is that simple.

Bob offered to make tea for us just now. I reminded him that I hate tea, and only drink it when I'm sick. He went back to the couch, back to *Bartlett's*.

I should have let him make the tea, I know. He just brings out the jerk in me. (I know what you're thinking. Thanks a lot.)

Distractions, distractions.

You tie a noose for yourself, but before you can put your head in the loop, a circus passes through your apartment— tigers, elephants, clowns in a Volkswagen. A high school marching band comes to rehearse in the living room. An ambulance driver knocks and asks for directions.

Where was I?

19.

Every day, my situation changes entirely. It's really starting to annoy me.

Eka's son has arrived. At the moment when she buzzed, Bob and I were brainstorming. Who would hire him? The want ads were useless. A search for *alternative careers* led to the EPA and the National Park Service. *Unusual jobs* gave us glass sculptor, drawbridge tender, and artificial inseminator of zoo animals.

We were getting nowhere, in other words, when Eka came to say that Davit had gotten his visa and would be landing in an hour, and she had to pick him up, and could I drive her?

(Her cell phone has been dead since Thursday because she accidentally sliced the charger cord when cutting fabric for a seat cushion, and she didn't have a chance to buy a new one until this morning, and she only heard her mother's messages a few minutes before she came to us in a panic. Didn't they e-mail her? Yes, but she's been "low feeling," and hasn't looked at her computer.)

She couldn't leave Mrs. N unattended, and I hesitated to abandon my depressed brother. Happily, the two problems solved each other. Bob offered to stay with Mrs. N, and Eka gave him two minutes of training. She showed him which pills to give her with her small bowl of applesauce, and told him how far up the block she should walk, holding on to his arm, and that she liked her rye toast medium brown, with no butter, at three P.M.

At last we were off. After years of longing to hold her son again, Eka found the reality overwhelming. "What he does when I die?" she asked. Good question. I'm not sure how Davit will manage on his own—unless he goes to work for the cousins in Brooklyn, slaving with a floor sander.

Rather than commiserate, I suggested she calm herself, enjoy the reunion, and make long-range plans later. (It's so easy to give sensible advice, and so hard to follow it.)

On the Turnpike, we passed the bristling smokestacks and skeletal refinery towers that make *The Garden State* such an amusing nickname. It was early afternoon: iron sky, clear highways, specklets of mist on the windshield. "He has all the money in socks," she confided. "I worry, because he changes the plane in Munich. Maybe he don't stay in airport, maybe they rob him."

As she envisioned the dangers of international travel, her lips closed down to the size of a grape.

On the Goethals Bridge, she wept. "All the years I should be with him and I am here. I don't see him grow up. I made wrong decision."

She may be right. Perhaps it's better to tend one's tots than to improve their lots. I'll never say that to her face, though.

Reminding her that she has finally achieved her long-cherished goal, I said it was pointless to regret the past, which she can't change. To keep her from arguing, I asked questions about Davit.

What is he like?

"Happy, friendly. All sport he loves. Not so much loving school, but good boy."

How did he pay for his ticket?

"I send money to bank for him. He must have money in bank so they see he don't need money. If he is poor, they think he comes to America for work."

Was it hard to get a visa?

She shook her head, as in, *Don't ask*. "I tell him how to answer all questions. 'You have family members in United States?' Say No. 'Where you going?' New York, for tourist purpose."

Her hands and head trembled. I couldn't tell how much of it was emotion and how much was her illness. She'll have to explain this to him. *That* ought to make for a touching reunion.

I caught myself feeling crabby and jealous. With Davit here, there'll be nothing left of her for me. I don't know what I was hoping for—a morsel of companionship for the last few weeks of her life?—but that won't be happening now.

I dreaded meeting him. In my experience, the best defense against scornful teenagers is preemptive contempt. High school teachers learn this quickly, or drown. But I couldn't treat Eka's son as an insignificant minor. That left me uncomfortably unsure how I'd respond when he looked me up and down, wondering why his mother was hanging around with this jumbo-plus American.

We didn't speak as we crossed Staten Island. I considered driving into a concrete pillar, thus solving many problems at once, but that seemed an extreme remedy for a lull in the conversation.

Skirting the hem of Brooklyn, out past Canarsie and the marshy salt-air wastes, we saw jets coming in low for landings. Eka put her cheek against the window and peered out at them.

Davit called as we were entering the airport. By then he'd gotten through customs, and was waiting at the food court in Terminal Four. I told Eka I'd drop her off and circle back, assuming she would want privacy for her reunion, but she was afraid of getting lost, so I put the car in the lot and we went to meet Davit inside the terminal.

I had a hard time keeping up. She talked even faster than she walked—asking if she looked all right, remembering the day she'd said good-bye to him as the bus waited, weeping at the memory. She tripped on the curb; I caught her by the arm, and the soft flesh reminded me of my folly.

"Davit!"

The name, shrieked, sounded like a crow's cry.

My first impression of her son: standing near the doors with a bright green backpack at his feet, playing a game on his cell phone, bigger than I'd expected, he seemed child and adult at the same time, with black corkscrew curls and wisps of novice beard on chin and cheek. The baggy jeans, logoless baseball cap, Nike sneakers, and leather jacket thrown over his duffel bag made me wonder, Is he a drug dealer back home? (She explained later that she sent him these clothes. This is how she spends her days off, shopping for her family and shipping the goods.)

Hearing his name, he looked up and grinned exuberantly. His teeth are just a little crooked, exactly like hers.

Until this month, I considered Eka a calm, pleasant woman who seemed to have purged the passion from her soul. How wrong can a guy be? She trotted over to her son and embarrassed him by kissing him like a baby and sobbing. Davit impressed me by allowing it, patting her back and never rolling his eyes.

A song bubbled up from long ago: *No, I would not give you false hope on this strange and mournful day, but the mother and child reunion is only a motion away.* I never understood what it was supposed to mean, but the words seemed eerily apt. *False hope. Strange. Mournful.*

Davit turned out to be a firecracker—excited to be here despite his exhaustion (he'd left Tbilisi at four A.M.), muscular, with an accent half-Georgian and half-British, he shook my hand vigorously, happy to meet his mother's *good friend,* not at all horrified. "How do you do, sir?" he said, which made me laugh, and he laughed along with me. (They've been pumping English into him since the fourth form, he explained.) Although his chunky Lakers championship ring inflicted some pain, he made a good impression.

Sleek cars in the parking lot caught his eye, I observed, as did attractive girls.

He noted the dimply dings in my Buick Park Avenue, which lost its sheen many years ago, but politely uttered not a syllable on the subject.

In the backseat, Eka held both of his hands as she interrogated him. I couldn't even guess at the gist. I assume he asked about her tremors; whatever she told him must have been a lie, because his cheer never flagged.

During a gap in their Q&A, I asked to share in some of the news from home, and Eka reported that a young couple from Gardabani will soon be moving into Davit's room and paying rent. Also, he has changed all of his lari to dollars. He has, in other words, no intention of going back.

Awed by the Verrazano Bridge, Davit commented, "*Ras astsorebs*" (pardon my spelling if I got that wrong), which means, *That's so straight*—not a compliment to the bridge's engineers, he explained, but slang for *cool*.

He was so intrigued by everything he saw that I decided to give him the grand tour. Instead of prudently returning via Staten Island, we crossed the Brooklyn Bridge into Manhattan. "I recognize this," he said. "Many times, I saw it on the telly."

Like triumphant astronauts, we took the ticker tape parade route down lower Broadway. Historic façades loomed above us on both sides, but he commented only on the holiday display of shooting stars, made of lightbulbs and mounted on the lampposts. "These are pretty."

Personally, I found them cheesy, but new arrivals have their own aesthetics.

Putting his head out the window, he said, "I thought the buildings would be more tall."

"These are just the little ones," I replied. "We moved the big ones to the Bronx so the terrorists can't find them." I assume he understood I was joking.

Pre-rush-hour traffic mired us as we swung back up-town toward the tunnel. Davit pointed out his favorite building, a plain cube draped in red lights with flashing white sparkles: Century 21, the clothing store.

"The old World Trade Center used to be right across the street," I said.

He nodded respectfully. I'm not sure he knew what I was talking about.

Eka pressed his hand to her cheek and kissed it. Glancing in the mirror, I saw the city lights shining in her wet eyes.

Davit gave me a smiling nod. He thought he understood her maternal excess. Alas, the lad understands nothing. But he'll find out—too soon.

He fell asleep on Route 3, and didn't wake until we reached my street. The little houses must have disappointed him after Manhattan, but he didn't let on.

In Mrs. N's kitchen, we found Eka's employer at her table, telling my brother stories. Each of them had a small red teacup. Bob seemed calmly attentive; Mrs. N kept going as if we hadn't walked in, telling how she used to ski to her childhood house from the road, pulling groceries on a sled.

Introductions all around. Sleepy Davit shook hands with Bob. Mrs. N, peeved at the interruption, croaked, "Welcome."

Bob taught Davit my landlady's name, Riika, which I haven't heard in years.

"I'm hungry," Mrs. N announced: two words I doubt she's ever said in front of company before.

"Should we all have dinner together?" I proposed.

"Yes, we can do this?" Eka asked her boss.

The crabby frown lasted only a moment. "As long as I don't have to cook," Mrs. N said.

I fetched the Chinese takeout menu from downstairs. Panting from the round trip, I took orders and circled numbers. Davit asked if he could watch American TV, and Eka set him up in the living room with the remote. Seeing him slouched on the sofa, surfing through Spanish news, British news, a lecturing nun, a chopping chef, and *Hogan's Heroes*, no one would have suspected that he'd ever lived anywhere else.

As the counterwoman at Top's Chinese swiped my Visa, I pondered a philosophical question: what happens to a dead man's debts? When the bill arrives but the addressee has departed, what then?

It was my first pang over my own death. Bruce Lee, bare-chested and fierce, showed no sympathy.

Davit was showing his mother photos from his farewell dinner when I got back. Each new image on the camera's screen brought a fresh flurry of emotion as she recognized faces she will never see again. Davit seemed to find this amusing. I hope he doesn't feel bad about that in hindsight.

"Come and get it," I said, reluctant to interrupt but starving.

Eka served Mrs. N first, then her son. When we were all ready to dig in, Bob asked if he might say a nondenominational prayer, and Mrs. N said, "Keep it short." Despite his shaky state, my little brother thanked the universe on our behalf for the force that draws families back together after long periods of separation.

Over dinner, he recounted some of what Mrs. N had told him. (Her throat is still sore from the feeding tube, and she wore herself out delivering her stories the first time.) As a girl, she used to build igloos out of snowballs and put a candle inside so the light glowed through the snow. On the day in 1939 when the Soviets bombed Helsinki for the first time, she was picnicking in the park with her sister, and no one ran because no one understood what was happening, even though they saw the bombs falling through the sky.

My brother, subdued, told these stories slowly and deliberately, as if reciting the teachings of a Finnish master.

The weight of his despair seemed to have diminished by a few pounds.

Davit is a storyteller, too, it turns out. His tale about the old Greek priest who helped him fill out his Customs Declaration form on the plane, who drank two cocktails and murmured the word *Toyota* in his sleep, made even Bob and Mrs. N laugh.

One absorbs bits of wisdom over the years. *When you're hungry, eat.* Keep it simple—enjoy the taste of your Scallop with Lobster Sauce, and leave everything else for another time.

I was hungry and I ate. A cold wind moaned outside, but Mrs. N's kitchen was warm. For minutes on end, amid contented talk, I forgot about Eka's illness, and Mrs. N's damaged brain, and how Bob will ever earn a living again, and what Davit will do when his mother is gone.

I even forgot my own plans.

18.

The longing grows. I find myself gazing at her pale fore-arm: the two dark birthmarks, the fine black hairs. What, exactly, do I want? Not sex—too fraught with peril. What, then?

Her head leaning against my shoulder. Her hand on my arm again, as we walk.

Go ahead and judge me. You can't think me more of a dumb-ass than I think myself.

Should Davit start school right away, or take time off for freedom and tourism? This was the topic of debate today in Mrs. N's kitchen. While Eka's son slept on a cot in her room, I argued that he deserved a chance to breathe before joining the masses in bondage. (Unspoken: *Let him spend time with you while you can still walk.*) Ever my opposite, Bob thought Davit might be happier in school with kids his own age than hanging around here, i.e., with the living dead. Eka wasn't sure. She wanted him to enjoy America, but not if it meant falling behind.

Davit had his own ideas. "I want to play with the school basketball team," he said when he joined us, in baggy yellow Lakers shorts and a T-shirt with *Tupac* spray-painted across the chest. "I don't want to lose the season."

She stroked his knuckles. And so it was decided.

I doubt the team roster includes any white players, or that he'll make the cut, but I kept my mouth shut. Let him have his dreams for a day.

With his last bite of egg still in his mouth, he asked if we could visit the high school now. So much for freedom.

The building, which I'd never seen before, is a low concrete box that keeps going and going, window after window. I found it dismal, but Davit grinned ecstatically, perhaps because we'd arrived during an early lunch period and found hordes of his peers outside. Kids in hooded sweatshirts lined the ledge by the side door like starlings on a wire. A girl twirled on the ball of one foot, playfully; others texted on their phones. Most of the females looked like children, though extremely sexual children. A few wore tight tan pants and black boots, like horsewomen, a style one doesn't expect to see in a blue-collar town. The world has changed since I shut myself in my basement twenty years ago.

Davit courageously let his mother hold his hand. He soaked in the spectacle around him, studying sneakers and exposed bellies. Some laughing Latinas bumped into us as we entered, excused themselves, checked out the new kid holding mom's hand, and broke down in giggles. Whether they were laughing at him or attracted, I can't say; either way, Davit gave them an exuberant smile that set off a fresh round of hysterical titters.

A pancaked woman informed us pleasantly that Davit can start as soon as they fill out an application and provide the necessary documents. She asked if he was excited about coming to a new country, and he said, "Yes, very much."

In order to apply, however, we needed to go to Central Registration on Belleville Avenue.

Before we left, Davit told the secretary that he wanted to join the basketball team, and hoped to meet the coach. His friendly assertiveness surprised us, and got results. The coach didn't answer his phone, but the secretary sent us to meet the athletic director, a woman with JFK's haircut, wearing a tracksuit. She asked if Davit had played for his school team in Georgia.

"My school has no team. I played for Academy Tbilisi—the youth team. You have heard of it?"

She smiled. "Sorry, I haven't."

"Viktor Sanikidze played for Academy Tbilisi before NBA."

Perhaps because we were with him, she didn't shoo Davit away. "If you're really good," she said, "then you'll be very welcome. I have to tell you, we're not exactly a power."

She told Davit to check back with her on his first day of school. The season has already started—practices, not games—but she'll make sure the coach gives him a tryout. "We had a kid from Bosnia a few years back. What a shooter. He could sink three pointers from midcourt. I think it's because they didn't have iPods over there—they had nothing else to do."

If Davit was excited before, he bubbled over on the way to Central Registration. Humming to himself in the backseat, he tapped what I assume was a hip-hop rhythm on the window. His eyes, in my mirror, saw past the little houses with their flags and aluminum awnings, past the tract of new condos, past the spooky, broad-shouldered cancer hospital, straight into the future.

Central Registration had other ideas, however.

Though housed in a mundane tan trailer behind Belleville School Ten, the tiny office wields as much bureaucratic power as the IRS. The documents Eka will need to produce include Davit's school and immigration records, and legal papers stating that she has full custody and the authority to make all decisions regarding his education.

"I have no legal papers," Eka protested. "His father leaves when he is born."

"It's a state law," the weary registrar said. "Who was he living with before he came here?"

"My mother."

"Then your mother can sign a notarized letter and fax or mail it."

"Where is notary?" Eka complained. "I never hear of notary in Georgia."

The woman patiently explained that they've had cases where divorced parents brought their children to the United States without the other parent's permission, basically kidnapping them. That's why this law was passed.

Eka didn't say so, but I think she doubted her mother's ability to procure the necessary papers. Davit encouraged her in Georgian, and rubbed her back as if he were the wise parent and she the anxious child.

So he'll have a bit of freedom after all, whether he wants it or not. "Now you'll have time to do some sightseeing," I told him.

"Excellent," he said, and gazed somewhere beyond the pink and yellow notices stapled to the bulletin board.

I had a short-lived fantasy of taking him around Manhattan myself, since his mother won't get another day off for almost two weeks. But my knees, ankles, and lungs won't allow it.

The drive home was deafeningly quiet.

Eka fixed Mrs. N her afternoon snack and left her with Davit and Bob in the kitchen, watching one of the *Terminator* movies on the little TV on the counter. After calling her mother about the required documents, she joined me on the living room couch for another interview. This was her idea, not mine: with Davit here, the need for posthumous income has become more urgent than ever.

I learned that she went to the university and worked as a nurse in Georgia, in a hospital radiology department. She wanted to work as a nurse here, but first she has to take the licensing exam, in English, which presents a formidable obstacle. She has the book, she's been studying it ever since she arrived, but she's so tired at the end of the day, she can barely keep her eyes open. "Sometime I am discourage," she confessed.

She learned German in school, not English. When she first came here, it was stressful, not speaking the language. In the street one time, without her dictionary, she had to call friends at home and ask them to look up an English word she didn't understand.

Before coming over, she arranged to stay with her cousins in Brooklyn for a short time. A friend of theirs told her about an agency that places Georgian women as home health aides. The agency charged a hundred dollars just to send her for an interview. Once the family hired her, she had to pay the agency three weeks' salary in cash.

They didn't train her. She has back problems now, from "lifting ladies."

She had hoped to learn English by talking to her elderly employers, but none of them talked to her much. Mrs. Prestifilippo said she couldn't understand a word Eka said. So she ended up watching TV with them—"to keep brain alive." She still watches *Law and Order* in all its varieties, and many shows involving medicine, some with living patients, others with corpses that serve as clues. (I could have been teaching her English for the past four years. I could have helped her study for the nursing test. Had I known, I might have volunteered. Or, sigh, I might not.)

Picture me beside her on Mrs. N's overstuffed sofa: pen in hand, notebook on thigh, scribbling a note now and then, like a suitor with one eye on the chaperones through the doorway—imagining Eka imprisoned in the homes of the taciturn elderly—tenderly questioning this woman twenty years my junior (but no longer young), who has come to rely on me, striving to concentrate on her words, in vain because the other feeling kept pushing through, insistent as a dog's snout in your crotch—reminding myself that I am, as they say, old enough to be her father—burning to rest my hand on her pant leg, while in the kitchen tires squealed, a shotgun blasted, glass shattered, and Davit laughed.

"Sometime," she said, "they want too much. I have one day off, but they call to tell I must return early. They don't buy the food I ask to buy. I don't got car, I can't go buy it. What I should eat? Sometime we make conflict, arguing. Always I am tired. And missing family. This is great country, but work is hard."

Her eyelids kept twitching: symptoms of something more serious than emotion or fatigue. She leaned back and rested her head against the loud roses.

"You haven't told Davit about your sickness?"

"I told him I have little flu."

If he believes that, then the human capacity for self-deception is greater than I knew.

"Have you gone back to the doctor since your diagnosis?"

The corners of her mouth pulled back, a resigned pout. "He can't do nothing. He tells me he is sorry."

"Still, you should be under a doctor's care."

She looked at her lap. "I don't got insurance."

While I brooded over the failings of our health care system, she turned to a more immediate concern. "Do you know how can I get insurance for Davit? For if he is sick?"

Mrs. N barked Eka's name. She left me to escort her employer to the bathroom.

I daydreamed. I still have my health coverage, presumably. If she were my wife, she'd have it, too. And Davit. I should offer to marry her, just for that.

(*My wife*. Two words we haven't seen together before. They look wrong, side by side—like *enraged walnut*.)

What would she say if I proposed? I could make it clear that I'm just trying to set her up with medical care. Even so, she might refuse—claiming that she never legally divorced, while privately fearing what I might demand in return.

Imagine: she's my wife, but I'm not allowed to touch her.

Did she do this intentionally? Smile at the lonely slob until his common sense melted, with precisely this goal?

No, I don't think so.

The Shitmobile finally died, outside Quick Chek. A dainty young mother, Brazilian, I think, strapped her twins into her Chevy Blazer and hooked me up to her jumper cables. She suggested I drive straight to the mechanic a few blocks down.

They think I need a new alternator. In the instant before I gave them the go-ahead, I considered letting them scrap the car, but reconsidered. If I keep it in working order, I can bequeath it to Davit.

The walk home, a hellish half-mile marathon, almost finished me. The weight of the milk and grapefruit juice in the plastic bag cut off the circulation in two fingers. Reaching home was not guaranteed. A logician might scoff: What's the worst that could have happened? That you'd drop dead en route, and be done? But logic misses the point. Dying when and how I choose is one thing; collapsing on a public sidewalk like a tuna cast up on the beach is another entirely.

Panting and cursing, ankles in agony (imagine a splintered bone pressing into your flesh with each step: that would have been comfortable by comparison), I ran into Bob and Davit at the corner of Stephens and Holmes. Davit had a little Kmart bag. Bob had walked him over there to show him a bit of America, and Davit had bought a candy bar and a 50 Cent CD from the discount rack. Sourly, I thought, *He should be saving his money*—especially since his mother earned it through grueling servitude, and won't be earning much more.

We were about to enter our separate mouseholes when Davit pointed to the old backboard behind the house. "I can use this?" he asked me.

"I don't see why not"—a challenging phrase for him to disentangle, but he managed.

"There is a ball?"

I directed him to the faded blue tub by the tool shed, where Garrett used to keep a basketball and a pump. With steady effort, Davit turned the flabby, faded rubber into a firm sphere that rang when bounced. Bob played with him— not exactly energetically, but with remembered skills—and Davit went easy on the old monk, letting him take jump shots until he sank one. Turning away in envy, I saw Eka at the kitchen window, watching her son while washing dishes.

Beatified is the only word for that face.

Kai or Ahvo stopped by awhile ago. Somber in his dark overcoat, he trod the creaky boards up to the back door. He had come to tell Eka that Davit can't stay with her. Their mother is old and sick, he said. She's entitled to some privacy and comfort. Also, Eka abandoned her twice in the last two days, leaving her with an untrained stranger, i.e., Bob. The Nieminen family understands how much it means to Eka to be reunited with her son, but this can't go on.

They're Huns in Social Democrats' clothing, these twin Finns. Bland, pudgy, with thin sandy hair, they cultivate an image of reasonable pleasantness. Meanwhile, they pillage without mercy.

She told me about the eviction in my vestibule. There were no tears; she'd cried already, and dried her face before coming to me. The evidence was still in her veined, red eyes, however. My first impulse was to stalk the sonofabitch to his home and drive through the living room window. I went with my second idea instead: "He can stay with me."

She hugged me for that. I should have luxuriated in the pressing of flesh, which may never come again, but all I could do was stand stiffly, a model of probity, and deny that I crave this and more.

Recollecting her breasts pressed against mine, I also recall the vibration that passed from her to me. This reminder of her condition sent dread all the way to my fingertips, even as I told her, "Everything will be all right."

What I said the other day about the circus coming through: add to that an Eastern European basketball player, sixteen years old, with a knapsack and duffel bag, camped out on my living room floor. Inexplicably, I don't mind. What's one more body in the cellar? The more the merrier.

17.

I'm a dead man with a crush on a dead woman. Why not ask her to marry me? There's no chance of our losing that magic spark after too many years together, or getting on each other's nerves.

Why not ask? Because she would say no.

And if she said yes? Then I'd be responsible for her son after she's gone. Something to consider before proceeding.

This isn't the sort of romance one imagines in youth.

But let's be practical for just a moment. I'd better make sure I still have health insurance before I go any further.

"I just quit my job," I explained to the Blue Cross representative.

"Oh. Then I'm sorry, but your coverage has stopped," she said, with genuine regret. (You expect a surly bureaucrat, not a kindly granny who should have retired years ago but has troubles of her own.)

"I thought I could keep it if I paid on my own."

"I wish you could. That's only if you're laid off."

It occurred to me that Jerri may not have terminated me on paper. Maybe she waited, hoping my madness would pass and I'd come back to my senses.

Before crawling and asking her to take me back (dire step!), I called Hendricks House and requested a phone consultation with a social worker. My question was this: If

I marry someone, how long will it take before my health insurance covers her, assuming I still have any?

The woman they connected me with had a voice unlike any I've heard before: not a whisper, exactly, but a silky, sibilant breeze, lightly sweetened. Each S softly stroked my spine. With soothing compassion, she asked me to explain my situation; I obeyed as if commanded by a hypnotist.

She stopped me. "But you realize she has a preexisting condition."

I hadn't thought of that. One more proof that my brain is shriveling.

Wait, though—doesn't the new law cover this? They can't turn her away, right?

"That provision hasn't gone into effect yet. We're still governed by the state law."

Which is . . . ?

"There's a twelve-month waiting period for coverage on the condition she already has."

According to this knowledgeable counselor, Eka's medical options are these:

• Hendricks House's free clinic (but they can only offer routine care and basic dentistry)

• emergency Medicaid—they can enroll her at the nearest ER

• an Urgent Care clinic, where they accept cash

• NJ Family Care, if Eka's salary is low enough—but, again, they might not cover a preexisting condition. She wasn't sure.

Though I'd called for Eka's sake, I found myself distracted by this unique voice, which breathed peace and reassurance even as it delivered woeful news. "What's your name?" I asked. "In case I need to call again."

"I'm Tami Driscoll."

Tami D! One of Dr. Jones's clucking fans!

"Thank you, Tami. You're very kind."

"I wish I had better solutions to offer. Call any time if you think we can help."

It's ridiculous. As I prepare either to marry a dying woman or take leave of this impossible world, I'm coming down with a crush on every lamppost I bump against.

The dregs of a twenty-ounce Sprite went down the kitchen drain, making room for a few shots of Old Crow. What I really wanted to do was drive, accelerate, and hit a tree. Since the mechanic still has my car, I exited on foot.

Sipping the anesthetic, I surveyed the houses of my neighbors: the teensy lawns, the dented aluminum siding, the rust on the fence poles. How I ended up here, I can scarcely remember. Like a horned toad on an ice floe, I could spend decades in this town and never belong. In fact, I've done exactly that.

Beneath these musings, a dark conundrum throbbed. *I must help Eka—I can't help Eka.*

Wheezing, fearful that my ankles would crack before I reached the end of the block, I caught the toe of my shoe on a broken sidewalk flag. As I struggled to stay vertical, Eka came flying toward me from behind, groaning my name. Dark snakes of hair, still wet from the shower, danced around her face; her satin blouse clung to her damp belly.

"Davit is in arrest for steal."

Her face resembled a furious baby's: red, distorted, shiny. After the initial confusion (*Davit is in a rest, for steel?*), her meaning emerged. My heart, like hers, took a nosedive.

Fortunately, she had overstated the case. They had him in the security office at Kmart—but they planned to call the police unless his parents showed up within fifteen minutes.

☞ And my car's in the shop.

☞ And Eka is too hysterical to make a convincing plea for leniency by herself.

☞ And I can't walk the two long blocks in the allotted time.

☞ And Bob hasn't owned a car in years.

Don Quinones saved us. Driving by in his battered pickup, silver ladders shining in the sun, he waved to us and perceived misfortune. The short version: he gave us a lift in his burgundy Taurus, while Bob babysat again for Mrs. N—tempting the wrath of Attila the Finn, but we had little choice.

(A scenelet: before we left with Don, Bob took distraught Eka's hand in both of his, looked deep into her eyes, and said, "Whatever happened—whatever happens—there's no need to worry." For a mesmerized moment, she seemed to calm down. His mystical malarkey irritates the hell out of me, but for once I was glad to have him around.)

Don still had dirt under his fingernails and particulate matter thickening his hair. Eka, back in panic mode, sobbed as we entered the parking lot, "They deport him." No, no, no, I told her, they like to scare first-time offenders but rarely prosecute. I based this on the fact that they didn't send my cousin Gary to Rikers Island when they caught him with *Sticky Fingers* under his Arctic parka at Klein's on the Square.

She sniffed the Old Crow on me—I'd deposited the Sprite bottle discreetly in Don's front hedge—and seemed less inclined than usual to believe my assurances.

"It's not same like for you. We can't make no trouble. They throw us out, no chance."

"Not for something as small as this. I really don't think so."

She dug her nails into her scalp, mumbling, "Davit, Davit."

The Loss Prevention office at Kmart hasn't been redecorated, I'd estimate, since Jimmy Carter was president. Taped to the blue-green paneling, curling mug shots of ethnically diverse shoplifters—each printed on copy paper and cut out with scissors—made a sloppy wall of infamy. Two red Ping-Pong paddles and a package of three balls sat on the desk, resting on a chaotic sea of paperwork. The room reeked of tuna salad; the crusty edge of a sandwich on white bread sat in the open trash can.

The man behind the desk had a more protuberant gut than mine. It jutted out over his belt, and you could see his navel imprinted on his tightly stretched white shirt, a bas-relief tortellino. (Mine doesn't look that repulsive, I don't think. Better check.) He wore his sandy hair in an archaic, sprayed-in-place, laughably perfect swoop, and had loosened his tie like a sweaty juror. Clouds of vexation dominated his sky.

"You can't all come in here," he told us. "Who are his parents?"

"I am," Eka said.

"I'm his stepfather," I interjected. "And this is his uncle. We're here to translate."

Davit, meanwhile—angry and sullen, unlike the boy I'd known for two days—concentrated his death stare on the vinyl floor tiles.

"I'm not thrilled with his attitude," the paunchy loss-prevention guy told us. "He seems to think I'm bluffing. He may force me to prove I'm not."

"He is good, honest boy," Eka said. "I don't believe he steals. I think someone mistaked."

"If that's what you think he took—" (I nodded at the red paddles) "—it's highly unlikely. We don't have a Ping-Pong table. We barely have room for the paddles."

A lumpy hag sat in the corner. Owner of a memorable Karl Malden nose and a pair of artistically drawn, hairless eyebrows with curled ends, like a musketeer's moustache, she gurgled, "I maintained observation until he exited the store."

"We've got it on video, too," the boss said. "If you don't want me to call the police right now, don't waste my time with denials."

I pointed out that Davit had just arrived in this country. "He doesn't know how things work here. He doesn't deserve to have a rap sheet."

"So, where he comes from, shoplifting is legal?"

Eka questioned Davit in Georgian, whispering, not wanting the enemy to hear. Without understanding any of the words, I can say with confidence that their dialogue went something like this: *Why do you did this? Why?/ I don't know why. It was stupid./ How could you do? This is why I bring you here?/ He's an asshole. He's been threatening me this whole time./ You must show to him you are sorry./ I won't apologize. He's a dumb shit./ If police come, they send you straight back. You want? Apologize!/ Grrrrrr.*

Our host observed them as if through a fluoroscope, examining their souls at work. "He doesn't seem to get the point. Maybe you should explain that he broke the law."

There was plenty that I would have gladly explained— to our host, not to Davit. *Your job has turned your brain to sludge. Kids do these things; I'll bet you drank your share of beer in your underage day. We're not talking about a felony. You're a disgrace to fat men everywhere.*

While I worked at keeping these insights bottled, Eka pried an apology out of her son. "I'm sorry," he muttered.

"See, that's the attitude I'm talking about."

He had a white pencil between his index and middle fingers, like a cigarette, and he twiddled it nervously, tapping the eraser against a green Pendaflex folder on his desk.

"What country are you from, anyway?"

"We come from Georgia."

"Part of Russia, right?"

He might as well have jabbed her with the point of his pencil. She contained her resentment, however. "No. Two different countries. Different language, everything different. The Soviets took Georgia with force, but we never lose our culture."

This seemed to amuse him. "She gave me a social stud-ies lesson," he told the hag. "That's a first."

Eka ignored this and took her lavender wallet from her purse. Removing two twenties, she said, "Sir, in respect . . ."

She placed the bills on his desk, atop the sea of papers.

If not for the video camera up in the corner, who knows? He might have said, *I'm glad your son finally understands.* Instead, he said, "Take that back, Ma'am," rolled his chair closer to the desk, and picked up the phone.

"Hold on," I said. "He's not a hardened criminal. He's a high school athlete, he's never been in trouble before."

My plea fell on deaf ears. He used the pencil eraser to peck out a phone number.

"Hey—" I argued.

"Holly, hand me the Incident pad."

Without moving from his place by the door, Don said mildly, "Excuse me. I think what all of us really want to say is how sorry we are about this."

The pencil paused; Don kept going.

"My brother-in-law's an LP manager at Target—I'm sure you've heard every sob story there is. There's no excuse for stealing, we all know that. But his mom is going to give him a pretty good talking to when we get out of here. She's an honest, hard-working person—she just misunderstood the situation. Believe me, by the time she finishes with him, he'll never do this again. You should know, though—it's really not her fault. She's been working here for years, sending all her money home to support her family. She didn't have a chance to teach him her values. But this could be the start. We're just asking you to see it from her point of view. If he gets labeled as a bad kid, that's going to give him a push in the wrong direction. I don't know the legalities, but it might mean they'll send him back where he came from—after she saved all these years to bring him here. But if you're will-ing to give him a second chance, she'll straighten him out,

I guarantee it. Really, this is the deciding point. His whole life is in your hands."

I expected our shrinkage specialist to sneer, *You should be a lawyer.* Instead, he hung up the phone. "I'm not a merciless guy. I like to give people a break—when I see they deserve it."

He inflated one cheek to help him think, and scrutinized Davit without visible sympathy.

"Do me a favor," he told Don. "Make sure he doesn't come back to this store. He's free to go anyplace else in America, just not here. If he does, he's trespassing." He got up to retrieve a photo of Davit from the printer, and taped it to the wall. Some of the other faces in the rogues' gallery were crying, I noticed. So was Eka.

"You can explain to him that he didn't fool me. I'm doing this for his mother's sake. I just hope she can get the message through. He won't get off this easy again."

Underappreciated. The word rippled on a banner high above us: a paean to Don Quinones, our hero.

As soon as the car doors were shut, Eka went to pieces. Where is the placid health aide who used to live above me? Gone forever.

Don pulled out of the lot and headed home. I wanted to ask Davit why he'd stolen Ping-Pong paddles, of all things, but couldn't risk pushing Eka deeper into grief.

"Did they handcuff you?" Don asked.

"No."

"What happened," I asked, "did they grab you when you stepped outside?"

"She said at the door, if I give back the things, she will let me go. So, I gave them to her, and she took my arm tight and pulled me in."

"You could have run," I said.

"I thought they would chase me with a car. And the school would forbid me on the team."

Eka's grief turned to mourning. She faced the window, not her son. Her head kept oscillating, a small but steady tremor; every two or three seconds, it took a bigger jump to the left, as if saying emphatically, *No*. What was she thinking? Something along these lines, I believe: *If I'd never left home, he wouldn't have become a thief. I shouldn't have left. And now it's too late. I wasn't there to teach him, and I won't be here long enough to teach him now.*

Davit slunk downstairs by himself, and Eka went to relieve Bob. Don accompanied me to the rear of the house, saying how bad he felt for both of them.

"Kids, huh?" he said.

"Yup."

We found Garrett shooting hoops by himself, which he hasn't done in years. He'd just gotten home from work; his sports jacket peeked out beneath the bottom of his down jacket.

Why Don came and stood with me on the wrong side of the hedge, I'm not sure, unless it was to postpone returning to his wife. I couldn't just walk away after he'd saved Davit's hide. So the two of us watched Garrett play, bouncing the ball waist high and then shooting with both hands on the rear of the ball.

Cindy came down to fetch her son for dinner. As if she'd never said a word to me about Don, she asked how us fellows were doing.

I told her that Don had just saved Eka's son from getting deported.

"Really?!"

"Really."

Don swatted away the acclaim. "Naw, he just got himself in trouble shoplifting. We went over to vouch for him."

"Ahhh."

At that unexceptional moment, Don casually yanked the concrete from under my feet. "Cindy, would you come for a little walk with me? Just for a minute."

With a good-natured smile and a zigzaggy brow to indicate puzzlement, she said, "Sure." She asked me to let Garrett know she'd be right back, if he asked. I agreed, stumbling a bit over my knotted tongue.

Garrett never noticed that his mother had flown the coop, which was fortunate. If he had, he might have blared, *Where are you going? Why are you going with him?* But his attention stayed on the ball: chasing it after each missed shot as if competing with an invisible rival, and then dribbling back to the faded foul line. The pathos of his fantasies reminded me of the pathos of mine.

I wonder what Don said to her. Given what we know about him, what could he possibly say? *I just want you to know, if I were free, there's no one in the world I'd rather be with.* I suppose that might be a relief—a bit of romance, without breaking his vows. They remind me of a pair of cats, locked inside a house and watching the birds flock on the lawn outside: teeth chattering, crazed with desire but trapped by walls and windows. Talking about it might not cure the itch, but—like scratching all around your chicken pox—it's as close as you can get.

16.

She's sleeping now, in my bed. I find myself calmly bliss-
ful at the thought of her there. The things that happen in
this world. The outrageously improbable, laughably unlikely
things.

I'd just come back from picking up the car. Not yet
recovered from the hike to the mechanic's, I gripped the
handrail on the way down, only to hear the buzzer blast as
I reached the bottom. Ordinarily, I would have ignored it
and collapsed on the couch, but I thought it might be Davit,
locked out. And so, up the steps I went, light-headed, panting, pissed off—and found Eka, her forearm bloody.

"I throw up," she whispered.

I couldn't tell if she meant in the past or the future. We
made our way down the narrow stairs together, her leaning
on my arm, me dreading that my knees would fail and we'd
tumble together and I'd crush her.

I brought a chair to the bathroom. She sat leaning forward
over the bowl, making gagging sounds. Nothing came up.

We retired to the living room. Bob and Davit were outside in the street, tossing around Garrett's old football, the
red rubber one.

She had stumbled on her way down Mrs. N's back steps,
and scraped her arm on the railing, thus the bloody arm.
The reason she felt so ill and weak was that they'd fired her.
She dropped a pill bottle again last night; Mrs. N snapped at
her to be more careful, and Eka, still distraught over Davit's

near-arrest, blurted out in self-defense that she has mercury poisoning. This morning, Ahvo came (apparently she can tell which twin is which) and asked questions about her condition. She answered honestly, and he gently informed her that, apart from her medical issues, she had left his mother with "unqualified substitutes" too many times. He had already interviewed a new girl, and she would be arriving later today. In gratitude for Eka's past help, they would pay for a hotel room for her and Davit, up to two weeks.

The burning wish to call and tell him off yielded to the need to wash her wounds. I cleaned the blood away with a damp cloth, picked out a long splinter, applied peroxide—not a sound from her, only rigidity—and covered the red patch with three Band-Aids. Touching the soft underside of her arm, even in this nurse-like way, brought me contentment.

"Have you told Davit about your sickness yet?"

"I don't like he worries. Let him be happy some time."

She seemed so weak. I asked if she wanted to lie down, and she agreed. After I'd straightened the covers and discreetly swept away the bits of mystery-grit, she climbed onto the bed and asked me to turn off the light. Her eyes were too tired, she said. She didn't frown in distaste at lying where I lie, and I thanked her silently for that.

Outside, Bob called out numbers—his spirit seems lighter today, more lifelike—and then Davit took a turn as quarterback, imitating Bob, "Twenty-nine, seven, two hundred forty-three, hike!"

I squeezed myself into the director's chair. (Garage sale, 1980s, never used before.) Having her lie on my bed made me happy as a boy with an injured sparrow in a shoe box. "You know you can stay here," I said. "I'll sleep in the living room."

Her belly rose and fell at an accelerated rate. I imagined she was overcome with gratitude—until she said, "I don't have time with my Davit. How I can be good mother, if we have so small time?"

While she snuffled, my gaze traveled to the gleam in the bookcase: my bumper pool trophy from seventh grade, the only prize I ever won. A mockery, since my team never let me play in competition. Did that have any bearing whatsoever on the present moment? No—except, I suppose, that it proves I'm good for nothing—including comforting a friend in her last days.

"I don't like it that he will see me more sick and more sick," she said.

Her corneas reflected the high window. Outside, Bob told Davit, "Go out for a long bomb," and Davit asked, "Excuse me, what?"

Eka turned on her side, away from me. "He will be alone, without any mother. When he will fall in trouble, he won't have nobody."

Counseling the afflicted is a new role for me. The darkness helped.

"Are you afraid?"

No answer.

If I held her hand, I thought, that might calm her—or, if unwanted, the gesture might seem intrusive and insensitive. Despite the uncertainty, I pulled the flimsy chair closer and put my hand around the fist that lay behind her on the bed.

She rolled onto her back again, resting her hip against our joined hands. The involuntary trembling passed into me through our fingers. The vibration terrified me.

Turning away from the buzz of mortality in my hand, I called her attention to Davit outside, practicing his football English: *"I am open!"* I told her, "I think he'll adapt to America very quickly."

She covered our hands with her free one, and squeezed. "I wish . . ."

"What do you wish?"

"I wish I don't become sick."

Her hands were rougher than mine. Her sweat smelled like chicken soup. I imagined that I heard an added meaning in her words: *If not for poisoning, I would be a companion to you.*

"Go deep!" Bob shouted.

Because there might never be another chance, I rose from my chair and kissed her damp forehead.

"Angus?"

I groped behind me for the canvas seat, so as not to follow the kiss with a pratfall.

"Something I want to ask, but already I ask too much."

"You haven't asked too much. What is it?"

"For my Davit: will you help him?"

Though I made my face neutral, my silence exposed my dismay. The involuntary thought was, Am I nothing to her but a bottomless aid-dispenser?

"I'm sorry, sorry. Please, I shouldn't say. I will ask cousin in Brooklyn."

The one who will enslave Davit and prevent him from going to school.

"I assume he wants to go to college."

"Oh, yes. In Georgia, education is most important thing."

Realistically, it wouldn't be forever. Just a few more years. And he's a pleasant kid, when he's not committing misdemeanors.

"One way or another," I said, "we'll make sure he has a place to live. And we'll help him go to college."

(*We*? Who's *we*? Bob and me, I guess: the Brothers Grim.)

The little curved windows in her eyes sent me such a grateful light that I didn't regret my promise.

I'm not sure I can keep it, though. Not sure of anything anymore.

Bob and Davit and I moved her things, following her instructions because she preferred not to set foot in Mrs. N's living quarters again. We packed her clothes and books in her two suitcases—including half a dozen stylish dresses I'd never seen, because she never had a chance to wear them—and put the various shoes in a cardboard box, along with CDs of Frank Sinatra, *Scheherazade*, and Vahtang Kikabidze. From the fridge we liberated her yogurt, feta cheese, and a tomato; from the bathroom, her cucumber melon shampoo. The little TV belongs to the Nieminens, Mrs. N told us—a shame, after I'd gone to the trouble of unscrewing the cable. Bob wrapped her glass figurines (swan, angel, butterfly) in newspaper before carefully arranging them in a shoe box. Davit transported her mini-shrine in a shopping bag: framed postcard-size icons of Jesus and Mary against gold-leaf backgrounds, along with their respective doilies and a tall yellow beeswax candle.

I emptied two of my dresser drawers, put the sweaters and pants in trash bags, and told her she could put her things there. She protested, relented, and reassembled her shrine on top of the dresser, which gives the room the touch of sanctity it has always lacked.

She's still sleeping. Peeking just now, I found her with a limp hand to her forehead, palm out, a silent movie heroine fraught with woe.

New voices outside—American girls, breathy, giddy, laughing. Out the kitchen window, I see six unfamiliar legs: black tights, clean jeans, and striped, baggy pants. One of them recognized Davit from our school visit, I heard her say. She asked if he was new, and he said, "I come from Georgia. The country, not the state."

They laughed at that—with him, not at him. I take this to mean they think he's cute.

Bob, chopping apples for some outlandish vegetarian dinner (he's had a pot of pinto beans soaking on the stove for hours), is smiling like Buddha at the scene outside.

The girls ask if Davit knows any American music. "Hey, ya," he sings in a reedy tenor, "Hey, ya-ah."

"I remember that!" says one of the girls.

He can do no wrong. Lucky boy.

In some ways, at least.

As far as Jerri White is concerned, I no longer exist.

I told her I'd met a dying immigrant without insurance, without the means, even, to obtain prescription painkillers. (Speaking of which: is Eka in pain? I've never thought to ask—but will tonight.) I told Jerri I wanted to do one last column, to raise funds for this woman's medical care.

"I'm on deadline," she replied.

Brrrr.

She reminded me, briskly, that Hendricks House supplies the subjects. If I want to help this person, I'll have to ask Wanda Cagle.

Unfortunately, the executive director despises me. (I showed up tipsy at their holiday party a few years back, and—etc., etc.) I could ask Tami D to intercede, but I fear they'd put Eka at the end of the queue, just because she's with me. By the time the article came out, she'd be gone.

Outside, under the yard lights, Eka's replacement is helping Mrs. N out of her son's Honda Pilot. This new woman is small, dark-haired like Eka, but darker in complexion, and younger. Her lips form sharp angles: a Gypsy, perhaps, or Turkish. It occurs to me that Kai and Ahvo, those stolid, married Scandinavians, have been stocking the house with desirable women for a long time—first Cindy, then Eka, now this one. Ah, the secret yearnings of bland, pudgy men.

Bob has gone to sleep. Listen to him snore, the son of a bitch. (No offense, Mom.) He sounds like a narwhal, drilling his way through the Arctic deep.

Davit's watching *CSI* here in the kitchen with me, with the sound down low. It's hard to think straight with all that criminal evidence flying off the screen, but I don't mind. We may be spending a fair amount of time together, Davit and I. So far, it seems doable.

I sound so serene, so accepting. It's a false front. Here's what's really simmering inside:

Pride has always hidden just beneath my skin. Privately, I believe (without evidence, like all devout believers) that I'm a superior being, in unspecified ways. But look at me now: ignorant as dirt, I understand nothing about Eka's illness. I can't help her in any way. My pride may always have been misplaced, but now it has become a sad joke.

There's one last call to make. Only one person can help her. It's too late tonight, but in the morning, I'll grovel and beg him to do whatever he can for her.

What a world, what a world.

15.

It's not fair. The bargain is coercive, merciless. A pound of flesh in exchange for a morsel of help that won't really help.

(If you're thinking I can easily spare the pound, then you're a shit, like me.)

Good old Old Crow, help me through this day. Lend me your amber warmth, let it serve as my inner compass, a small but constant flame glowing from throat to gut, lighting the inner darkness, reminding me that all pain is temporary.

But *arrrghh!* I quit my job in order to free myself from pious lying—yet here I am again, locked in my room until I've composed two pages of inspirational excrement for an audience I despise.

The laptop is burning my thighs. I've got a splitting backache from sleeping on my new $29.95 Kmart exercise mat. Or, not sleeping, while Bob shnizzled and snorted and Davit rolled around on his towels.

All so I can pretend to be her white knight: one of history's more pointless gestures.

Bob is sautéing garlic. Eka was just telling him about a palace that impressed her as a child, with its many paintings of *mare-maids*. That led, somehow, to him telling her about the monastery, and how hard it is to keep your mind focused on your koan, and how, even though he never completely succeeded in quieting the noise of random thoughts, the long hours of stillness heightened his senses. Colors looked more vivid, and he heard music in the most ordinary sounds: footsteps on the wooden temple floor, water filling a tub.

"I would like it, this experience," she said.

In the quiet that followed, I assume that she and Bob realized she would never get the chance.

Freezing in my undershirt, behind the house—the only privacy available—I called Dr. Jones this morning. He was about to leave for the hospital, but he listened. Could he intercede on Eka's behalf, so I can profile her in the *Register*? The donations would pay for medical care in her last days.

He asked about her illness. I explained, and then shivered while he pondered.

"It's funny you should call just now," he said. "I wonder if you might reconsider our invitation to speak at the Hendricks House gala. It's tonight, by the way."

The benevolent doctor had me over a barrel, strapped by the wrists and stripped naked. No, I thought, I'll pay for her care myself, with my credit card. But I'm already near the limit, I fear.

In the end, I agreed to his terms—the rental of my soul for the evening in exchange for a phone call to the executive director—and asked whether I should hand him the column tonight, at the gala.

"Hold off on that," he said. "Let me try something else first. Can I reach you at this number in a few minutes?"

"Of course. But understand, this is urgent. From what I can tell, she doesn't have many weeks left."

(My own words pierced me. They're still there, stuck between the ribs.)

"I won't waste time," he promised, and he kept his word, leaving me to clap my arms in the damp, cold wind for no more than six minutes—in which time I met Nino, the new health aide. A Georgian like Eka, she was returning from a slow walk with Mrs. N, who told me, "You should put a coat on."

Another day, I might have asked Nino why her parents had bestowed an Italian man's name on her, but other business preoccupied me.

When Dr. Jones called back, he told me to deliver Eka to the office of Dr. Lawrence Oh at Newark Beth Israel Medical Center at four P.M. today. "He's a toxicologist, a rising star in his specialty, and a personal friend. I've explained the circumstances. He'll see her free of charge. Meanwhile, find out where she was treated and have them fax her test results to Dr. Oh."

The words *Thank you* caught in my throat. All I could bring up was a retch-like, "Well done." It was not lost on me that he'd accomplished, effortlessly, what I couldn't have achieved in a lifetime.

Davit's immunization and school records arrived in Eka's e-mail today, along with a notarized letter attesting to her custody of her son. Her mother, a surprisingly capable woman, had taken the documents to a private translation agency and then had them scanned.

Mrs. Heiner at Central Registration accepted the papers and said a guidance counselor will make up a schedule for Davit. He may be able to start by next Wednesday—which sounded soon enough to me, but not to Davit, who scowled like a prisoner denied parole.

Better things awaited, though. We stopped at Walgreens for toothpaste (something I thought I'd never have to buy again), and a girl called Davit's name. One of the three who'd stopped out front yesterday, she had on black tights that showed off her ripely bulging behind and muscular calves. Her knowing, flirtatious manner made me very happy for Davit—although it also seemed inevitable that she'll be pregnant before she's eighteen, and the father may be Davit, and he may be my responsibility by then.

But I'm getting ahead of myself.

Undeterred by his mother's presence or mine—or by the kneeling store clerk restocking the bottom shelf with Stay-free Maxi pads—the girl invited Davit over to her house. Eka weighed her son's happiness against the risks, and decided to let him have his candy. She insisted on taking young Sophia's number, however, and poked it into her cell phone. After a few urgent murmurings, which Davit tolerated cheerfully, she sent them off on their own.

Be very careful. Like a dad, I fervently wished I could tell him that.

Eka dressed her best for the visit to the toxicologist: a modest silver-white blouse with soft black slacks; a slender malachite pendant, prettily marbled; mascara that made her eyes striking, a word I wouldn't have used to describe them before. The lipstick was too brightly red, it magnified her pallor, but that was her only mistake. I suppose all this was her way of thanking the doctor for treating her gratis. To me, the effect was tragic. I wouldn't have called her beautiful before today: now every twitch of her head or hands drives a barbed hook into my chest. It's wrong, I know, to mourn more because she's lovely, but that's how it is.

Dr. Oh, a delicate young man with a thick black pompadour, still has a pimple or two on his otherwise smooth cheek. He examined Eka in a curtained-off room at the Emergency Department. A dandyish doc, he wore a mauve necktie with a full Windsor knot beneath his lab coat.

If, for an instant, he betrayed a touch of annoyance (*charity . . . favors . . . bah!*), it vanished with her first tremor. Fascinated, staring almost rudely, he peppered her with questions and noted the answers on his clipboard chart. Although he had her test results, he insisted on taking blood and urine samples for retesting. She had to put on a paper gown; he squeezed her abdomen, ankles, hands, and throat.

Most of his questions focused on her symptoms (yes, pain was one of them, mainly in her calves—from the muscle spasms, he explained), but then he turned to her exposure to toxins. "Did you ever live near a farm? Did you ever live near a chemical factory? Do you eat a lot of fish?" Stiff-backed, tensely smiling—bedside manner seems not to be his strength—he reviewed her CT scan and x-rays, and told us it was very interesting that the EDTA had brought down the level of methyl mercury in her blood yet the tremors had grown worse.

She put up with all of this politely, passively, but the visit distressed me almost to the point of explosion. We'd come here to make Eka's last weeks as comfortable as possible, not to raise false hopes; apparently Dr. Oh hadn't gotten that message. I wanted to explain, but couldn't with Eka sitting there.

"I'll have the results in a day or two. I'll call you as soon as I get them. All right, Eka?"

Something about this man made her uncomfortable. (His Asianness? His unrelenting attention? His apparent homosexuality?) She evaded his eyes and mumbled, "Thank you."

I wanted to throttle Dr. Jones for conveying my message so half-assedly.

Wait.

Is Dr. Oh Dr. Jones's lover? Is that the eminent neurosurgeon's dark secret?

On the other hand, who cares?

Davit was still out with his new friend when we got back. Eka called him, but he'd turned his cell phone off. Fortunately, she had Sophia's home number.

The mother answered. From Eka's side of the dialogue, I learned that this chatty woman is a divorced hairdresser who emigrated from Bulgaria when she was eight.

Eka's words to her son were unexpectedly tender. She seemed to be asking if he was having a good time, and savoring the sweetness of his social success.

Meanwhile, she kept nodding, yes, yes, yes, yes, yes.

"She shows him her Facebook," she told me.

Her smile seemed a wistful world away.

I've put it off as long as I could. I now have half an hour to write the odious speech, stuff myself into a suit, and embark for the gala.

How does one say, *I would rather eat large stones* in Georgian?

"Please, Angus," she said to me just now, interrupting my queasy concentration, "one thing I must say. You should reduce. Please, this is my wish, health for you."

"I'll consider it. Thank you."

Maybe I'll pop the question later tonight. *How would you like a fat fool for a husband?* And then, when I'm introduced as a widower, people will size me up indulgently: *Poor man, he must have let himself go after she died.*

The Second Worst Night of My Life

(A close runner-up to Krzysztof Borglund's wedding, when my humorous toast got me thrown out of the catering hall, but not before the matron of honor slapped me— which taught me that it's best not to rhyme *pulverize* with *her vulva's size* at a family gathering.)

You try to do the gallant thing, sacrifice for thy sweet lady's sake, and sheer horror ensues. I'm too old for this.

The memories are a vest of thistles. Claw them away!

Drinking: help or hindrance? It's impressive that I reached the gala without crashing into a single guardrail or lamppost. I'm a weak man; we've established that. Couldn't sell my soul without the aid of a liquid solvent.

WHEN WORLDS COLLIDE

WHIPPANY—Wealthy do-gooders and striving unfortunates rubbed elbows this evening in the Marriott's lavishly appointed ballroom, disregarding inequalities of income, education, and status. Hearty bonhomie and mandatory egalitarianism were the order of the day.

All so she can be retested but not cured by Dr. Oh. The pinnacle of futility—yet I had no choice.

(Nagging memory: Eka patting my chest, saying, "Very handsome." She reminded me, for that instant, of the cheery Playmate bride of a geriatric Texas billionaire. Which again raises the question, Am I her knight or her chump?)

Who was there? Who *wasn't* there? Cardiologists, bankruptcy attorneys, portfolio managers, social workers—a nanny, a supermarket cashier, a car service dispatcher—black men in strange, long-jacketed church suits (royal blue, purple), ample women with straightened hair pulled back tight, clad in snug fuchsia and balancing precariously on spike-heeled velvet boots—a disproportionately blond crowd of prosperous wives (the cost of whose wardrobes would feed all the children in Sierra Leone for a year) and their kindly, silver-haired husbands.

Oops! I'd entered the wrong ballroom! This wasn't the gala, but the wedding of an ambassador's daughter and the son of the pastor from the Living Word Baptist Tabernacle.

I wish.

For much of the evening, I sequestered myself in a stall in the men's room. Far from dulling the pain, the alcohol sent me on a free-fall elevator ride to the subbasement of self-pity. The smug board members I was dodging had stature; I had none. I couldn't even close my pants. (I had to hope no one noticed the undone button behind my belt buckle.) Look where my superiority had brought me: hiding while unseen men shat on both sides of me.

What could I do to avenge myself? For one thing, I could visit the Hendricks House Facebook page as soon as I got home, and tell yet another tale. (*I met Dr. Jones this afternoon at the December luncheon of the Garden State Necrophilia Society. He seemed a pleasant man, despite his regrettable table manners.*) Or, I could tear up my speech and deliver a different one—surprise my audience with some true tales of Les Misérables, the details I couldn't find room for in print— Sonia Herrero disciplining her dachshund with an extension cord, Claude Dutalier's odd beliefs about Chinese people.

Back in my seat for the presentation of the Ronald and Sylvia Krentzler Leadership Award, with my tormentor at my side, I savored the possibility of rebellion while tucking into my prime rib and Chicken Florentine. Dr. Jones's wife, a psychoanalyst and cookbook author, leaned across her husband to praise my work, and I gave back a sickly nod.

A salsa band took the stage after the awards, and a gaggle of wives hauled their compliant husbands onto the dance floor. I took the opportunity to slip away again, stopping at the bar en route to the loo, and was accosted by a chatty pencil in a shimmering silver sheath. "My husband never missed a dance before his stroke," she confided, wizened yet plucky. I nodded and sipped, and noted the purple bruises on her forearm—but the nodding cost me my equilibrium. Vertical and horizontal bent and blended; I hit the carpet rolling, like a paratrooper.

A security guard with a square head, who smelled of baby powder, helped me to my feet. When I pointed out that he'd squeezed my arm long enough, he said, "Speaking of enough, maybe you ought to go back to your seat."

The temptation was too much. "Speaking of seats," I said, "kiss mine."

He seized my arm again, less compassionately, and had me halfway to the door, amid the lewd blaring of trumpets— *I've done it*, I thought, *I've escaped*—when Dr. Jones blocked our way and reminded me that I was the next speaker.

Another rescue. Could he be more tiresome?

As the fragrant goon unclamped my sleeve, a pug-sized fellow with a Latin lover's mustache strode toward us and pumped my hand. He reminded me that I'd written about his battle with testicular cancer; the resulting donations had enabled his children to go to camp for two summers in a row. Shaking his head in bewilderment—the point being, I think, that my abilities boggled his mind—he said, "I wish my wife was still around to say hello."

I censored the impulse to ask if she'd left early. Under the watchful gaze of Dr. Jones, I replied, as if through a muzzle, "Best wishes."

Realizing that his hero was drunk, the good man covered up for me by proclaiming my talent to the doctor, the security guard, and the silver pencil woman.

I yearned to wander out the door, but wretched refuse found its way to me as space dust sticks to a massive planet. They were an unsightly assortment, all of whom I'd helped in their time of desperation, none of whom I wished to see again. First came Mordy Chodorow, the Orthodox Jew from West Orange, who'd been struck on the head by an errant golf ball while walking home from temple, who'd needed months of speech and physical therapy when he came out of a weeklong coma. Then there was Hazem Kamal, the Egyptian barber, who had cracked his jaw in a courthouse bathroom during a seizure while on jury duty . . . and then Henry Quezada, the Guatemalan housepainter who'd fallen through the floor when he saved a neighbor's dog from a fire. Yes, everyone fortune had screwed in northern New Jersey in the past decade seemed to have come out for the evening.

I suppose it was too much to ask that my stomach accommodate Bob's tomato curry along with the beef and chicken, as well as three shots of Canadian Club, two Rob Roys, and the earlier Old Crow. Like Eka at my doorstep, I feared I'd spew in public view. All I wanted was solitude and a clean, flushable bowl, but the grateful profilees weren't done with me. Mrs. Obote of Clifton—who'd lost a hand in ethnic warfare back home, but now works as a medical receptionist, using the prosthesis I helped her obtain—reported that her son was now at Rutgers, and thanked me again, "a thousand thousand times."

(I wish I could believe that I deserve this gratitude. I wish I could believe that my articles accomplished worthwhile things. But I find it impossible, knowing all I know, to esteem myself as highly as they seem to.)

We were a sizable gathering by then, a crowd within a gala. I sensed that my unfortunates wanted me to say a few words, but the trumpets scattered my thoughts like pollen in a hurricane. A hair's breadth from puking, I leaned closer and closer toward making a dash for the exit.

They may have mistaken my silence for heart-swollen emotion. Mr. Chodorow began to clap, and the virus spread until the entire southeast corner of the ballroom was a noisy, percussive pit of appreciation.

I found the small, bespectacled face of Dr. Jones among the clappers. Had he orchestrated this outpouring? Had he coached my luckless subjects to cheer me, so my leathery heart would soften and I'd get misty-eyed on stage?

If that was his plan, it backfired. They'd get no choked-up oration from me. I claimed the right to speak the offensive truth. They owed me that much, after ten years of coerced treacle. *Ladies and gentlemen, social workers and clients—for a decade now, I've played along with your game. I've flattered you for a living, omitting your faults, painting you as noble when most of you were far from it. I left out so much: the primitive religiosity, the foul cooking odors, the colossal TVs. I left out the truth, and disrespected myself for it. But that's all over now.*

Whoever you may be, reading these babblings, you must assume that I caved at the last minute. You can't imagine that anyone would cruelly insult the hapless proletariat to its face. But you don't know Angus Truax with three varieties of alcohol in him.

The time had come. Dr. Jones escorted me from the mob of admirers toward the stage. Along the way, he said softly, "I spoke with Dr. Oh just before. He found your friend's case very interesting. He promised that, if anything can be done for her, he'll do it."

And then I was alone on the stage, as a black-clad banquet-staffer rolled a wooden lectern in front of me. The doctor's quiet reminder enraged me. He could at least have said it straight: *Watch what you say, or your lady friend will die without the benefit of palliative care.*

Waiters served dainty desserts. A sickly codger coughed weakly. Far away, across the room, a pair of exit signs glowed red, beckoning.

You were right. I caved. Reading from my prepared script, I delivered my speech and never looked up.

A farmer breaks his leg. The harvest begins in two days. A widower, he has three young children to feed, and not enough cash under the mattress to hire help. No one knows about his leg except the doctor who set the bone, and the farmer is too proud to ask his neighbors for help.

Now, this doctor happens to be something of a gossip. Every patient who sits on his examining table hears about the broken-legged widower. On harvest morning, the despondent farmer looks out his window and sees an army of children, dispatched by their parents to help out.

This is a true story. It really happened—in the metaphoric sense—and it's still happening. All over northern New Jersey, readers of the Register *send their children—their dollars—to rescue neighbors in trouble. I guess you could say I'm the gossiping doctor.*

What do we owe our neighbors? As far as I can tell, absolutely nothing. But something inside us refuses to believe that. We still live by the pioneer's ethic. Today I help you, because you need it; tomorrow, or the day after, the tables will almost certainly be turned.

And so on, bla, bla-bla, bla-bla.

The applause that followed my speech was polite, far from thunderous. I told myself they were thanking me for stopping. Dr. Jones patted my back as I sat down.

The Hendricks ElderSingers came next. After climbing cautiously onto the stage, they started clapping hands and singing, "Celebrate good times—come on!" The crowd joined in, clapping and cheering—grateful for the chance to live again after my tedious homily. I ate teaspoons of melted ice cream as the decrepit chorus kicked mildly with their white sneakers.

In exchange for my self-abasement, I calculated, Dr. Jones owes Eka full medical care to the end, in a private room.

Someone tapped my shoulder. An unfamiliar face: near-black irises, soft, pale skin, gray pixie hair. The round dark eyes reminded me of Don Quinones's late dog, Cutie-Pie. "I have a strange question to ask," she said, smiling apologetically. "Did I speak with you recently about a sick friend?"

The unmistakable voice was Tami D's. I'd imagined her twenty years younger.

"You did."

"Why didn't you tell me who you were when you called? I wish I'd known."

Her respect brought me back from the dead. "Would you have told me something different?"

"No, of course not. But still."

Dr. Jones pointed out that at least a dozen of the people I'd profiled had been Tami's clients.

"You have no idea what your articles meant to them," she said. "It's not just the donations—they take such pride in the things you say about them. Your profiles were a high point in every one of their lives."

Like a vampire confronted by a crucifix, I had to look away from her sweetness.

The pendant of her necklace was a turquoise sun, radiating blue beads of light. Her purple dress seemed to have come from Guatemala, or some other color-mad locale. This girlish social worker with soft wrinkles and lines on her forehead had never stopped being a hippie.

"You have the most extraordinary voice. It's mesmerizing."

She enjoyed the compliment, and admitted that people sometimes said she should have been an actress.

"Or a radio personality," I suggested. "Imagine the visions you'd have inspired in your audience."

"And they'd never have to see the ho-hum reality."

"Not a drop, not a drop."

I'd forgotten this, but long ago, I used to lapse into British whenever I met an appealing woman. (Tiresome affectation, that—and years since the last flare-up.) Already, I was asking myself, What if we'd met in my twenties, before I inflated to this size? Under her influence, I might have become an entirely different man.

I was already discounting that alternate history (she wouldn't have gone out with me more than once; and I couldn't have swallowed her sugar for long) when she waved her husband over. A pleasant but distracted fellow who blinked constantly—new contact lenses?—he shook my hand and said, "I enjoyed your speech."

"Sir, you strain my credulity."

Behind us, the ElderSingers segued into "For Once in My Life." The pangs re Tami were minor. That's one of the few consolations of late middle age: what once would have bled now merely throbs.

Upon my return, I found Davit and his new friend snuggled together on the couch, listening to a song on her iPod, the white cords from their ears forming a quasi heart. The bottle of plum wine Jerri White gave me for Christmas last year stood on the coffee table, along with two coffee mugs. I'll have to talk to the lad about birth control. Maybe there's an educational cartoon on YouTube, featuring a condom that floats down from the sky onto a dancing penis, while woodland animals sing in harmony.

Eka lay in my bed, asleep, her mouth open as if saying *Ahh* for the doctor.

Davit didn't know where Bob had gone.

All I wanted was to lose consciousness, alone. I returned to the car and closed my eyes in the backseat.

But couldn't sleep—worried about Bob, and about Eka. I assume I'll be with her at the end, unable to help in any way.

A car door thunked. Red taillights pulled away. Davit, alone, went around the back to my door. (Make that *our* door.)

I went in, too, and found Bob brushing his teeth. He'd been upstairs talking to Cindy—listening to her troubles at the kitchen table with a warm mug of cocoa in his hand while Garrett watched *The Matrix* for the 800th time in the other room. Here's what Bob learned: she's looking into supported housing for Garrett, so he can have more independence and a social life. The idea of coming home to an empty apartment every night scares her to death, but she has to let him fly with his own wings.

Bob also informed me that she was a champion ice-skater in childhood, and still has a shelf of trophies . . . that she wishes she'd had the chance to study ballet . . . but she enjoys her job, because her patients are incredibly appreciative. I, meanwhile—peevish and already starting a hangover—thought, Are you the whole world's therapist?

As we turned out the lights, I told Bob, "I wish someone would come along and make her dreams come true."

He murmured his reply, to keep it secret from Davit. "She's having an affair with Don, next door. Didn't you know?"

14.

Everything has changed, it's a whole new ballgame, I'm jumping out of my skin, don't know where to start. This is what they mean by *happiness*, I think.

See what a bit of good news can do to a guy? I count four clichés in just that last paragraph. I've turned into a sap, running down a hillside, tossing dandelions, tra-la-la-ing. This is why you can't trust a cheerful man's view of the world: it's clouded by laughing gas.

I'm a balloon that never left the ground before. All right, a blimp. I've been chained down, but today the chains broke. Up I go, swimming toward the light. Wheeee!

How different everything looks from up here. There's more green than I ever suspected. It's not so bleak a planet after all.

The morning gave no hint of the changes to come. I dressed in the bathroom, for privacy. By the time I opened the door, Davit had already left for Sophia's house. My thought at the time: If Eka doesn't tell him what's going on, I may have to. Otherwise he won't spend a minute with his mother, and then it'll be too late.

Bob played basketball with Garrett—a favor to Cindy, who had to go "out." Eka and I used our time alone to tape another interview. Though I lost faith days ago in my ability to write her book, and though I yearned to take some aspirin and climb into my own bed, I questioned her diligently about her life as a home health aide, and learned some things I hadn't heard before. Her agency said she was entitled to two hours off per day, when the client napped or watched TV, but she usually didn't take the time because she worried that Mrs. N would hurt herself. "I say to her, 'Don't get up, please, stay just here,' but she don't listen." The doctor said Mrs. N should exercise, so Eka took her for a walk every day; she always wanted to turn around before they got halfway down the block. "Each day, she says, 'I can't do this,' but I say, 'You can, you can.' She is more strong than what she believes."

Scribbled notes, furtive glances at her pale wrist with its subtle blue veins. I kept badgering myself to ask her to marry me—wishing for a gaze that said, *Yes, what is your question? Ask and I will say yes, no matter what*—but couldn't meet her eyes long enough to receive encouragement.

It wasn't just the standard failure of nerve. I didn't ask because I dreaded what it would be like to share my basement with her and Davit after she said no.

Lunch. The bacon fell out of her BLT. Mrs. N's chair scraped the floor loudly above us. Eka said she wished she could have tried fashion design as a career.

The unspoken question swelled in me like a tumor, until I couldn't bear to sit with her. Citing a just-remembered dental appointment, I fled, and spent the next hours at the Newark Museum, viewing colonial silverware and twentieth-century pottery while urging myself to forget my fantasy of connubial bliss.

She was on the phone when I returned. She seemed stressed, but relieved to see me. "Now my friend comes— yes, we can go to hospital. Yes, we come now."

Dr. Oh wouldn't say why he wanted to see her again, only that it was urgent and he would meet us at his office. By then it was past three, on a Saturday afternoon; I was terrified.

"How did he sound?"

"Very serious."

I imagined him telling me confidentially, *She's going to die this week; you have to have her admitted.* In case I've been wrong about God's existence, I prayed: *Don't let her die.* Then, in case God turned out to be a legalistic bastard, I revised my prayer: *Let her get better. But if she can't, then don't make her suffer through a long, agonizing death. And don't punish her because this request is coming from me.*

Dr. Oh had on a magenta polo shirt and neat black slacks. He sprang to his feet as we entered—the reception area was deserted except for him—and shook Eka's hand vigorously, then mine, less so. After leading us to his office, he commanded us to sit, and spewed his report while pacing. "I knew it couldn't be the mercury. The chelator brought the levels down, and you were still tremoring. But there's another toxin that produces the same symptoms. I wrote a paper on it. Have you ever heard of parathion? It's an insecticide—an organophosphate. Farmers use it all over the world. When the runoff gets into a river, and the river is used for drinking water, or if people eat fish from it, some will develop your symptoms."

I couldn't understand why this had him so agitated. One poison or another—what's the difference?

"I did a broader screen than the first one, I took blood cells and centrifuged them down, looking for an enzyme called cholinesterase, which is inhibited by this toxin. Guess what? The lab called me just before—and they confirmed that you don't have mercury poisoning."

He beamed, and seemed to expect us to cheer; we must have disappointed him. Eka watched him, uncertain, her head bobbing.

He came alongside her, put a hand on her shoulder, and laughed. "Your condition is reversible. You're going to get better."

While we tried to absorb that, he took what looked like a ChapStick and a Magic Marker from a drawer.

"These are auto-injectors, atropine and 2-PAM chloride. As soon as I administer them, you should start to feel the difference. I'll also give you 2-PAM pills to take home. You'll take one a day for five days, just to be thorough. By the end, you should be back to normal."

He didn't waste time. After ordering her to roll up her pant leg, he swabbed the side of her thigh, then squatted, held the first injector like a pen, and pressed it into her flesh. Eka looked at me like a confused fawn as the needle went in. Dr. Oh held the injector in place for a few moments— "You're allowed to breathe," he told her—then carefully withdrew it and massaged the site.

"This doesn't happen often," he said. "I've only corrected a mistaken diagnosis one other time. And that case was incurable."

After he'd repeated the procedure with the second injector, he asked how she felt.

She looked like she might cry. "I have fear I understood wrong what you say. Please say again, slow."

Dr. Oh grinned, beside himself. "*You're not going to die.* Your tremors will go away. You'll have a normal life. The medicine will make you better."

Without asking whether or not she understood, he went to the electric keyboard on the table behind his desk, and expertly played a yearning, Russian-sounding waltz. Maybe he meant to evoke Dostoyevsky, sentenced to death, hauled before the firing squad in his pajamas, then pardoned at the last moment, a cruel Czar's terrifying lesson: *You were to die, but I, in my mercy, let you live.*

Or, perhaps he generously meant to provide our story with a sound track. Tragedy defeated at the last possible moment, leaving the two lovers an unexpected future together.

As we waited for him to finish, Eka's head kept nodding— sobbing, I thought, but no, it was still her poisoned nervous system. I put my hand on her back, and felt her bones, her breathing, her heat.

"I want to see you again in two days," he told her, "to make sure the medication is working."

"Please, you have tissue?" she asked. He handed her one, and she wiped her eyes.

I asked for one, too. Just in case.

"Thank you, Doctor," she said, fervently sincere. Searching in vain for a more eloquent tribute, she added, "Thank you."

Delirious with joy—thunderstruck—I was tempted to thank God. But, as always, there was a shadow. An hour before, she might have married me, but with half a lifetime miraculously restored, she will almost certainly hold out for someone better.

"How could they get it so wrong?" I asked Dr. Oh, funneling anxiety into outrage at the incompetent ER docs who'd handed her a false death sentence and then almost fulfilled their own prophecy. "She would have died if she hadn't come to you!"

He seemed to find both my praise and my blame-throwing distasteful. "It was a difficult distinction to make. Many specialists would have gotten it wrong."

I've noticed this about doctors. The terror of malpractice is so pervasive, they shut down the first hint of accusation, even when the criticism is aimed elsewhere.

"Still . . ." I grumbled.

"What's it like?" I asked her in the car. "To think you're dying and find out you're going to live?"

We had just left the parking deck and turned onto Lyons Avenue. The sun was a pale region in a watery gray sky.

She put her hand on my upper arm. "How it feels? Grateful. To you, Angus. You saved me."

A van vacated a parking space at the next corner. That was enough of a sign for me. I pulled into the empty spot and, without hesitation, without dithering, unbuckled my seat belt, ignored the steering wheel pressing into my side, and leaned over to kiss her.

She didn't pull away, didn't turn to escape. Instead, she made her lips soft. I kissed her for maybe fifteen seconds, until a muscle in my neck cramped from twisting.

It's been years since I kissed anyone, and longer since I wanted to. The awkward position distracted me, but those soft lips: I never dared hope for such an extravagant gift.

Back on the road, I asked how she wanted to celebrate.

She shook her head. Her wet eyes shone. "Davit—I call him."

That was her celebration. She called her son and spoke to him quietly, in Georgian. At one point she guided a stray lock behind her ear with one finger. It was the gesture of a teenager—of a woman from whose shoulders old age has been lifted.

"He babysits with Sophia," she explained. This amused her: "My baby babysits."

Smiling, sniffling, she blew her nose.

"My mother, I will see again."

That burst the dam. Sobbing followed.

I kept driving. It seemed like the right thing to do.

If I ask her to marry me, why would she accept? She's young(ish), attractive, and can work to support herself. She has a son to love and take care of. Why would she marry an obese, unemployed pessimist? Gratitude has its limits.

Her book is unwritable now—you can't tell the tale of a lovely woman poisoned by pollution if she recovers—but also unnecessary. The emergency is over.

How Bob took the news:

Overcome, he hugged her and cried with her. Why didn't I think of that?

She's resting, watching *House* on my bed. (There goes the tormented physician with his cane, limping and snarling. How nicely he incarnates the hidden suffering of us all!) Now Eka will stop twitching, regain her strength, study, and become a nurse. And I . . . ?

If I lose eighty pounds, exercise, give up misanthropy, and find a job, maybe there's a chance.

(Yet here I am, eating Little Debbie Swiss Rolls as I type.)

The last time I tried to get myself in shape, by walking in Branch Brook Park, my knees hurt so much that I had to sit on a tree stump, because I couldn't reach a bench.

Okay: this time I'll join a Y and swim instead.

Am I willing to relinquish laziness, scorn, and overeating in exchange for her company? Let's say she accepts my proposal. Could I really behave myself forever? I'd have to submerge my opinions, my antisocial impulses, my fundamental nature.

And then there's the other matter. Can I accept *her*, for the rest of my life?

Can't stay long. She's waiting for me.

Davit visited with her briefly when he came home. I found him sprawled across the foot of my bed while she, resting against two pillows, listened to him dotingly.

"What did he do all day?" I asked after he'd excused himself.

"Sophia babysits on three children. He made clay food with them."

On TV, a righteous detective grilled a slimy, darting-eyed worm. Eka asked, "Angus?"

Her gentle tone heralded a tender rejection, I assumed. She'd thought about my kiss, and wanted me to know that, although she never will forget the too many helps I give to her, her feelings on me don't go like that.

"Yes, Eka?"

"You don't have to sleep on floor tonight. The bed is big for both."

So you see, I've been proven wrong once again. I wish I could freeze-dry the elation, to nibble on in leaner times.

Why am I typing this instead of lying beside her? Because I had to tell you.

Wish me luck.

Sunday

A day of rest—from pessimism and the assumption that all is for the worst in this worst of all possible worlds.

This would have been Day Thirteen in the countdown, but that seems to be over now. Abandoned. Aborted.

She's napping. We've had a busy day. I could use some sleep, too. Didn't get much last night. I wonder if she did.

What was it like, to open my eyes and find her facing me in her flannel nightgown, again and again and again? A joy, but also ungraspable. Like a wet bar of soap, it kept slipping out of my hands. Nothing could be better than this peaceful affection, but I can't help assuming it will be snatched from me the moment I stop worrying.

Her wrists between us in the dark seemed delicate as a child's next to mine. (My arms must remind her of slabs of beef. Yet she doesn't flee.)

Gray morning light seeped around the edges of the shade. I watched her stir from sleep, and prepared myself for the startled face, the unguarded horror. When her eyes opened, though, she reached across and rested a limp hand on my shoulder. What a gift!

Emboldened, I touched her hair, her ear, her forehead. My tenderness toward her surpasses any feelings for past partners, by far. It must be that she nearly died—or else, that she thinks I saved her.

"Thank you for inviting me," I said.

She laughed comfortably. "The guest invites owner."

Her face is twitching less already. Savor this!

I made a cheddar cheese, onion and tomato omelet for the four of us. Haven't done that in decades, but one remembers.

Our happiness was not shared, alas. Bob and Davit both seemed down, distant, dismal. I expected, of course, that Davit would resent my sharing a bed with his mother. I have to give him credit, though: at no point was he surly to either of us. But the hearty, joking new arrival has gone away, leaving a large, silent brooder in his place.

Hoping to remind him that I'm still the same friendly host, I asked Davit if he could connect with his old friends on Skype. It seems, though, that he was the only boy in his crowd with a computer. No one else had a mother in America.

Paddling against the current of gloom, I asked Eka what people ate for breakfast back home. She said, "Everything. Soup, mashed potatoes, chicken. Before school in mornings, my mother always was making cucumber and tomato salad."

During cleanup, she took Davit into the bedroom to talk privately—perhaps to explain that she nearly died, and I helped save her, so cut us a break why don't you? Bob, meanwhile, asked for a loan of twenty dollars, so he could take the bus into the city and visit the Metropolitan Museum of Art. Risking an outpouring, I told him he seemed a bit downcast. He said he's realized something: he needs to live abroad, because "I'm starving for an environment that will nourish me." He can support himself by teaching English. At his age, he said, there's a strong undertow dragging him toward comfort and away from new challenges—a tendency he equates with giving up on life. He wants to throw himself into a foreign setting, absorb the culture and the language, and wake his wilting soul.

It sounded to me like a recipe for loneliness and disintegration. I didn't want to kick him when he was down, but neither could I encourage him to run off to his doom.

He asked what I thought of his plan.

"It fits the pattern of your life: always extreme. I'll be honest, I don't see it as a solution—sitting alone in an attic in Cairo, swatting mosquitoes and contracting cholera. Wouldn't Roshi say the enlightened man can find spiritual nourishment anywhere?"

Like an elephant hit by a dart, he barely blinked. "I'll keep thinking about it," he said.

Low-grade worry has been buzzing around my head since he walked out the door. I really don't want him to jump in front of a subway train. But perhaps I'm projecting.

Sophia called Davit while I was talking to Bob, and he left (without enthusiasm) to meet her up on Washington Street. I told Eka, "It must be uncomfortable for him—you and me." She said, "No, no, no. He misses friends. He is sad, thinking he never sees them again. Today he realizes this, first time."

I feel for them both, Davit and Bob: yanked out of their familiar worlds, dumped in my mildewed basement. Who wouldn't be depressed?

But enough empathy—this is the tale of a joyous day. Our futures suddenly restored to us, Eka and I had an entire Sunday to fill with spontaneous pleasures. To delight her was my mission and my only wish. Trawling for ideas, I made a catalogue of other people's Sunday fun:

> Broadway matinee
> Read entire Sunday *Times*
> Brunch with inoffensive live jazz
> Football on TV
> Test-drive cars with no intention of buying
> BBQ with extended family
> Sit in church

The only criterion: I wanted to see her face light up. But I doubted that my list held the answer.

I asked if there was anything she wanted to do today, anything at all. She said, "What makes you happy, I will enjoy also."

I could only think of one truthful response: What would make me happy would be to go back to bed and have your hand on my shoulder again, all day long.

"No, this is *your* day," I insisted.

Yielding, she pondered. "To look at stores in the mall will be good. With you."

And so we visited one of the last places I would have chosen, and shared the best day I can remember. Neither the jostling nor the Christmas music nor the sight of the suffering children on the snaking Santa line could spoil the pleasure of stepping out with my lovely Eka in this crowded carnival, this melting pot of immigrant shoppers, this American dreamland.

But I never told you about last night. What could have left me so contented, so attached to my partner?

Not what you think. She's still weak, and her legs still ache. She hinted at the ground rules before I climbed into bed: "You can sleep if I turn and turn around?"

I said I'd try, and appreciated the clarification, because until then, I wasn't sure what the invitation included.

Arranging myself along the edge, keeping my back to her so as to give her privacy, I wistfully envisioned things that might have been, had I maintained my former weight.

"Tonight is cold," she said. "I move close, okay?"

"Please."

I rolled onto my back to welcome her, and she curled up into my shoulder and side. The arm resting on my chest, chastely sleeved in thick flannel, weighed so little.

"Is nice," she said, sweetly.

"Very nice."

She moved her cheek along my upper arm, just half an inch and back. The soft contact, combined with the fruity scent of her shampoo, created an awkward problem. The last thing I expected: a standing wiener that would have turned the comforter into a shallow tent if not for my raised knee. She never noticed, except when her hand went to scratch her leg and brushed against the rude organ—but she discreetly ignored it and went on snuggling as if nothing had happened.

How does one sleep with El Exigente standing vigil, mutely pleading for relief? One can only remind oneself of what happened the last few times (how many years has it been? I've lost count) and that Eka is still recovering. No man could nod off, though, with this torpedo crying out, *Put me to work, boss!* (Sure, he puts on a big show, but he'll always let you down when it counts.) That's how most of the night passed: in bliss and torment, as I gave thanks for her damp cheek against my shoulder and, despite my fears, devoutly wished for consummation.

The day was knife-cold and cloudless. We saw Don and his wife getting back from church, he handsome in his Sunday suit, she box-like in her dress and sour in the puss. Eka had dressed up again, in a black silk blouse and white pants, the reverse of yesterday's outfit.

Near the entrance to the mall, we came upon a kiosk selling framed prints. I'm not an art guy, but an Andrew Wyeth picture caught my eye: white snow and bare trees through windowpanes with cracked paint on the mullions. The fine tracery of the trees against the pale sky reminded me of the austere landscape we'd just driven through, minus the strip malls. The picture appealed to me—the world pared to its sleeping bones—but Eka said, "Why someone makes so depressed painting? Where is color?"

You're thinking, There it is, the seed of difference that will grow into a thick root and crack us apart. But you don't know everything. If living with her means covering my walls with pictures she likes—yellow daisies on a pink tablecloth, a kitten cuddling with a chimp—then, like the man said, Bring it on. I wish I could believe that someday, I'll be lucky enough to share a home with her, decorated with as many garish, sentimental posters as the walls will hold.

We spent most of the day in women's shops. Few things interest me less than feminine fashion; the endless succession soon turned into a blur, but I enjoyed myself overall. New York & Company, Ann Taylor, bebe, Guess, J. Jill, J. Crew, Express, The Limited, Old Navy, H&M, XXI Forever, Love Culture: Eka's taste knows no boundaries. She can find contentment (and bargains) in a ripped-jean/strobe-light/throbbing-bass teen emporium, a mature women's blond-wood skirt-and-sweater mart, and everything in between. I found it charming, watching her shove hangers along chrome racks to get at a ruffly fuchsia blouse or a simple white jacket, unconcerned with the ages and styles of the shoppers around her. She didn't want to buy anything, she explained in advance, only to try things on "for the fun," and she did exactly that, at least two items per store. I've never seen her smile as much: enjoying her costumed reflection in a zebra-striped top, a puckered black minidress, a coral sweater, a pashmina scarf. To me—the admiring sugar daddy, sans sugar—she looked stunning in everything. Again and again, I savored the wondrous fact that I was her companion. The miracle of it far outweighed the backache.

We both needed to rest often. Fortunately, they had anticipated our visit and placed benches everywhere. While sharing a Wetzel's pretzel outside the food court, she startled me with a bit of reality: "I go back to work soon."

"You should give yourself more time. To get your strength back."

She shook her head as if shooing the temptation to pamper herself. "I need money."

I referred in code to a hypothetical honeymoon. "It might be nice to take a vacation first. A trip. Together."

With a grape-colored fingernail, she pried a bit of pretzel-dough from between two teeth. "Yes, I would like. Someday."

I considered proposing to her then and there, to free her from financial anxieties, but I'll need a job myself before I can do that.

The subject of money was a leaden bummer that sent me crashing to earth. I counseled myself to resist gravity by letting go of fear. Don't worry, be happy! Forget the future and enjoy the strange, swirling present—the mothers and daughters exiting Victoria's Secret together, the Chinese grandfather pushing a tyke in a little green frog-car, the white gull sailing across the blue in the skylight above, the specialty kiosks selling nothing but red Christmas stockings or Zippo lighters, the shoppers talking on cell phones in languages I couldn't identify. (Arabic? Farsi? Tagalog? Hindi?) The wonders of the mall! Our own bazaar, *mercado*, *souk*—or, if you're a refugee from poverty, violence, and open sewers, plopped down amid the festive lights and gorgeous bounty, then you can simply call it heaven.

In our new intimacy, I asked Eka what she and her mother argued about. At first she said they never argued, but I reminded her that she often raised her voice on the phone. She explained that they sometimes disagreed over important decisions—whether or not Davit should come to America, for example. "Is usual for Georgians to discuss with passion. Here is not the same."

But there was more shopping to do. She ended up buying a black blouse with powdery gold stars for her mother and a radio-controlled helicopter for her nephew, and allowed me to treat her to a snug white sequined top. By then we were both exhausted, but she insisted on buying something for me. There's really nothing in the world I want—nothing for sale at the mall, anyway—but, while passing through the narrow aisle of a toy store (her whim), the stacked Monopoly boxes sent me hurtling back to childhood. My father, an overeducated civil servant who never gambled so much as a nickel, had discovered the secret of winning, and he used it against his children ruthlessly on rainy weekend afternoons. His strategy was to buy up the cheapest properties and put as many houses on them as he could afford, thereby bankrupting the rest of us before we could buy a single house on our fancier real estate. (Check the property cards in your old Monopoly set. See how little the houses cost on purple and light blue? And how the rents jump once you have three?) I didn't figure out his system until I was a teenager—just in time to never play with him again.

The memory of Dad snickering as I mortgaged my railroads to pay him rent bothered me anew, but the resentment came encased in nostalgia. I asked Eka for the game, and looked forward to teaching her, Bob, and Davit my father's method. I would caution them not to overspend, and help them along. I'd be a better father to them than my father was to me. Maybe I would finally win—with pleasure, but without gloating.

Too tired to reach the car, we recuperated on a wicker bench near Sears. The piped-in music reminded her of Christmas back home, of singing "Alilo" with her family as they walked through the street—a carol that tells the story of the basket, the stable, and the baby. Their Christmas comes on January 7th, she told me, because they use the Julian calendar, and their Santa is called Tovlis Papa. Even during the Soviet days, when religion was suppressed, they used to light a candle, say a prayer, go to church. Last year, she found an Orthodox church in Manhattan and stayed all night, praying, a custom called *Litonioba*—everyone standing, energized by the service, and then feasting at a long table, on *khachapuri*, wine, and fried chicken. "It was so great feeling—so safe and friendly. So good spirit."

As she told her holiday tales, I worried: did she understand that I can't write her life story now? The question nagged at me until I had to ask it aloud.

She sighed. "I know this. But I like too much telling stories to you."

On the way home, she asked if I'd ever traveled. I told her my stock anecdotes from England, Paris and the Bavarian Alps, but withheld the sudden memory of Lena. (Touring Neuschwanstein together, listening to the tour guide discuss the mosaic swan in the floor tiles, obsessively yearning to hold her hand: let go, Angus. The memory is pointless now.) "You saw so much places," she exclaimed.

I quickly corrected her misconception. "I've only set foot on two continents out of seven."

She followed up by asking where I'd like to travel next, and I thought of the mountains of China, those eerie, phallic spires.

I didn't speak, though. My traveling days are over; my knees won't carry me much further. This may have been the first time I've faced that fact—or, at least, the first time it upset me.

"What about you?" I asked. "What would you like to see?"

Uncharacteristically impish, she said, "I would like to see, right now, beautiful big houses."

"And so you shall," I announced. One exit later, I pulled off Route 46, a veritable genie, and gave her a driving tour of Montclair's mansions.

The vast-lawned villas and multigabled manors delighted her—the pompom shrubs, primeval trees, elephantine wreaths—but they sickened me. This is what she covets, and I'll never be able to give her more than a toolshed.

She asked if something was wrong. I told her feebly, "I wish I could give you everything you ever wanted."

She read my mind and chased away my fears with a laugh. "I don't need big houses. Little things I love more. A cabinet on wall, all filled up from small glass animals—*this* I want someday."

I said, "I believe we could manage that," and made a mental note: *glass animals, display case*. I'll start searching online as soon as I finish up here.

Though I worry that she'll flee at the first opportunity, she hasn't yet. It seems she may actually stay with me. But I'm afraid to believe it.

✳ ✳ ✳

My innards are shaken. Calm yourself, man!

Returning from a Thai dinner run, I found Denise Quinones frowning downward on the other side of the fence. She had on a gray sweat suit and blue rubber gloves, and I worried that she knew everything, including my role in wrecking her life. "I can't stand this," she said.

If you stood Denise next to Cindy, it would be cruel. One gives off sparkling light and indestructible hope. The other glowers beneath unnaturally black hair, her haunted eyes charging you and all the other bastards with conspiracy to disappoint her. Squint your mind and you can imagine it was Don's love—bestowed on one, withheld from the other—that made the neighbor bloom while the wife withered.

She had a paper towel in one gloved hand and a yellow ShopRite bag in the other. A rotten-meat, summer-garbage stink reached me across the little hedge, informing me that it wasn't Don's infidelity that had her down, but a small dead animal by her feet.

"Would you like some help?" my guilty conscience said.

"I shouldn't ask you to do it. But please, would you?"

She let me use her rubber gloves, which barely fit my hands. The dead squirrel was soft, unmangled, dense, and heavy. (There's more packed into those tiny torsos than their nimble springing suggests.) Into the ShopRite bag it went.

I suppose a large cosmic hand will dispose of me similarly someday.

The gloves tugged sadistically at my hand-hairs coming off. Punishment: if not for me, her husband would have been here to do this dirty work.

"Don's out on a job, I guess."

"Leaky dormer. It happens all the time."

Terse. Half sour. Layers of frustration built up over decades, covered with sardonic scar tissue. *He stays away because she's angry. She's angry because he stays away.*

"Water damage can't wait until Monday," I said in his defense. "He'd end up in small claims court."

"Oh, he's already been. There are lots of lunatics out there."

Having never exchanged this many words with her, I'd thought of Denise as barely animate, a harridan and nothing more. Her tone was more wry than complaining, though.

Asked about her daughters, she turned chatty and enthusiastic. They went to pick out a wedding dress yesterday. The fiancé is a paramedic. He'll never get rich but he's solid as a rock, one in a million.

"How's Don's back? I remember he got hurt last year."

"He should retire, but he's putting it off. He can't stand sitting still."

"He was home for a while, right? That must have been hard on both of you."

She cawed: her laugh. "That was the best time we've had in years. We watched the World Series together. I like having him around."

She might as well have plunged a knife in my forehead. I wanted to flee, but she had a question. "I haven't seen your column in a while. Are you on vacation?"

"I took a leave of absence. I needed a break."

"It's a funny thing. I used to read that column, before I knew it was you, and I had a picture in my mind of what you must look like. It was nothing like you."

"What did you picture?"

"An older guy, in a jacket and tie. With a mustache. Do you remember David Niven? Like that."

I.e., an urbane professor. No need for either of us to comment on the discrepancy.

I excused myself, explaining that my guests were waiting for the dinner I'd set down on her asphalt.

"And I'm going back to my figure skating. Thanks." Into the trash went the weighted shopping bag. Into her side door went Denise.

And down the chute I slid, a sulfurous wind in my face, speeding toward hell. For love and happiness are commodities like any other, and if Don has transferred his affection to Cindy (thanks to me), then he has withdrawn it from his wife. She doesn't know it yet, but she's about to become a wretched, miserable woman.

Thai food in hand, I descended into my pit and found Eka at my open laptop, reading this.

Her own laptop had frozen, something it does from time to time, and she'd wanted to keep searching the Help Wanted ads, so she had borrowed mine, and found a document called *Last Words* on the desktop. Some sort of symphony was playing on the radio; she hadn't heard me coming.

Lit only by the screen in front and the stove-light behind, wearing the white sweater I'd bought her (which glinted like snow in moonlight), she stared at me moist-eyed, her mouth a small arch of disillusionment.

She was up to page five.

Without subtlety, I closed the laptop as if herding the world's evils back inside. Then I took it from the kitchen table and shut myself in the bedroom. I would have turned the lock, but there isn't one.

On the edge of the bed, slumping, I simply breathed. The slim black shell sat across my thighs, hot as plutonium.

She knocked shyly. Receiving no answer, she opened the door.

"I'm sorry, I shouldn't read, I know."

She explained how she stumbled on my "docooment." I couldn't look at her.

"To be unhappy, I understand. But this idea, to end life—you would do this?"

"I was depressed. It was before you came to see me."

She shut the door behind her, though no one else was home. "What you wrote, how you don't like the people with so many problems—you feel this truly?"

I shrugged. *Sort of.* I refused to lie to her, even if it meant the end of us.

Her forehead folded with compassion. "To me is too sad. You help people, you do good to everyone, but you don't want to live."

I appreciated her willingness to talk to me, despite the things she'd read. But I couldn't tell whether she had changed her mind about me on a deeper level.

Wait—didn't I describe her voice as ugly?

Opening the laptop, I searched for *Eka*, and found the name on page five, one screen past the paragraph she'd reached. *That grating voice.*

"Please, Eka. Promise never to read my files again."

Her thin lips became thinner. Chastened. "I promise, never."

But will she keep her promise?

She was leaning against my door, hands clasped at her belly, prayer-style. No tremors at all: no longer sick, no longer dying. At least I accomplished that.

"I can ask question?"

Nod.

Oh so softly, "You want to die still?"

"No. Things have changed."

"Please, now you promise to me. Like I will live, you will live."

Bold as a man on a ledge, I asked, "Together?"

It was too much to demand. I knew that as soon as the syllables escaped. Too late to call them back, though.

Her smile was small: not exuberant, but accepting. "If you want. Yes."

Because I'd coerced her, I couldn't believe she meant it— at least, not until she said, "You should come to kiss me."

As I held her hands and kissed her forehead, she leaned a cheek against my shoulder.

I believe that was my first experience of contentment.

MONDAY

I couldn't quit while I was ahead. Like a drunk playing Russian roulette, I had to keep pushing my luck until I shot a hole in my skull.

Everything seemed good, better, best; then she changed. Shadowy, preoccupied, secretive—she has turned into a different person. I don't know what's going on. She won't say.

It's not losing her that's made me frantic. It's not knowing whether I've lost her or not. And, if I have, what the fuck happened?

Where is jaded detachment when you need it?

I proposed to her like any earnest Ernest. She wouldn't answer yes or no, only *wait*. Which, in the hindsight of the dark kitchen after midnight, sounds very much like, *I will let you gently down.* Because a vow of eternal fidelity was just too much. Who can promise such a thing? To me, especially.

She'd already agreed to stay. But I had to ask for more. Idiot!

Remember, though: it wasn't my asking that made her change. It was her changing that made me ask. Seeing her drift away, I groped desperately to hold on.

If the verdict goes against me, then the sentence is solitary confinement. Can a misanthrope be lonely? Apparently, yes.

She can't do this to me. The urge to scream these senseless words comes raging from my gut. Like other jilted jerks before me, I'm finding it hard to maintain my aplomb.

Would positive thinking make a difference? I don't see how.

I shouldn't have stuck my neck out. (The origin of that phrase becomes starkly clear when awaiting the headsman's axe.) If I'd just kept my mouth shut, we could have gone on as we were indefinitely.

Except that she'd already changed.

A corrective thought: all she said was *wait*. Possibly I'm overreacting.

(Don't be a sap. Don't start wishfully thinking that darkness doesn't always mean night and light doesn't always mean day. That's like betting on neither heads nor tails, but a sudden whirlwind that will blow the coin away.)

We dropped Davit off at the high school for his English assessment, and returned to Newark Beth Israel for Eka's follow-up visit. This time, there was an older couple in the waiting room, and a receptionist, a frail woman with a sweetly nun-like smile, who told us that Dr. Oh wanted to see the patient alone today.

(What did he say? The little shit! Did he come right out and tell her, *You're too attractive to throw yourself away on that behemoth—I may be gay but even I can see it—you don't owe him the rest of your life just because he did you a favor.* Or was it something more sinister, that I can't even imagine?)

While waiting, unsuspecting, I opened my laptop and read about her homeland. Admittedly, I'd held an attitude of amused disdain toward this presumably backward republic; reading the facts chased away some of that smug superiority. Natural resources: forests, hydropower, nonferrous metals, manganese. Industry: steel, aircraft, machine tools, foundry equipment. The Georgian language, unrelated to any other tongue, is one of the oldest in the world that's still spoken. They have their own alphabet, a collection of loops, hooks and squiggles that reminded me of earrings.

Georgia was the second nation to adopt Christianity, around the year 300; ancient monasteries are hidden in the Caucasus Mountains. Queen Tamar of Georgia presided over a golden age in the 1100s.* Stalin came from Georgia; his real surname was Djugashvili. Georgia formerly supplied all of the Soviet Union's citrus fruit. Georgian hospitality is world-renowned.

The author's love of homeland reminded me of Eka's:

> Pure Georgian air, unique coniferous forests, clear mountain lakes, Alpine meadows and healing mineral springs; sacred places of early Christian culture, and numerous resorts known over the world . . . such attractions call to tourists across the globe.

The lightly accented rhapsody awakened an urge to travel again to take Eka back home, to reunite her with her mother and witness her joy.

And then she reappeared, and everything fell apart.

Useful Georgian words and phrases:
Hello—*gamarjoba*.
Thank you—*madlobt*.
I want—*me minda*.
I love you—*miq'varkhar*.
Sorry—*bodiski*.
I don't understand—*ver gavige*.
Good-bye—*nakhvamdis*.

Actually, my waiting room reverie didn't include such delicate poignancy. It went more like this:

---

*Confronted with a rebellious nobility, her father had its leaders killed or banished; the pretender to the throne was castrated and blinded, and died of his wounds. I confess, I worried that some vestige of medieval melodrama remains in Eka's blood. If only that were my worst problem!

I would love to take her back—to see this church, this Tsminda Sameba, glowing at dusk like a honeycomb. But it can't be. An hour and a half hike to the peak of a mountain? Not likely. And there's the other thing: we're not really a match. Even Mr. Magoo could see that.

Dr. Oh's other patient came out before Eka. She had waxy skin, a white head scarf, and a grotesquely swollen neck. I've seen sick and dying people before, and managed to accept their fates philosophically, but this slow-moving, benignly smiling woman terrified me. The sight of her made me want to bow a thousand times to whatever power had granted Eka her recovery. (*Yes, I'm helpless! Yes, I'm nothing! Yes, I cower in fear before Your whims!*)

Eka had been fairly calm when she went in for her checkup. When she came out, though, her eyes were moving everywhere, like those of hunted prey.

Stab of fear: Doctor Oh's diagnosis had been wrong. The ER doc had gotten it right after all.

"Is there a problem with the medicine?"

She shook her head. "No. Recovery is good."

"What happened? What did he say?"

"I will be like normal, very soon. Come, we go now."

"But something's wrong."

"No . . ."

Doctor Oh is exceptionally fastidious and fairly effeminate; it's unlikely that he demanded sexual favors as payment, or groped her. I couldn't imagine what secret she was keeping, and still can't.

How pretty she looked in her red and black dress, and how troubled. "What did he say?" I asked again in the elevator.

"Only, he is happy because I am better."

Which was certainly *not* all he said, but who am I to demand that she cough up her secrets?

Tiny white flakes hit the windshield and melted. Inwardly, I compared the lifespan of a snowflake with that of my happiness.

A few blocks from home, she asked gravely, "Can you lend to me please fifty dollars?"

I laughed explosively—the hearty, bitter laugh of one who has lost everything and has no recourse but to pretend amusement at the unfairness of the game.

"Why you do laugh?" she asked.

Because you're confirming my fear that, to you, I'm just a walking ATM.

"What do you need the money for?"

"You will think it is waste. I want lottery tickets. I give back the money when we come in the house."

"Do you do this every week? Are you a gambling addict?"

"No, never, never before. Please, Angus. I want to buy these."

She pleaded so urgently that I couldn't keep up the teasing. We parked outside Gigi's Luncheonette and spent nearly a half hour picking numbers for tomorrow's Mega-Millions drawing. I asked if she'd share any of the sixty-eight million dollars with me, should she win.

Solemnly: "I promise to you, I will share all."

She didn't specify a percentage, but even 1 percent would come out to $680,000. And if I marry her, I get half.

I swear, though, that's not the reason why, once we'd buckled our seat belts, I said, "I don't suppose you'd want to marry me, would you?"

The dome of my gut eclipsed the bottom of the steering wheel, and that was where I kept my focus. Even without looking, though, I could see the tepid nature of her fondness for me. Put that together with the rarity of marital happiness in general, and you've built an argument that should have made me shout, *Just kidding.*

Her quiet reply: "I don't know how to answer."

"That's all right. No need to say any more about it."

She wouldn't let it drop. "You are so good person to me. But too much things happened to me, all at once together. I am confused. Please give time. Okay?"

What changed since the other day, when she said, *If you want, yes?* Beats me. Factors hidden from view are at work here.

I should do as she asked and give her time, instead of guessing. But I doubt I'll have the fortitude to wait patiently, neutrally, for her decision. Fear will infect me—it already has. Soon I'll start peppering her with wisecracks. *Might today be the day? Has Her Highness decided?*

This can't end well.

Unable to sit still while she questioned Davit about who knows what—he kept stretching his arms behind his back while they talked, in preparation for his tryout later today— I grabbed my brother and left the apartment.

We drove aimlessly. Bob stared out his window, showing me the back of his head. (Where once an elastic secured a flaccid ponytail, a gray field of bristle now stands.) I wanted to pour out my disappointment, and my dread of losing her, but pride turned my fear into sarcastic complaint: how brilliant I had been to propose marriage just as she was distancing herself, etc., etc.

I hoped my brother would work his therapeutic magic and calm me down. His mind was elsewhere, though. All he had to offer was the oldest of chestnuts: "You should tell her how you feel."

Brilliant! Why didn't I think of that? Thanks a lot, Bob!

We had reached Paterson by then. Cruising past the brick factory ruins, we came to a little building with a sign announcing, *GREAT FALLS.* I'd never seen the falls and had little interest in seeing them now. But my irritation with Bob drove me to tourism, just to escape being sealed in the car with him.

We parked in the lot and followed the thunderous noise to a view of two slimy spumes pouring between fractured rocks. Discontented, I kept seeking a closer vantage point, until we stood on an arched walkway watching the water spill into the canyon below. The noise drowned out the car radios blaring on the streets nearby, but failed to blot out my fears about Eka.

White mist rose from the gorge. Bob stared into it. Why had he grown so dismal again? What the hell is going on here?

Could it be that, like Cindy, he has a secret to hide?

It wasn't a long leap from there to the suspicion that's still chewing at me. What if my brother, like Don, has betrayed the person closest to him—by falling in love with Eka?

And what if the feeling is mutual?

I'll murder him if it's true. I swear, I won't let him do this to me. (Is it really possible that, of all the men on the planet, she would fall in love with my half-wit brother? My guts are howling!)

A faintly foul odor reached us from below, where the plummeting water bashed its head against the river's green surface. The pieces seemed to fit: Eka's guilty evasiveness, Bob sneaking his way edgewise into her heart by playing football with Davit. Scummy foam floated on the river's surface; my soul crashed along with the dirty water.

They couldn't come out and tell me about their affair, if that's what's going on, because neither of them has any place to go if I throw them out. Also, give them credit, they're considerate people, and neither one wants to hurt me.

Even if they haven't done the deed, Bob may be miserable at the thought of her sharing my bed.

The sudden, volcanic urge to push him over the railing was checked by a last remnant of sanity, which whispered that I may be (must be) completely, preposterously wrong.

Davit still hadn't returned from his basketball tryout by the time we got back. He had his phone turned off, and Eka was starting to panic. "Too long time he is gone. If someone robs and hits him, we don't know."

I pointed out that such things rarely happen around here. She replied that, in the years after independence, such things happened every day in Georgia.

I offered to take her out and search for him. She accepted, but before she zipped her jacket, he came bounding down the stairs—the whole flight in two floor-shaking leaps.

His tryout had gone well. Apparently he has a better outside shot than anyone on the team, and is more consistent from the foul line. The coach praised his hustle and his willingness to pass.

He must have thought those were tears of joy in his mother's eyes.

At dinner, Eka eyed her plate like a prisoner staring at a life sentence. (Am I that life sentence?) Davit told further tales of his tryout. Bob drifted in and out, listening at times, then departing for continents unknown. And I considered what I would do if Bob married Eka. (*That's* why he wants to transplant himself—so she can follow and I'll never know. God damn him!)

Considering the mood of the house, I'm not sure why I inflicted an after-dinner game of Monopoly on my guests, or why they consented to play. Mostly, I hoped the game would distract me. I suppose they felt obligated to humor their host.

We set up the board on the kitchen table. As I explained my father's strategy, they listened so distractedly that, midway, I had an urge to walk out the door.

The dice knocked hollowly on the cardboard, again and again. I pointed out how the battleship token I remembered from childhood had turned into a bag of money; the observation sank like a pebble in a well.

There were no furtive glances between Eka and Bob. I would have been grateful, had I not been so busy wrestling with rage and dread.

Bob left first: out for a walk, "to get some air."

Eka pleaded exhaustion soon after, and disappeared behind the bedroom door.

That left Davit and me to move our die-cast cannon and dog around the board. He followed my advice diligently, and we clashed in a brutal real estate war until he said, "Sorry, may I leave? I don't really like this type of game."

With a royal sweep of the fingers, I set him free and he exited the apartment.

More relieved than disappointed, I bundled the property cards in a thin red rubber band, gathered the money in one sloppy stack, and put the lid on the box. I doubt I'll ever open it again.

Advice to self: accept that she won't marry me. Then, when she breaks the news, I can say, *Tell me something I don't know.*

Tuesday

Sheer insanity.

The guests will arrive in one hour, they'll tromp down the steps and fill up my dank brown living room. But I'm unequipped for the task of entertaining them. Sure, I can put out chips and alcohol as well as the next guy, but making guests welcome is a skill I never bothered to cultivate.

Yet I must not fail. I can't tell if my fears about Eka and Bob are on target or absurd—but it seems I'm still in the running, and her decision may depend on what she sees tonight. If I prove myself a congenial host, a man who can get along with others, then she may say yes after all. If I fail, I'm doomed.

I can't do this.

But I'll try. When one who can't swim is thrown in the ocean, he splashes to find air. That's what I'll do, too.

When *can't* meets *must*, what then?

How it happened:

After we dropped Davit off for his first day of school, she asked if I planned to look for work again. I may be thick, but the underlying meaning penetrated. She was taking my proposal seriously; she can't afford to hitch her wagon to a falling star.

I told her I'd call the paper today and see about the possibilities.

As soon as she got in the shower, I took a deep breath and phoned Jerri White. I found my ex-boss in a candid mood. "If you're calling to get your job back, don't bother asking. Everyone's very happy with Terrence."

Pride was my undoing. If I'd said, *A pox on you, too,* and hung up, that would have been that. But I refused to admit she'd pinned me to the wall and named me like a butterfly. "That's not why I called," I claimed. "I just wanted to invite you to a little Christmas party. Are you available tonight?"

The silence went on and on.

"I'm so sorry," she eventually replied. "Yes, of course. May I bring something?"

"Just your lovely self."

Something small fell on Mrs. N's floor just now, a dull thump above my head. More than anything, it sounded like the first shovelful of wet dirt hitting my coffin.

I've never thrown a party before, and wasn't sure how to begin. Logic helped: first, I reasoned, one needs guests.

My address book, rarely opened, includes a few relatives, assorted doctors, friends I haven't spoken to since the Clinton Administration, and most of the women I ever went out with. (*Went out:* a curious euphemism. I supposed *stayed in* would come too close to the sordid truth.) Finding these long-ago partners, these Debbies, Susans and Julies— once the names of young classmates, now the names of retirees—filled me with wistful satisfaction. I may be vastly overweight, jobless, and incapable of sustaining a bond with any living mammal, but at least I slept with a fair number of women in my time.

Other names in the book cast darker shadows. It's not exactly news that I've become a recluse, but their remembered faces depressed me. I'm thinking of Frank Czerniak and our trip to Boston, where he got drunk at Fenway Park and risked our lives by proclaiming he was Mickey Mantle's son . . . and shy, sly Ed Feig, my colleague at the *Raritan News*, who worked harder than I did and now covers City

Hall for the *New York Times*, damn him. The details of our drifting apart don't matter—they're gone, that's the point. I can't call them now.

But I digress.

The guest list included my brother and sister; Cindy and Garrett; Jerri White; Neil the physical therapist (who has done more to ease my pain than anyone on earth); and Marty the computer repairman, a chatterbox who charges so little per hour that the bill usually comes to half what I expected. I called each of them by phone; only Cindy couldn't make it. (They're having a celebration at Garrett's old school tonight, she claimed.) I left a message for Don and his wife instead.

Eka heard me leave the message as she dressed in the bedroom. When she emerged, still red-faced from the shower, she asked, "You will make party? Tonight?" Yes, I admitted, I'd done something crazy and invited seven people to a Christmas party. Covering my tracks, I added, "I wanted to celebrate your getting better."

She gave a small *tsk!* and shook her head as if I were her irresponsible-yet-lovable pal. "Too much to do! So small time!"

Bob had gone to the library, job-hunting. By the time he returned, we had written a menu, set up music, bought food, liquor, and festive doodads, and done most of the cooking.

On my own, I would have bought beer, salsa, and two bags of Tostitos, but Eka planned a feast, including baked ziti, stuffed cabbage, a Georgian cheese pastry called *khacha-puri*, tomato and cucumber salad with feta cheese and onions, red wine, vodka, and a round sponge cake that she called a holiday *specialitzi*.

The apartment has never smelled so thickly of supper. I imagined coming home to this meaty, oniony aroma every night, and chuckled inwardly. Maybe I'll grow a mustache like Stalin's.

Sous-chefing, I chopped tomatoes while she lined a pot with cabbage leaves and told me about New Year's back home, when they would eat for days, visit family and friends, and set off fireworks. As it happened, she met her husband at a New Year's party. He was her cousin's friend, and he brought fireworks to the party. This was after independence, *in chaos time*. They were all sad because no one could get fireworks this year, and then Zura showed up with a shopping bag of *shushkhunas* and *khlapushkas* and little dynamites. Eka's father called him Promete, or Prometheus, a reference she understood because her father had read Greek myths to his children. Zura wasn't a criminal himself, but he had friends who became successful gangsters after independence, and through them, he provided her family with many things. *I was only fifteen, more young than Davit, but Zura couldn't think of nobody, only me.* The attention made her uncomfortable. But when her father's factory closed and he couldn't find another job, and her mother's boss had a stroke, and they had no salary—after they sold all the good furniture, Zura was there, bringing groceries to the apartment every day.

She had wanted to be a doctor, not a nurse, but *he loved too much me*, and he kept pushing her to marry him.

"But you must have liked him," I said, only distantly jealous. "You must have found him appealing, if you ended up marrying him."

"He is handsome, but I don't have interest in marriage. I am fifteen, sixteen. And my parents say always, 'Don't marry if you don't love, we will find a way.' But we had hard days. People are hungry, they killed you for six hundred dollars and rob your home. This happened to us. I ask myself, 'How I can be so selfish? He is considerate person. I can love if I try.' So, when I am seventeen, we marry."

She was stirring the meat sauce for the baked ziti, stirring and staring. I intruded. "And then Davit was born . . ."

"I cry, I cry, I cry. Everything what I hoped for, I lost. Sometimes he scolded, 'Grow up! You are not little girl now.' My parents see me unhappy, they say, 'You can come home.' And what do you think happens? After Davit, Zura found a different girl, fifteen like I was before. So, he disappeared forever. I told to myself, 'You were bad wife.' But now I know, I was too young for this."

The story demanded a response, but I couldn't speak, because the subject—a man who pushed her into a marriage she didn't want—touched too close to my own wounded, gasping hopes.

"I talked off your ears," she said.

"No, you didn't."

Once she had the ziti in the oven and the stuffed cabbage simmering on the stove, we set to work converting my dark cave into a festive party space. We moved the kitchen table out to the living room and covered it with a tablecloth from Party City; the red poinsettias seemed to pop out of the vinyl. We hung golden garlands, a 3–D paper snowflake, and a Santa cutout with elbow, knee, hip and shoulder joints. We filled a basket on the table with fleece snowballs. She hummed unfamiliar melodies as she worked, her face glistening with an angelic sheen. I tingled as I watched her. It was so easy to imagine us together at the supermarket . . . attending weddings . . . shopping for furniture . . .

By the time we finished, the apartment looked like a nursing home on Christmas Eve and smelled like Eastern Europe at dinnertime. A sweet memory: Eka setting the little tinsel Christmas tree on the table, and carefully, contentedly arranging the tiny fake presents beneath it.

She's napping now, resting from her work. In a few minutes, the first guest will press the buzzer. Dare I say it? I'm almost optimistic.

My eyeballs hurt. So does the brain behind them. I doubt I'll finish this.

I was right all along. Sadistic gods dangle shiny objects before your eyes until you give in to desire, then yank them away.

Last Night's Party

- Introductions, cordiality. Bob subdued, disengaged.
- With her doctor's permission, Eka drank wine. In her simple black dress, she was the most desirable woman in the room, by several lengths.
- Bob planted himself on the couch with Greer all night. He seemed to be venting the frustrations of a lifetime, but I also overheard him say there's an opening for a clerk at the library, and he may take the job.
- Remembering that *Georgian hospitality is world-renowned,* I exhorted myself to be jovial with the guests, individually and collectively. After introducing Don and Denise to Neil the PT and Marty the computer guy, I detected Jerri White's discomfort, and went to drink punch with her. Not too much, though. Mustn't get sloppy, I warned myself.
- Overdressed in burgundy velvet, she asked how I knew everyone. I said, "Answering that would bore us both to tears. Instead, tell me something about yourself that I don't know." I congratulated myself that Eka would approve of my hostly charm—but Jerri said, "It's a little late for that. After so many years of not wanting anything to do with me."
- *Is this it?* I thought. *The ugly scene, the outpouring of unsuspected resentment that will taint me in Eka's eyes?*
- In self-defense, I met blunt with blunter. "Jerri, did you know that the job nearly drove me to suicide? I didn't want anything to do with *anyone.*"
- With Jerri, you never know whether you'll get the moist eyes or the bayonet. "Nice try."
- If I stayed with her, I knew, the daggers would only sharpen. Solution: "Don, I want to introduce you to someone . . ."

• Once that fire was under control, I had a moment to reflect: *These are, more or less, the people who'd show up at my funeral.*

• Or, one could view the room as a picture of the life I might have with Eka: hearty food, companionship, friends. And family, including Davit, this friendly boy carrying around an overfull plate and chatting with Neil, then Denise, then Marty, then Jerri. Of the many stepsons I might have landed, he seemed the cream of the crop.

• I'd set up an eclectic mix of archaica in the CD carousel—Bossa Nova, R&B, Herb Alpert. When "Dancing in the Streets" came on, Eka took my hand in hers, put my other hand on her waist, and rested hers snugly on my shoulder. She sang along as we danced, with da-da-da's in place of words.

• I wonder when I danced last. Greer's wedding? Considering how fervently I wanted not to make a spectacle of myself, and how unconducive that fear is to dancing, I think we did nicely. The pleasure of her touch more than made up for the agony in my joints.

• After our dance, Eka turned the music off and called for everyone's attention. "I want to make toast. Everyone take to drink something. In this room is a very good man. He saved my life. One doctor said I will die from poison, but Angus found for me a different doctor. Now I got strong and healthy again. For me, he is a great, kind man. Please, everyone—cheers to Angus."

• Whistles, yip-yip-yips. In my own living room, with golden garlands all around.

• She gazed across the room at me as if through a private tunnel. Everything I'd feared seemed, in the light of that gaze, clearly wrong. I thought her eyes were saying, *Yes, I'll marry you.* And I confess that a prick of fear hit me in the chest like a dart. What had I gotten myself into? (You'd think I was a menopausal trapeze artist, swinging from one extreme to the opposite—but wait. You ain't seen nothing yet.)

- Someone put the music back on. Eka went to work wrapping leftovers in foil. I found myself alone with Don in the kitchen, setting up a pot of coffee. After checking that no one could overhear, he told me softly, "Cindy and me are talking about where we should live."
- I hadn't expected so much so soon. We both peeked out into the living room, making sure Denise was out of earshot. (She was telling Davit stories her girls had told her about our local high school in days gone by.) "I want to thank you," Don said. "If it wasn't for you, none of this would have happened."
- He went on to explain many things. *I can't see how I deserve her—haven't felt this happy since I was nineteen—everything about her is so sweet and soft and clean—I feel bad about my hands, they're like sandpaper—I missed out on so much.*
- His babbling doused me with flammable guilt. I asked how soon he expected to move out, and he tossed me this lit match: "I thought I would talk to Denise later tonight."
- My half-conscious reasoning went this way: when forced to choose between the supreme happiness of Person A and the prevention of crushing, mutilating pain to Person B, you have no choice, you've got to rescue Person B. "I hear your daughter's getting married," I said. "How do you like the guy?"
- The change of subject threw him, but he tried to seem unfazed. "He's a good kid. He used to work for a landscaper, but now he's a paramedic. And Autumn's very happy."
- I willed Denise to come into the kitchen at that moment and join us in singing their future son-in-law's praises. I wanted Don to see her happy—to show him the smile he'd once loved, just above the neck he was planning to snap. Sorry, Cindy.
- Since Denise didn't come, I led Don out of the kitchen. I congratulated Denise again on her daughter's engagement, and she played her part masterfully, bubbling with delight as she told us how much fun she and Autumn were having

together, shopping for the flowers, choosing the menu and the hall. Eerily, I could see in her face the teenager she must have been.

• Don listened with bowed head and sober mien. At one point he cast a long, forlorn look my way: *Why are you doing this to me?* Rarely have I felt so powerful an urge to apologize.

• Jerri ducked out first. "Thanks so much for inviting me!" "Thanks for coming!" "Happy Holidays!" "The same to you!" We were enemy ships firing cannonballs of courtesy at each other.

• Don, as he left, seemed blasted and uncertain. Denise, on the other hand, was cheery, fulfilled, and only slightly tipsy.

• And Eka: cleaning up when all but family had gone, the dedicated hostess and (I thought, warmly) wife-to-be.

Greer stayed to help. She, Bob and Eka brought the debris in from the living room while Davit sent text messages and I washed dishes. First time in years my siblings and I have all been in the same room; vestigial sentiments gurgled within. *My family*, I murmured inwardly, trying on a revised attitude.

Eka, sprinkling baking soda on a grease spot on the carpet, asked Greer what I was like as a child, and heard about the backseat car game I made up where we would each put out one or two fingers, and whichever one didn't match the other two could call them any insulting names he or she devised. She claimed I'd once called her Zombie Child of the Damned.

The story reminded Eka of her own siblings, and she went to the bedroom to call one of them. I wonder what time it was there—nine hours' difference, says timetravel.com—i.e., seven thirty in the morning, but here was Eka, weeping on the phone behind my bedroom door while a groggy, far-off brother or sister sipped the Georgian equivalent of black coffee and listened. *Let her be missing her family*, I prayed. *Let the crying mean that and only that.*

"She's nice," Greer said.

"Did you expect me to shack up with Lady Macbeth?"

"I'm saying I never pictured you with someone like her. Are you thinking about marriage?"

"Incessantly. We'll see."

"Will you invite us, if there's a wedding?"

"Of course. Unless it's very small."

Nuptial imaginings: same guest list as tonight's party, same party space. Myself squeezed into a suit. Eka in a pastel summer dress, the hem rippling.

Looking back, it's hard to conceive that such a Hollywood ending still seemed possible half a day ago.

By the time of the MegaMillions drawing, Greer had gone. The Whirling Balls of Fate flew in their spinning drums and rolled into place—five white and one gold. We wrote down the winning numbers and examined her tickets one by one. We did this on the bed, with the door closed: for undisclosed reasons, she didn't want her son to know what we were up to. As far as I was concerned, the search was mere play; for Eka, though, it seemed like serious business. Her hunger to win was unlike her: greedy, unrealistic, unnecessary. We had each other, after all. (Ha, ha, ha.)

Her picks yielded no more than two matches on any one ticket. I went around the bed to her side, to remind her of our nonmonetary riches. After her toast and our dance, a comforting hug seemed only appropriate.

She stood up, however, dodging my arms, and broke the news from the doorway. "Angus, I don't know what should I tell you. Dr. Oh invites me, he wants me to go in his house to live."

. . .

I had to pause there, after setting the words down. The End of the Dream, Relived. She stopped me cold when she said it, and here I am again, destroyed anew.

There was more. "I know, this is crazy. But I have terrible fear for money—so Davit can go to college. Maybe my mother I can bring here. I don't know what is right to do. This rips me up."

I should report what I did as she was speaking. There's a postcard of the Grand Canyon taped to the wall by my dresser, sent to me by Barbara, a girlfriend, during a period of fond-hearted absence. To convey the canyon's immensity, the card is twice the normal width. Since I couldn't look at Eka, I focused on the pink and tan strata, and the wide void between the steep walls. The space seemed inviting: a good place to see how far a fast-moving car can fly.

Dr. Oh—the devious little androgyne—has only met her three times. What sort of maladjusted geek asks a woman to live with him before they've had a half hour of conversation?

Suppressing more bitter replies, I asked what he'd said, exactly.

"He knows it is crazy. I don't remember all of the words—he said too many. He wants to know me, and to waste no more time. He is so . . . urgent."

Oor-gent.

He may change his mind once he gets to know her. He may throw her out on the street. She'd be taking a risk. Still, there are reasons why she would be insane to choose me over him: my lack of an income, my excess weight (how many years do I have left, really?), the troubling question of what sex would be like, and my corrosive spirit, to name just the highlights. She's still relatively young, and shouldn't have to nurse me as I fall apart. She would be wise, in other words, to ignore any loyalty she may feel and go for the gold.

"You can tell anything to me," she said. "I will listen."

Her gaze was unbearably direct, unblinking, possibly beseeching. What she wanted from me, I still can't say. (Permission?) All I knew was that I couldn't compete with the well-groomed, well-heeled doctor. And that it would have been criminally selfish to argue on my own behalf.

"You're free," I said. "You have no obligation to me."

'Tis a far, far better thing I do now, etc., etc.

She looked at me as if I'd shot her. To preempt an unbearable scene (which wouldn't have changed the final outcome anyway), I walked out. Bob and Davit, brushing their teeth—in the kitchen and bathroom, respectively—watched me take my laptop and a near-full bottle of Wild Turkey. Farewell, family.

(I took the laptop so she wouldn't find everything I've ever written about her. Let her think of me with keen pangs of remorse, not hurt and disgust, when she's Mrs. Dr. Oh.)

If I were a recovering addict, I would have relapsed then, with a vengeance. Having no particular addiction, however, I searched for anesthesia by driving nowhere, taking slugs of Wild Turkey and watching Eka announce her news, again and again.

You think I should have pleaded my case. But here's the thing: if she really cared for me, she would have told Dr. Oh, *Sorry, thank you, I already got guy. And my guy is twice the man what you are.*

I found myself on Central Avenue in East Orange, a wide, deserted boulevard floodlit with superbright anti-crime streetlights. Gray gates sealed most of the storefronts; nothing looked open except a Wendy's, a Laundromat, and the Exxon station, whose monumental sign would have looked just right on a hundred-foot pole above the highway. Holiday lights blinked in only one window of a brick apartment building. A wailing wind drove a sheet of newspaper down the street, faster than my car. A hand-painted sign on a little shop advertised *Oxtail, Jerk Chicken,* and *Curry Goat.*

Funny how you can tell, without seeing a soul on the street, that you're driving through a ghetto. Unless it was a matter of memory: because this bright avenue looked familiar. I'd interviewed someone in an apartment near here, not that long ago, though I couldn't remember whom.

Next door to a long-deserted furniture showroom with seventy linear feet of empty windows, I found what seemed to be a bar. The sign said *Club Lagos* in yellow, hand-drawn capitals, outlined in black. As a venue for self-obliteration, the place seemed as good as any.

Puddles had frozen in the hollows of the uneven sidewalk. Tottering along, I sang to myself, "Fools rush in where white men fear to tread." Though already staggering, I remembered to bring the laptop with me, so as not to return to a smashed car window.

The words *bitch, slut, whore* occurred to me, but I'm not the kind of monkey who flings dung around his cage.

Inside the bar, colored lights outlined a wall of mirrors. Ancient images returned to me, unbidden: I half expected to find menacing Africans in ceremonial dress. Instead, two very dark gentlemen in white cardigans were working together on either side of the bar, inserting sheet music into plastic sleeves and then into binders. They stopped what they were doing when they saw me.

Into the startled silence I tossed an apt quotation: "Strange visitor from another planet."

"Sah, this is a private club," the bartender said. A tall, handsome fellow, he had a perfectly straight hairline, as if he'd shaved his forehead with the aid of a ruler.

"May I join for the night? I'll sit quietly in the corner."

"Sah, this club is not open to the public."

That was the other one, a short, round-headed man with semicrossed eyes.

"All right, then. You'll find me in the morning, frozen outside your door." A sighed addendum: "No room in the manger?"

They conferred, and disagreed. "This is non sense," the short one said, breaking the word in two. I'd heard this accent before—the syllables crisply divided, the *th*'s more like *d*'s—but couldn't remember where.

"If you promise not to talk," the bartender said, "you can sit there." He indicated a table near the door. "But if you disturb us, I'll have to send you out."

I accepted his terms, and made my way to the table. An unlit candle with a blackened wick served as centerpiece, a glass globe encased in waxy mesh. *Out, brief candle*: a clear message to anyone who knew his Shakespeare.

I liked this dark, quiet room, and enjoyed listening to their softly spoken African English. They shared an exasperated amusement—at how little they would earn at their upcoming gig, and how likely it was that the drummer would once again show up late. I wished I could stay there indefinitely, and never have to think about the Other Thing.

(The Nigerian bookkeeper, the widower whose daughter had to write about Thanksgiving—he was the one who talked like them. What was his name, though?)

Other men in white cardigans arrived, unless I dreamed them. One held a trumpet. I didn't belong here—I had neither cardigan nor instrument—and I'd already overstayed my welcome. Where to next? A park nearby, if I could find one. Sit back against a tree, drink, and sleep forever.

Adesina.

"Does anyone here know a man named Adesina?"

I can't say how they replied. My head was on the table by then, my eyes closed.

THE END

No longer living but not quite dead, I sit peacefully in this temporary way station, alone. Waiting. A pale wooden mask hangs on the wall, thick-lipped. Beside it, an unfamiliar green and white flag hangs from three thumbtacks. A wrinkled plaid sack dangles from a doorknob by its wrinkled plaid handles.

I've been asked to stay until evening, and so I postpone my exit. Courteous even at the brink of eternity.

Empty minutes make long hours. I'd like to get on with it, not wait here all day. But sitting still isn't so bad. It feels like the right thing to do. And I'm not capable of much else.

For now, the stillness soothes me.

The couch was coarse-textured and bone white. My feet, up on the armrest, stayed asleep while my head awoke. A small girl was complaining, "I don't want to go alone." A wide woman scolded her in a whisper, "You're big now, you're old enough. Now you go!" "You have to come." "We have a guest. I can't leave before he wakes up. Ssh! Be careful crossing!"

They were both very dark. The little girl wore glasses. By the time I understood where I was, she had left.

The woman—Adesina's fiancée, the hairdresser—wore a yellow robe. I watched her through a doorway as she gave herself a new face at a vanity table in the bedroom. The ritual took time, and she performed it patiently. When she was satisfied with the metallic green that covered her eyelids and the two shades of red on her lips, she removed her head—or, the elaborate, ringleted hairpiece—and scratched her shorn scalp behind the ear.

She passed through the living room en route to the kitchen. I said, "I'll get out of your way in a minute or two."

The sound of my voice provoked a scowl. "He wants you to eat dinner with us. But I work from eleven to five. If you stay, you'll be alone until the children come from school."

She didn't hide her displeasure. She wanted me gone, but Adesina wanted the opposite.

"I apologize for the inconvenience," I said, closing my eyes to shut out the uncomfortable light.

"Do you know what time they called here last night? Close to midnight."

"Again, apologies."

"Hm!"

She closed herself in the bedroom. A small mercy.

I was looking for my shoes, planning to try walking, when she came back out. "Don't think I didn't notice how you left me out of your story." She was hissing like a viper, and puffing herself up to an intimidating size. "'Here is poor Adesina, raising his children all alone after his little wife died.' I am nobody—just the housekeeper who cooks and cleans for him and makes lunch for his children every day and nurses them when they're sick. I know: you wanted people to feel pity for him, so they would send money. Do you know how much they sent us? Three hundred dollars— four coats and a coffeemaker. For that he put his poverty on show for all to see. I told him he should come with me and sell underwear at the flea market on Sundays, but he wanted his day of rest. Why not? He has me to slave for him while he puts his feet up. Why not rest?"

I could have defended myself, I could have said I was only trying to help a man who'd lost his wife, whose daughter needed expensive glasses, who had unpaid bills. But she didn't give me a chance.

"My mistake was to agree to live here and help with the children before he married me. Why should he hurry now? No reason what-so-evah."

She disappeared behind the bedroom door and spent the rest of the morning watching television and talking on the phone, emphatically and conspiratorially. I went back to sleep, and woke to find her mopping the kitchen floor in a royal blue dress that displayed every contour of her belly. She was still bitching, now with a Bluetooth headset hooked over her ear. "I'm tired of wasting my time. Why did I come here? Not for this."

When she left, she told me, "If you go, be sure the door locks behind you. A thief could walk off with everything."

Alone in this alien space, I survived the hours by recording last night's events. The task left me flattened. Returning to the couch, I sought refuge in sleep but couldn't find my way there. I didn't see the point of eating, but eventually had to. In addition to Gatorade and ketchup, the refrigerator held a bag of okra, a tub of orange rice, and a jar of hot pepper sauce. There were also blackened plantains, a KFC box containing two leftover pieces, and a package of frozen spinach defrosting in its own puddle. In the end, I ate a tomato from a bowl on the counter and some corn flakes.

I've now brought this account up to the present instant. Here I sit, beached on the sofa until my host returns. My belly inflates and subsides, a mechanism that has served me for half a century. I am a slow pump: up, down, up, down. A coarse machine, emitting foul smells and revolting substances. Slowly running down, coming to a stop.

If I seek a subtler, intangible self—my soul, my me—I find nothing. Which leaves me, again, with my creaking, aching body.

Nothing more to say.

* * *

Why (the bundled woman must wonder as she walks her fuzzy pooch) would a man sit in the backseat of a car parked on a dark street with the motor running, on an Arctic December night, lit only by his monitor's screen?

It's a long story.

* * *

The two older brothers came home from school, arguing, and found me snacking on Oreo Cakesters in the kitchen. They turned straight around and answered my mouth-full "Good afternoon" with polite "Hellos" as they fled.

The little girl arrived later, along with the youngest boy. She pestered her big brothers to play Barbies with her, a hopeless cause, while Tiny played a handheld electronic game that beeped roughly every half second. As soon as I returned to the living room, the four of them ran to hide in their father's bedroom. I wished I knew how to show them that I'm not a white devil—but even more, I wanted to be left alone.

There was no peace to be had. Behind the closed door, the brothers seemed to be playing a video game—rifle fire, explosions, death-metal soundtrack—until one of them said, "Stop leaning on me," and then a littler voice said, "*You* stop." Then came the thump of a small body landing on the carpet, and a wrestling match with squeaks of smothered fury, until the girl reminded them in a whisper, "That man is out there."

The dull pain of recognition: Cain and Abel, Angus and Bob. This is one of those insights you have repeatedly through the years, that illuminates but doesn't help. Like these two boys, I've lived the archetype forever, never transcending it for a minute. One more failure.

If I had more time . . . I still wouldn't do better.

It seems that, as Adesina and his white-sweatered friend helped me up the stairs, I said to them, half conscious, "Don't eat me."

I can't tell if my little joke offended my host or not. He recounted the moment with an inscrutable smile.

Let's be coherent, though. Begin at the beginning.

Adesina clasped my hand in both of his, welcoming me like a long-lost brother. (An opposite archetype: Castor and Pollux to my Cain and Abel. Black to my white.) The vein in his forehead bulged with enthusiasm. While the loving girlfriend made dinner and the children did their homework, we drank orange soda in his living room and nibbled on homemade plantain chips and fried doughy bits that he called chin chin. We ignored the sputtering noises from the kitchen, only half of which came from the frying pan.

One of Adesina's eyes had an alarming blood spot in the white, which I didn't comment on. As we snacked, I wondered whether he would lose the eye, but checking now, I see that the blood spot fits the description of a subconjunctival hemorrhage, caused by straining, and should go away in two weeks. I'm glad.

He delayed with silly pleasantries, but reached the obvious question soon enough. "How did you happen to find that club, of all places?"

I couldn't answer with his children in the next room and my enemy frying tilapia on the stove, and not a closed door in the place.

He held up his pink palm. "If it's personal, I'm sorry."

"I'm concerned about my car," I said, dodging the question. "I parked in front of the club last night. They wouldn't tow it away, would they?"

"I think the police have better things to do. Don't worry—I'll take you there after dinner."

I complimented the chin chin, doing my part to fill the air. He told me, *sotto voce*, "You should have tasted my wife's. These have too much butter and not enough sugar."

He shook his head mournfully. For an instant, his loss was mine.

My fish stared at me blindly from a sauce of pureed tomato and red pepper. At the edge of the plate sat a glob of yam flour boiled in water. Adesina courteously steered the conversation away from me and my unspecified troubles. He told how his supervisor stood on a desk to change a light bulb and fell, breaking her ankle, and now she'll be out for weeks. The fiancée asked if they would promote him now, and he said, "No, but I'll have to do most of her work."

"And they'll pay you more?"

"No."

"Then why are you happy?"

"Because the company has laid off some people, and now my job is safe."

"You're so ambitious!"

Fortunately, it's not my job to recount the conflict that followed. Adesina can write his own diary.

As soon as the others finished eating, I said, "I should go."

"I'll take you," Adesina said.

He had tears in his eyes. (Rage? Embarrassment? I couldn't tell.) His daughter sat on his lap and tipped her head against his chin, to comfort him. He squeezed her shoulders, but his gaze went thousands of miles away.

His car, a gray Cavalier, is even older than my Buick. As he drove, he explained that he's an Anglican, but he fears that his wife's ghost is watching him, and he doesn't know if she's angry or pities him. He knows he should keep his promise and marry his fiancée, but something stops him. He tries to be a good father, but never knows what to say to his boys; his own father died when he was two, so he isn't sure of the best way to discipline them.

The houses we passed sagged forlornly. They pressed close to the sidewalks, and hid their tenants behind shades with curling edges. I pitied Adesina more than I pitied myself, and that's saying something.

To keep him company in his misery, I shared the saga of Eka. He made sympathetic clicks with his tongue as he listened; when we reached the club, he parked behind my car to hear how the story would end.

His first response surprised me. "These women are vampires! They suck everything they can from you."

I hadn't thought of Eka that way, although her accent does bear a resemblance to Béla Lugosi's. "I'm sure they see it differently."

"Look what they do to us! This one is never satisfied and insults me in front of my children and guests. That one will marry a man she doesn't know and throw away the one who took her in when she was sick. It's inexcusable."

I can't remember anyone taking my side so wholeheartedly, ever. Much as I enjoyed the support, though, I saw the limitations of his perspective. "I don't think Eka is ungrateful. She's just trying to take care of her son, and her mother."

He stared through the windshield, into the past.

"My grandfather used to beat my grandmother with his cane. I hated him for that. But now I think some women don't respect you if you treat them kindly."

"Your wife wasn't like that, I assume."

"No, she was a good woman. I wish you could have met her. She didn't deserve to die."

His eyes filled with new tears. If we'd had this conversation back when I interviewed him, I would have exploited those tears for maximum effect. Sometimes it's better to be unemployed.

Returning my sympathy in kind, he said, "We can never understand them. Who knows? Maybe your Eka wanted you to fight for her. It's something to think about."

I thought about it, but couldn't see Eka as Guinevere: dropping her handkerchief and exulting as a pair of knights slashed each other to bits for the privilege of returning it.

Unless that's exactly what she wanted.

With the suddenness of a storm cloud blotting out the sun, the mood of fellowship ran out. I had to get away from Adesina, back to solitude. "Thanks for everything," I said, and climbed out.

"Call me any time you want to talk!" he shouted as I closed the door on him.

※ ※ ※

Ten feet from my passenger door, on a lawn that's only slightly larger than a bath mat, an inflated snowman glows from within. Twinkling lights in four colors twine along the railings of the front stairs. My intention, since this morning, has been to pull into my rented garage, close the door, and start the motor—but I can't do that, because Eka would blame herself.

If there's a place for me on this Earth, I don't know where it is.

In the Land of Lost Typists

There are three others typing on laptops here, one old and two young. Breathing the nut-rich coffee air, we search for wisdom and relief through our fingertips, quickly clicking. I wonder what griefs they're analyzing and bemoaning. I wonder if they're making more progress than I am.

The boy barista tells the girl, "I can't believe I'm going to A.C. on New Year's Day."

"What, and, like, gamble?"

The boy has a wispy beard and a Devil's Tower of black hair. The girl has little hoops through her lip and nostril. I must be a thousand years old.

It's late, dark, cold. I don't know what to do, how to live. By keeping these words flowing, I hope to stumble on something.

Over my head, holiday songs play on a flat TV. Children sing sleepily, *Christmas time is here*. I remember the first time the cartoon aired. Charlie Brown and his meager tree, a squiggle above his head standing for his fizzled dreams. That's all I can retrieve, though. My memories, which once seemed durable as stone, are crumbling. The names of my early teachers have left me. Everything is falling apart, tumbling over the edge.

Where to begin?

With this: they worried about me. While I passed last night and today at Adesina's apartment, Eka and Bob called my cell phone (which I'd turned off), searched the neighborhood on foot, waited up for hours, called the police to ask about accidents, and finally reported me missing. I regret causing turmoil, and wish they'd written me off instead. Must I be made to feel like an inconsiderate asshole when I'm already drowning in woe?

The moment of my return was tricky. I couldn't tell from her up-sloping, sorrowful-saint eyebrows whether she wanted to come to me but was afraid I hated her, or simply pitied me. She watched from the bottom of the stairs as I made my way down. I had my own contorted longings; above all, I wanted not to lose hold of my self-control and beg her to stay. With a simple "Hi," I hung my coat over the newel cap, its accustomed place, and went to the kitchen for a beer.

Davit mumbled in his sleep. Eka and Bob questioned me quietly, and told how they'd searched the streets, etc., etc. I apologized and called the police to report myself found.

A thorny question arose. I waited until Bob stepped away, and asked it quietly. "Where do we think I ought to sleep tonight?"

"On your bed," Eka insisted.

Having used up my audacity, I didn't ask where she planned to sleep. I just went to the bedroom and left the door open.

She followed me in, but kept her distance. "If you allow, I sleep here with you. If you don't want, I go out on the floor."

As if it made no difference, I said, "No, no, you can stay, it's fine."

Once she climbed under the covers, though—as the poet said, oh, baby, that's when the heartache began.

Would we lie on our backs all night, separate as a pair of light switches, staring at the dark ceiling?

The scent of her perfume, dabbed on quickly as she changed into her flannel nightgown: cruelly inflammatory.

Her fingers in my chest curls: an almost unbearable joy.

The sound of our nibbling kisses in the quiet: a bit slurpy, and therefore embarrassing.

Her arms and shoulders beneath the flannel: tender skin and mature flesh concealing sturdy muscles underneath.

(Turn the laptop, so passersby can't read the screen—though how many nosy pedestrians are likely to pass a Starbucks in Nutley so close to midnight?)

The taste of her mouth: mint toothpaste with a stubborn hint of onion.

Most of all, her hands on my cheek, my shoulder, my scalp: miraculous.

It would have been hard to miss the message. She wanted to make sure I understood what I hadn't two nights before, when her report of Dr. Oh's invitation had shot me out of the house like a human cannonball. *Ask me to stay. The answer will be yes.*

The time came for words. She waited patiently.

Here's the thing. What she wants isn't the deciding factor. She has no idea what staying with me entails. I may never find another job. (Would *you* hire me?) I'll most likely have a heart attack within a few years. And what happens when the magic dust wears off? The Angus she wants to accept is the kindly soul who sheltered her and her son, not the cur who rudely mocks luckless amputees. She offered herself to me—but I couldn't let her doom herself.

Long after any other man would have accepted the invitation and fit his puzzle piece into hers, she paused in the half dark and asked with her eyes, *What is wrong?*

I love her, but couldn't let her choose me over Dr. Oh. I squeezed her upper arm under the nightgown's sleeve, and said nothing.

She moved away gently and carefully, so as not to rend her dignity, and spent the rest of the night on her side, very still, her back a defensive barricade. I don't think she was crying—she has survived harder trials than this.

I cared enough about her not to touch her again.

You think I'm deluding myself, that *of course* Eka and I belong together and I'm making every possible excuse to escape happiness, just so I can go back to saying that life sucks. What you haven't considered is that I may be right. I'm not even a poor facsimile of the man she should marry. She would never have conceived this misplaced affection if calamity hadn't dumped her in my lap. Not even true love can survive the disappointments of poverty.

I'm right. Admit it. Sometimes the shithead knows what he's talking about.

The two younger typists have gone. Only the gray woman is left. Serious, professional, mouth shaped by years of frustration, she's got her down coat on, her papers spread across the table in front of her. There's an impatience about her. She fidgets. Whatever her pain is about, whatever has led her to this dead end, she has my sympathy.

Eka called Dr. Oh early this morning, while I slept. He promised to come get her and her belongings at two P.M. He must have cancelled his afternoon appointments.

By the time she told me her plans, she had become a different woman: detached and monosyllabic. Lack of sleep had put creases in her face.

Because most of her things were in the bedroom, she couldn't pack until I woke. I heard the folded clothing going softly into the suitcase while I ate my toast.

The clatter of her framed icons returning to the cardboard box nearly broke my will. *She's getting away. You'll never find another woman. This is your last chance.*

To prevent an unseemly breakdown, I left the apartment. At Willowbrook, scene of our recent happiness, I found many mothers with strollers lunching at the food court. An aggressive beauty with an accent tried to sell me natural soap made with Dead Sea salt; I stared at her, wordless.

Upstairs, looking down on the shoppers, I leaned on the railing (*go ahead and break, let me come crashing down*) and tried to cultivate a sense of relief, because now I won't have to live up to her idea of me. When that failed, I reminded myself of the reasons why I hadn't asked her to stay. Sydney Carton found peace in self-sacrifice, but he didn't have to live with it for another twenty years.

I accept that I don't have the right to drag her down with me, but how can she be happy with Dr. Oh?

Below me, a small boy strapped into a stroller reached desperately for the toy helicopter fluttering around a nearby kiosk. His mother, busy chatting, never noticed.

I stayed away until three. On the way home, I let myself hope she'd still be there, having told Dr. Oh to go to hell. *You big dummy-dum*, she would scold me, *you almost letted me to get away.*

My wish came true in a twisted way, as wishes so often do. Approaching the house, I saw a black Mercedes in front, shining and clean, its trunk open. Eka was giving Bob a good-bye hug. Dr. Oh, tensely smiling in a blazer with a violet shirt, closed the trunk.

I guess the plan was to pick up Davit at school. Dr. Oh jingled his keys. Bob caught sight of me and pretended he hadn't.

I parked down the street and watched her like a wino gaping at a liquor store window.

Her face was neutral, which enraged me. Why wasn't she weeping? And why had she left the decision to me, a bumbling idiot?

Bob couldn't help glancing my way again. This time, she followed his eyes and found me. Nothing passed between us except a missed heartbeat on my side. She climbed into the doctor's car, and a crack opened in my chest, a gap that has widened in the hours since.

A dusting of snow had fallen. Dr. Oh pulled away from the curb a little too fast, and slid a bit before straightening out. *Incompetent*, I muttered, taking consolation where I could.

He drove past me, never noticing my face. The upholstery inside the Mercedes was dark tan, a close cousin to gold. Eka's posture was impeccable.

I couldn't go inside. I couldn't make myself move.

Bob came toward me, hesitantly. His Birkenstocks made bean tracks in the snow.

I lowered the window an inch.

"I'm sorry," he offered. "Do you want to talk?"

I was unable to produce a word—a syllable—a whimper.

"She told me you never asked her to stay," he said. "Why didn't you?"

I could barely breathe. "Go inside, Bob."

"She told me she wished she could stay. Did you know that?"

"Drop it, please."

"Why wouldn't you ask? Was it some sort of insane pride?"

"Get away from me."

He shook his head, but I was spared a lecture, because he had to get back to the library. Today was his first day at his new job. He'd taken a break to say good-bye to Eka, and stayed too long.

She thinks I don't want her. It's intolerable—I can't let her go on believing that—but would explaining the truth be more merciful? That I love her, but would rather Dr. Oh have her?

Bob's sympathy left my guts so agitated that I wondered: *Stomach cancer?* This was the state Don found me in when he came to pay his respects.

It must have struck him as odd that I kept sitting in my car in the midafternoon chill, after Eka had driven off with her dapper, ecstatic suitor—especially since he'd heard her toast me two nights earlier.

I rolled down the window again. "She's gone?" he asked gently.

"Yup."

He curled his lips in, gravely.

"You okay?"

"Peachy."

The thoughts that pop into one's head. Peach . . . Georgia . . . Eka . . . No, Duane Allman . . . He got run over by a peach truck, I think—that's why they called the next album "Eat a Peach." (Actually, no, Snopes informs me that this is a myth. One more lie I've gone around believing for eons.)

Don might have stood there nodding for the next seven years if I hadn't dismissed him. "I think I'll go in now," I said.

He blurted out what I mistook for his idea of consolation: "Sometimes it seems like we weren't made to be happy."

I didn't comment, so he elaborated on his own. "I told Cindy I couldn't leave Denise. I just couldn't."

At that instant, he became my only peer, my fellow sufferer, my best friend. "I'm sorry to hear that."

"No, it's all for the best. It was really something, for a little while—but I'm good. I'm too old to start over."

Snow was falling again. Ashes. Dust.

And then Cindy herself showed up, home from work. Seeing us as she left her car, she froze for a moment. Face clenched in grief, pale—now that I think about it, she wasn't wearing makeup, a first (nor was she smiling, another first)—she went behind the house to her entrance, turning her face away from us.

"Maybe you can check in on her sometimes," Don said. "Just to make sure she's all right."

A quick assessment. I'll ask Bob to do it. He's better at that. And climbing stairs.

"Listen," he said, "if you need anything, or want someone to talk to, just come on over."

I nodded, and he drifted back to his house. I went inside soon after—that is, I almost made it to my door, but a red and black Mini Cooper pulled up at the curb, and a mini person climbed out.

"You look like you've had a setback," Dr. Jones said.

A faint scent came off him, fresh, clean, citrusy. I suppressed the urge to tell all. "Nope, not me. What brings you to this remote outpost?"

"I called Dr. Oh this morning, to see how your friend was doing. He told me a surprising story."

He watched me for signs of imminent breakdown. I gave him nothing.

"I was afraid that what happened might be disheartening, from your point of view."

"You see all, don't you?"

He brings out the paranoid in me like no one else: had he plotted the entire course of events, in revenge for my online slurs?

We ended up standing outside for many minutes while he consoled and counseled me. "Quitting a job is a double-edged sword," he said. "Everyone wants to be free, but sometimes, if you cut yourself loose, you end up adrift. When you don't have a place to go every day—it's harder than people realize. Don't misunderstand me, I admire your nerve. But when you take a big gamble, there's always a chance you'll lose."

Listening to this eminent little fellow diagnose my difficulties massaged a tender region in my brain. I saw him, fleetingly, as the older brother I never had. Unconsciously hostile, subtly condescending, but having my best interests at heart.

"There's a vein of self-destructive unhappiness in you that I've never understood," he said. "I wonder if leaving your job has turned into more of a problem than a solution."

He puffed a warm cloud into his hands as if conjuring a magic snowball. I had already succumbed to his spell, but I kept up the appearance of sovereignty by maintaining aloof silence.

"What I wanted to tell you is, if you decide to come out of retirement, I'd like to help."

"And how would you do that?"

"Hendricks House has a branch in Fort Lauderdale. They'd like to replicate the arrangement we have here with the *Register*. I made a couple calls, to see what's possible. Would you consider a fresh start in a new place?"

Mr. Misery Goes to Florida. Heat. Flatness. Parents. Hell on Earth, with air-conditioning.

"May I ask you a question, Doctor?"

"Of course."

"Why do you keep helping me out of the holes I dig for myself? Or do you do this for all God's creatures?"

He calculated his answer carefully. "I think it's because, for all your problems, I envy the way you refuse to do what's expected. I wish I had the nerve to live as recklessly as you do."

Falling snow glinted in the gray light like diamond dust. Was he giving me honesty, or a ludicrous lie that only a broken man would swallow—because, really, all he wanted was to banish the Masked Marauder to a steamy penal colony a thousand miles away?

He offered his hand for a good-bye shake. "If you're interested in the job, let me know."

I'd forgotten for a moment how small he is. The hand-shake broke the spell; he became a munchkin again as he returned to his model car. It defies the laws of physics, that a person of such negligible mass can exert so much gravitational force.

"Thanks," I said as he drove away.

       ✳ ✳ ✳

It's almost closing time. My *compañera*, the other lost typist, has packed her papers and her laptop into a zebra-striped satchel. Now she's standing and zipping her long, quilted coat. Will she acknowledge me, her fellow sufferer, the only other customer in the place?

No. Slipping her wrist through the cuff of an aluminum crutch, she sways like a metronome, back and forth, out the door. "Good night, Kate!" the boy barista calls.

She sends them both a fond, maternal smile. "Get home safe, guys."

A gust of frigid air engulfs me.

I had hoped that, by the time I reached the end of this, the fog would have cleared, revealing the path I ought to take. No such luck.

Florida?

Why not?

2:07 A.M., NORTH CAROLINA WELCOME CENTER

This parking lot is an empty, pink-lit plain. The building is locked and dark, its white columns and pediment dusky. Evenly spaced trash barrels keep a somber vigil over the access road. BBQ grills stand idle in the winter grass. My windows are already fogging up, softening the light that shines down from above. I've been nodding out every minute or so for the past twenty miles. To preempt a crash that might leave me quadriplegic but still acutely aware, I'll nap awhile—as soon as I jot down a few notes.

Left home at six thirty P.M., took the Turnpike South through Delaware, Maryland, Virginia, dropping down the coast like a spider on a filament. The tall coffee has necessitated many rest stops. My vertebrae seem to be fusing: climbing out of the driver's seat hurts more each time.

The highway has been mostly empty since ten P.M., except for some trucks and a playful psychopath who stayed close on my tail from the Fort McHenry Tunnel on down. When he exited in Petersburg, Virginia, he left me both relieved and lonely.

A voice has been speaking to me. Like a temptation to sin, it repeats a simple message, endlessly: *Why are you doing this?* Every mile of highway I've put behind me has required a strenuous effort of will.

The voice is here again now, asking why I'm writing this. When I wake from my nap, it will greet me and say, *You're not really going through with this, are you? Relocating to a place you loathe, in order to take a job you'll loathe even more?*

The odds I'll reach my destination are so uncertain, I wouldn't bet the price of a vending machine soda.

Bob's going to stay and pay the rent and utilities. Mrs. N likes him. That worked out nicely.

A considerate fellow, he kept his doubts about my move to himself. When I shook his hand, he pulled me close and ensnared my shoulder with his other arm. Smell of almond soap and tea, close-up of nose pores: more of my brother's body than I wanted to know.

I asked him to check in on Cindy and offer her a shoulder to cry on. He promised he would. Imagine her weeping in his arms, and then looking up to see, blearily, a good man of an entirely different type. Not my intention, but hey!

Was there, on leave-taking, a throbbing appreciation for my flawed but loyal brother, whom I may never see again? A little. Mostly I was eager to get going.

I found a small wrapped box in my sock drawer while packing. She'd taped a note to it, all upper case, FOR ANGUS, FOR CHRISMAS, FOR EVERYTHING, FROM EKA. Inside was a weighty glass globe, baseball size, with laser-etched continents. A legend in script crossed the North Atlantic: *World's Best Friend*. I've placed it in the spare cup holder, behind the coffee, as a reminder that someone thought well of me once—though I may have to move it, to shield myself from the pain.

My computer said twenty hours to Fort Lauderdale. I should arrive in time for dinner, if I don't sleep too long.

Casimir the barber, hearing that I had a job interview, made me look like a middle manager. These thin strands have not lain so perfectly perpendicular to my part since I was ten. I don't quite recognize myself—but that may be the perfect way to start this journey.

Have I already said that long hours on a highway are to optimism what a bath of Coca-Cola is to a tooth? I've gone from wondering whether Eka only wanted to stay with me because she has a racist dread of hairless Asian men, to regretting that I didn't take those Benadryls and seal the bag over my head way back when, to also regretting what a piss-poor brother I've been. The closest thing I've had to a distraction was the black woman mopping up at the rest stop in Maryland, whose face and arms were covered with boils. She kept my mind occupied for a good half hour. *I'm supposed to think,* Gee, my problems aren't so bad after all—*but I don't think that. She seems to have adapted, she goes about her business without noticeable self-pity; if strangers gawk, that's life. We have this in common: others shrink from us in horror. Those same people might say I'm inflating my own burdens—that I'm pampered by comparison, and a stiff dose of adversity would set me straight. But they'd be wrong: I wouldn't learn my lesson. (Notice that I've shifted the focus from the boil woman to myself. Is there no end to my self-absorption? What's that you say? "Everyone is self-absorbed"? True, but they don't compare with me.)*

While listening to a comical evangelist on the radio, I remembered the other time when I set out alone and began again: arriving at college with a suitcase and a typewriter, on line for dorm sign-in, knowing no one, hiding my fear, and when the twerp in front of me peeped humorously, "I want to go home," I barked at him, "Stiff upper lip, man! They can crush our bodies, but not our spirits! Or is it the other way around?" Someone applauded, others joined in, I bowed, and for the next four years, I stuck with that winning formula, playing the sardonic curmudgeon, always good for a sharp shot of vinegar. Had I kept my mouth shut, who knows? In a different mood, I might have stumbled on a better alternative—sly lecher? lazy hedonist?—and carved a somewhat cheerier path through the years.

Heading into terra incognita again, I have a chance to reshape myself. But it's not easy to turn a ship this size.

Here's a song I made up along the way:

A fat old shite
Rode out one night
Into the dark unknown.

He'd lost his love
In Jersey, above,
He was sinkin' down South like a stone.

But I-95
Is a mighty long drive
And his heart wasn't up to the hike.

It's no great loss
In fact, you can toss
His carcass wherever you like.

I keep seeing her in bed with him. Making the best of it, she aims to please. (It's maddening, how adaptable she is to any man who'll take her in.) Pleading shyness, she requests lights out, because she's not so young anymore and doesn't want him to be disappointed. Mostly, though, she passively accepts his attentions—which, one could say, is exactly what she did with me. In the final analysis, we're not so different, Dr. Oh and I. Just a couple of misfits who couldn't resist the damsel we'd rescued.

(She didn't want to leave me. My poor Eka. Actually, I can't bear to think about that.)

No one sits here in the backseat, yet it's a pig sty. Broken umbrella, empty Pepperidge Farm bag, crushed Kleenex box, handleless ice scraper, unidentifiable crumbs. How did it all get here?

The Advils I bought in Virginia haven't done a thing. My butt is numb, my spine no longer bends, and my toes sprout needles each time I move my feet.

Like an orphan in a Dickensian melodrama, I wonder and worry, *What will become of me?*

INFERNO

I've made a terrible mistake. I chose the wrong path. It's what I do at every fork in the road.

The air here is toxic, deadly. Her home is one of the few places where the law still permits my mother to smoke, and she exercises her right ceaselessly. Up north, they used to open a window now and then, but here, my father has sealed the place ruthlessly against the heat; entering their house is like stepping into a diseased lung.

This beige-carpeted nightmare, this mildewed pit: this place will destroy me.

Tropical fish swim in turquoise water on the quilted spread that covers the narrow guest bed. A trapezoidal foam prism, in matching fabric, allows them to call it a couch. The popcorn ceiling, nearly thirty years old, has a long, erratic crack. These nubbles were bone white and new when they retired to this little cottage; now the ceiling is pale gray. Seashells glued to a jewelry box gather dust that their ancient eyes can no longer see. The lamp on the end table survives from my childhood: brown cork potbelly, orange shade. I hated it then and I hate it now, because it reminds me that all I've achieved in fifty-five years is a return to helpless dependence.

I shouldn't have called them. Thought I was being prudent for once. *If I'm going to keep living, I'd better not fuck up my finances more than I already have.* A hotel would have eaten up at least eighty dollars a night; therefore, I exited the interstate at Daytona Beach and called to say I may be taking a job in Fort Lauderdale, and might it be possible, etc.? Mother replied to each successive sentence with the same taut phrase, "That would be fine." Meaning it's anything but fine.

The gap beneath the door reveals the shadow of her slippers on the floor tiles. *Don't knock. Don't.*

The shadow moves on to the garage, where they keep spare supplies of everything on clean steel shelves. She passes my door again. Bedsprings creak. The TV goes on.

I fear I'll be a vegetable when I awake, after a long night of smoke inhalation. This is the worst possible end.

Magical thinking: if I stay up tonight, I may have a better chance of survival.

Was it this morning when I woke in that parking lot in North Carolina? What a day!

Naively hopeful, I took courage from the lightening sky as I drove. At rest areas in South Carolina, Georgia, and Northern Florida, in seldom-used, well-mowed patches of grass, I performed stretches dimly recalled from the month in 1983 when elfin Ellen the parole officer led me in a private fitness class. My exertions must have made an entertaining sight for arriving travelers.

A traffic jam trapped me for miles and hours, from Melbourne to Vero Beach. My right foot grew dangerously twitchy. Motionless, I stared at the concrete barriers strewn on the roadside like Scrabble trays after a giant's tantrum. A first for me: like a slaving cabbie, I had to pee in my empty coffee cup.

The source of the obstruction turned out to be a charred hulk parked on the shoulder and still giving off smoke. A fire engine's rear protruded into the roadway.

On the embankment, a shirtless young black man rode a noisy red mower between palm trees. *Say Yes to Life!* commanded a jolly baby on a billboard.

My exotic new home.

Sue Muenster, my contact at the *Sun Sentinel*, isn't the big cheese, she's just the Lifestyle editor. When I called, she bounced me over to the Sunday editor, Glen Geduld, who said, "I've read your stuff. It's not exactly journalism, but it'll do." He promised to carve out five minutes to meet me tomorrow, "just to make sure we're not hiring a three-eyed alien."

And when he sees me, what then?

Lunch at the Huddle House, alone. Table edge pressing into my belly. Healthy resolutions, broken as soon as the waitress (elderly, with cascading, piss-yellow curls) took out her pad. Country Ham, Country Sausage, Farm Fresh Eggs, Grits & Toast. Irresistible on the laminated menu, less so on the plate.

Leaving 95 at long last, heading toward the just-set sun, I exulted, but only for the length of the exit ramp. My torturous trip was nearly over, but something worse awaited. Along the broad, straight avenue, tidy strip malls and funeral homes alternated with lushly landscaped entrances to tropical-themed subdivisions, Coco Breeze, Sweaty Palms, and so on. Were those bougainvilleas or hibiscuses? You'll forgive me for not knowing.

Guided by uncertain memories, I turned too soon and drove along deserted, winding lanes of nearly identical homelets (no second floors as far as the eye could see), now and then spying a brown landscaper with a hedge trimmer. They've put up more of these houses since my last visit, and dug many miles of straight flood control canals, whose banks converge at distant vanishing points. One could lose one's way here for years.

As far as I'm concerned, it would have been better if they'd left the swamps to the alligators and egrets, instead of enticing Northerners here to play, wither, and die. That I've relocated to this hot, tidy wasteland seems the ultimate joke of the gods. Just what I needed: more cause to sweat.

I had to call them for directions out of the maze. You can imagine the respect that won me from my father.

Their home looks too small to hold two full-grown adults. They bought it new, but the stucco is dingy now and the chocolate aluminum awnings have faded to a shabbier hue. Across the street, a black woman in flowery nurse's scrubs helped a fragile, shrunken man from car to wheelchair. Twenty-five years ago, he must have stood here in white pants and admired his brand-new home in paradise. Quite a thought.

A concrete bunny in their screened entranceway greets guests and promises a whimsical welcome within. A small lizard perched motionless on the bunny's head, but darted away from my inquisitive forefinger, quick as regret. I was dressed for New Jersey, in long pants and long sleeves; fortunately, the temperature was a cool eighty.

The doorbell button glowed an unsavory amber. By pushing it, I lost the option of driving away and checking into the nearest hotel.

Mother wore a clean white blouse with a narrow, rounded collar, the eternal Catholic schoolgirl. She gave my wrist a squeeze with the hand that wasn't holding a cigarette. Her pinched smile and glazed, wet corneas made it clear that she'd had a cocktail or three to prepare herself.

What would Eka have seen if she'd been standing by my side? A petite, mottled woman with a bit of an osteoporotic hump. Hair tinted caramel, large honey-tortoise glasses two generations out of style. Bird-beak lips, and light brown teeth. What she wouldn't have seen was that my mother worked as a podiatrist's receptionist for years, that she had a double mastectomy a few years back, that she used to remind me of a hummingbird as she flitted about, and that she always seemed to view her children as chores to be finished.

Did unexpected tenderness well up at the sight of her, reduced by age and surgery, frail and vulnerable? No, it did not.

My father, straight-spined and put out, looked past me, into the driveway. "You have to move your car so I can get out of the garage," he said. "Just put it on the edge of the driveway."

His first words to me in six years.

He's still lean, still formal and fastidious in his dress. (No shorts for him, plaid or otherwise.) New on this visit: the tubular veins on the backs of his hands, and the black stitches down the bridge of his nose, where a malignant mole was removed recently. His mouth still forms a flat, disapproving line, as if he were perpetually witnessing a violation of the natural order and powerless to stop it. For someone who's lived in Florida so long, he's pale. But the external details matter less than this: each time I speak, his jaws clamp tight. It's not just the fear that I'll stay more than a night or two. He can't stand me. Never could.

Despite their disappointment in their first-born son, they enacted a pageant of civility. Drinks and catching up in the seldom-used living room, three sacks of aging flesh amid the shining glass and chrome. I asked about their health and activities, and learned that my mother plays cards five days a week with a group of younger Jewish ladies, in their seventies; her bronchitis keeps flaring up, but otherwise, everything's lovely. My father, she said (since he sat mute as a stone idol) should use his cane more, he's been losing his balance recently, and he doesn't like to wear his hearing aids; he still does his marquetry, but hasn't gone back to golfing since his rotator cuff surgery, which is a shame because that was his greatest pleasure.

Her chirping reminded me of someone waving her arms to keep the mosquitoes away.

She had made lamb stew with bacon, her old standby when entertaining. The taste brought back the memory of her hair in a flip, the little wings standing out left and right—and her teasing me in front of the guests for taking more than my share. *Other people have to eat, too, Angus.*

There are smudges and crumbs on the glass dinner table; my parents can't see as sharply as they used to. They keep their meds in two islands at the foci of the ellipse. I could murder them both by pulling a switcheroo in the night.

Over dinner, I told them about the Monopoly game, how I taught my friends Dad's strategy. He watched from a distance as I spoke, and said he had no memory of playing Monopoly with us.

No one else can reduce me to desperate small talk the way they can. By involuntary reflex, I jabbered about the traffic jam, the car that tailgated me, and the boil-woman. My mother said, "You're still the same old chatterbox."

She then shared with me the story of my father's near-fatal heart attack in October: left descending artery, 100 percent blocked; right coronary artery, 75 percent blocked. Luckily for him, they were visiting old friends in Sarasota, so he had his attack a mile from a major heart center; they had him on the table in under ten minutes. Greer had mentioned something about this, the day of her son's party. I suppose I should have called. I'm sure they hold it against me, while never expecting anything different.

The telephone rang. It was one of her card-playing pals. Instantly, she turned into Breezy Brenda, a character I'd forgotten. Out of sight in the kitchen, she told her friend that she couldn't play tonight because she had company, then told a joke she'd gotten today by e-mail, about a priest and a talking chicken. She dropped her voice decorously for the punch line, so I wouldn't overhear. I still don't know what the chicken said.

Trying on an alternate persona myself, I helped clear the table. After my first trip to the kitchen, she said, "You don't have to do that. Go and rest in the guest room. You must be tired."

And here I've been ever since, except when she called me out to show me my towels in the linen closet, and I glimpsed the stacked cartons of Marlboro Lights, a lethal cache packaged in appealing Caribbean teal.

My suit is hanging in the closet with her old winter clothes. (When did she ever wear a pink brocade jacket with shoulder pads?) The rest of my clothes are still in the suit-case, because I can't bring myself to unpack.

En route to the bathroom just now, I glimpsed my mother snoring alone in bed, propped up on pillows, while the television told her to ask her doctor if Flomax is right for her. In her long, lace-trimmed nightgown, she looked like a wrinkled Wendy, waiting for Peter Pan to return one last time.

My father was working at the dinner table with his back to me, head bent, using tweezers to place bits of wood veneer on a large board. His hair is thicker than mine: one more injustice. He glanced up at the window, stared inertly at my reflection, and went back to his work as if he hadn't seen me.

Which calls to mind a certain driving lesson. Near tears, I rolled my rage into a hard little ball and flung it at him, "I'm sorry I'm such a total disappointment." He replied, "Apology accepted," and we went on with the lesson.

Mister Dis, I once named him, looking back on my teen-age years. Displeased. Dismissive. Disgusted. The man who made me want to disappear.

This is better. Outside the front door, the air is free of menthol fumes. Maybe I'll sleep here, in this lawn chair, in the humid cool.

The concrete bunny keeps me company. A spider web connects his ear to the stucco wall; one of his shiny black eyes has fallen out, leaving a sad crater. Times are tough.

Here's what I remember from childhood: my mother saying, "Don't be a clingy thingy," my father saying, "Figure it out for yourself, I won't always be here," and a general impression that they might have been a contented couple except for their three young burdens. It's pathetic for a man my age to complain about his aged parents like an adolescent—but there they are.

A Farfetched Possibility

I saw a sign today. Someone had slapped a bumper sticker over the word *Drive*, leaving a terse rhyme: 55 *Stay Alive*. Because that's my age, and because I'd been thinking, once again, of letting go and being done, I took the slogan as a personal exhortation from the cosmos.

The bumper sticker, however, said, *El Decapitán*—a garage band, I'm guessing—which diluted the message somewhat.

On my way to interview Ellsworth Bardo this morning, I called Bob. Pulled off the road, stood pensively above a narrow canal while a gargantuan orange grasshopper traversed the gravel by my feet, and wished I had a friend. A surprising wish—I thought I'd outgrown the need long ago. Why do others have friends, but not me, not for years? You could say I lack patience for their annoying habits (the whinny, the thrice-told tale, the affected ascot)—or maybe I've got it backwards, maybe they couldn't stand *me* anymore. It may have to do with my preference for solitude, which doesn't require a false front. Still, sometimes you wish you had someone to talk to.

"Peace, brother," I said to Bob.

He'd been meditating, and sounded a thousand miles away. "You made it down there all right?"

The impulse to confide collapsed at the sound of his voice. "Yup, I'm here."

While I studied the alien grasshopper's painted armor, he told me, "Eka called just before."

I won't list the hopes this unleashed.

"And she said?"

Long-distance static.

"Why did she call?"

"Just to say hello. I told her you'd gone to Florida for a new job."

You moron! I thought. Now she thinks I'm trying to forget her.

"What did she say to that?"

He couldn't remember, exactly.

"What was the gist—the upshot—the general idea?"

"I think she said something like, 'It happened so fast.'"

I parsed those words for hidden meanings. She would have come back to me if I hadn't left. She hoped I would pine for her. I've let her down again.

"Did she say how she's getting along with the doctor?"

A small clearing of the throat. "I don't want to depress you."

"Go right ahead."

As he delayed, the flecks of sunlight on the muddy canal bank resolved into an alligator's scales. The predator basked ten yards away, but there was no room for fear with this greater terror hanging over me.

"I'm waiting."

"This is going to hurt."

"Tell me."

"She said he wants to marry her. Soon."

Save me—that's what she called to say. *I don't need this luxury. Take me back.*

Or, she wanted to say a last good-bye.

Which?

The grasshopper probed my shoe. The alligator grinned lazily. I had stepped out of civilization, onto prehistoric terrain. From this remote vantage point, I viewed my former life with aching nostalgia. Not so long ago, I presided over a household of four: my brother, my beloved, and her son. I could have kept it all, but chose not to.

Incomprehensible.

That scheduled interview with Glen Geduld never happened. He called this morning to say that the guy who writes the Sunday religion roundup is in the hospital with a ruptured spleen, i.e., he's in crisis mode, and to give me contact information for a Hendricks House client named Ellsworth Bardo. He also sent along a social worker's case summary by e-mail, and said there may be more work for me than he'd thought.

I'm his trusted pinch hitter now. When I promised him his profile by five, he actually thanked me.

Ellsworth Bardo's phone has been disconnected, so I came unannounced. He rents a gray hut west of I-95, behind a cement plant—as far from the ocean as you can get and still be in Fort Lauderdale. There was an old box fan on the front steps, presumably kaput, and a milk crate full of empty diet soda and Glucerna cans. Music was playing inside, Miles Davis, I think. Though he hadn't been expecting company, my story matched what the social worker had told him, and he let me in.

A retired algebra teacher and, until recently, an amateur sports photographer, he may be a light-skinned African American, an olive-skinned white man of Mediterranean descent, a mulatto, an octoroon, who the hell knows. I couldn't tell by staring, though his near-blindness gave me all the time in the world. What intrigued me about Mr. Bardo was that, in some ways, he could have been my fifteen-years-older twin. It was like gazing into a magic mirror at my future, if I'm still alive by then, and it wasn't a pretty sight. I don't mean just his physical state, I'm talking about the whole crusty habitat—the peas on the carpet mashed by his wheelchair, the finger-size water bug strolling across the kitchen floor.

After settling me on his couch (draped with a frayed bedspread), he offered me a Coke, by which he meant my choice of orange soda or Dr. Pepper. "I'm happy to serve as a poster boy if it helps Hendricks House," he said. "They've been like family to me."

"Actually," I explained, "the donations will go to you, not Hendricks House."

He'd been wheeling his way along the kitchen counter toward the fridge, but now he stopped. "They didn't make that clear," he grumbled, apparently reconsidering.

The social worker's report had included a catalogue of his unmet needs, including cash to pay for the 20 percent of his diabetes supplies not covered by Medicare, and the copays for his frequent doctor visits. I pointed out that his situation seemed a bit more difficult than the average Hendricks House client's. He admitted this might be true.

Here are the notes I took while he poured my soda:

- old LPs make bottom shelf of bookcase sag.
- silver Xmas tree, red garlands.
- snapshots of EB + wife at Bryce Canyon, the Parthenon (sunglasses), and Windows on the World (bridges in background below).
- gray dust on horiz'l surfaces, from cement plant.
- 8-lb. hand weights.
- gray rubber wheelchair wheels speckled w/crumbs. Sticker on back of seat: Ignorance Is the Worst Disability.

He confirmed the catalogue of sorrows I'd been given. He's losing the vision in the eye that still sees, due to temporal arteritis, which has blocked the flow of blood to his optic nerve. (Hendricks House has referred him to the Lighthouse; he'll start learning Braille next week.) Eight years ago, a drunk in a Jeep crashed through the window of the Bob Evans Restaurant where he was dining; he never regained the use of his legs. His wife, a school nurse, died of ovarian cancer two years later, and the two medical calamities consumed all of their savings. Long ago, in 1983, a school-bus accident claimed the life of their thirteen-year-old son.

He answered my questions tersely, but relaxed when we moved from past to present. He tutors the kids next door in math and anything else they need help with. In exchange, they wash his dishes and bring him dinner each night. The tutoring has gotten harder recently, since he can't read their textbooks even with his magnifying bar, but he won't stop because "it helps me more than it helps them." Though his home reeked of fried fish (a microwaved lunch), and though I doubt I'd have survived the blows he's endured, other evidence suggested a happy life. His walls are covered with photos he took of the Yankees at spring training, including faces even I can recognize. A former student had autographed an eight-by-ten of himself in a space suit, *To Mr. Bardo, Thanks for the lift!* And a framed newspaper picture showed some local dignitary shaking his hand while a gym full of teenagers in caps and gowns stood and applauded.

A leaning stack of *Scientific American* magazines threatened to come crashing down on us. During the hour I spent there, he told me about the quest to reach absolute zero (did you know that, as you get close, particles of matter behave like waves?), and that, Darwin to the contrary, some species have recently been observed to evolve within the span of a human lifetime.

Unlike my past profilees, he showed not a glimmer of self-pity. He finds endless fascination all around him, and is too busy to mope.

For my own murky reasons, I asked how he proposed to his wife. He had just brought me a plate of key lime cookies with green icing, and he snickered. "That's a funny story. I didn't think she'd accept. I'd been trying to get up my nerve for weeks. I lived up north back then, near the state line, and had a canoe. We used to explore the swamps and creeks off the Apalachicola River every weekend. I asked her while she was paddling, with her back to me. But the blackbirds were making a racket, and she thought I'd asked her about *carrying* me. She said, 'No way, not till you lose weight.' I just about died inside, but she had no idea, not till she glanced back. She said, 'Honey, what's the matter, I was just teasing.' So I said, 'You mean you *will* marry me?' She came close to tipping the canoe over, she was so surprised."

I suspect the story has been polished and perfected over the years, but who cares? I wish it were my story, my memory, my life.

An urge came over me: to tell him about Eka, and ask what he thought I should do. It took stern self-control to suppress the urge. I wish now that I hadn't.

He insisted on showing me home movies of his wife and son, transferred to videotape. When he turned on the TV, before he inserted the cassette, Jimmy Stewart showed up, leaping through snowy Bedford Falls like a merry madman. My host squinted at the screen. "I used to love that movie when I was young. Now I hate it."

I asked why.

"They engineered it for maximum lump-in-the-throat. I can't tolerate that anymore. Just a matter of taste."

A moment later, we were watching his son swing a plastic bat at a Wiffle Ball on a tee. His wife, in a one-piece bathing suit, hid her face from the camera. He knew from memory which images came when, though he could no longer make them out clearly. The furrows in his brow were deep enough to plant seeds in. Talk about maximum lump-in-the-throat.

"Right now," he said, "my main goal is getting Jihan into college. I've been tutoring her since she was twelve— no one in her family ever went past high school before."

I confess: I cracked, then and there. I admired Ellsworth Bardo the way a boy admires an Olympic champion.

Before leaving, I offered to help clean up in the kitchen. He asked, without irony, "Does it need cleaning?"

I didn't want to shame him. "Just a few crumbs here and there."

"That's par for the course. The kids'll take care of it."

I didn't want to leave, but had no excuse to stay. We shook hands at his front door. I told him I'd enjoyed meeting him. Intuiting, perhaps, that I needed more help than he did, he said, "Good luck to you, young man."

I wrote the profile at a diner on Andrews Avenue. Concentration didn't come easily. I kept imagining how Ellsworth Bardo would have answered the question, *What should I do about Eka?* I saw him smiling like the Dalai Lama and saying, in various ways, *Haul your ass up there and beg her to come back, before she marries the wrong guy.*

To do my subject justice, I resisted the usual tear-jerking. Each sentence required vigilance against sleazy habit. Interestingly, I found that the more adjectives I deleted, the more dignity I conveyed. *Because he can only see out of one eye—and the light is fading there as well—the floor is littered with crumbs he's not aware of. Offering a visitor a soft drink, he placed the can and a glass of ice in a homemade caddy on the arm of his wheelchair, and rolled himself back to the living room.*

Simple and unadorned. I'm almost proud of it.

Maybe I'll mail a copy to Eka.

There's an unpleasant matter I haven't mentioned.

As I emerged from the guest room this morning, my father summoned me into the kitchen. Mother retreated to their bedroom—sickly and decayed without her makeup, a bird plucked bare. I was still in boxer shorts and undershirt; my father had already dressed, in a wrinkle free white shirt and gray slacks. We sat at the small table, boxes of Grape Nuts and Fiber One forming a barricade between us.

"You're falling apart," he informed me. "It's disgraceful, how you've let yourself go." He wiped his leaking red eyes—morning blear, not emotion. "Babying you won't help. You've got to knuckle down and pull yourself together. I shouldn't have to tell you this, at your age. You're your own responsibility, not ours. You can stay here two nights, no more. We're too old for this."

His speech split me down the middle. One side asked, *Who is this man?* The other, scolded like a child, responded like a child. I imagined buying a small pistol—something you can still do at any Florida gun shop—and blowing my brains out in their guest bathroom. A small thank you for the hospitality.

He always wished he could throw me back, like a misshapen fish. And I've tried to grant his wish, by making myself scarce for decades at a time. It was a mistake to swim back here.

A memory: as Armstrong and Aldrin flew over the moon, searching for a place to land and running low on fuel, my father paused to watch with us and muttered, "I don't see the point. Why go there?"

That was his attitude toward other men's achievements: *All that effort, for what?*

And I learned it from him.

To think that one of my quintessential traits comes straight from him. It's as if the prime minister of Israel found out that his transplanted heart came from a cryogenically preserved Hitler. What do I do, claw the loathsome organ from my chest?

Figuratively, yes. Get rid of it. At least try.

The concrete bunny, blind in one eye, sits at my feet like a loyal pet. I can smell Mother's smoke even out here tonight.

If I were a man of discipline, a hundred pounds lighter and gainfully employed I would have asked Eka to stay, because I would have had a right to ask. To this extent, my father has a point.

Can I change? Slim down, keep this job, ask her to join me?

Possibly.

I'll move to a hotel in the morning. Perhaps look at apartments, with room for Eka and Davit. Find a place they'd be happy to live in—near the beach. Then I'll call her.

But she'll have grown accustomed to wealth by then. I should call sooner, not later.

Right now?

(A fantasy: we share a small Florida bungalow. There's no shortage of jobs for home health aides here. Every day at five fifteen, when she comes home from work, we head over to the community pool, where I carry her, weightless, her arms around my neck, her side warming me in the cool water.)

If I call, though, she may say, *Angus, I am so sorry.*

Doomed.

Glen Geduld on the phone just now—dissatisfied, harassed, barely containing his anger. I have one hour to turn Ellsworth Bardo into a standard sob story, just like the clips I sent, because *I didn't hire Hemingway, I hired you.*

Poor Angus. As soon as he resolves to improve himself, the god of Oh-No-You-Don't shoves a hot spear between his ribs. A man can't live like this.

Can't. Must.

Now what?

Decisions

Dearest Eka,

It's time to take action. That's why I spent the afternoon floating in the little pool at La Quinta. A good place to think, to let the mind drift, to find a way back to you.

A few possibilities presented themselves. Now I must pick one.

See you soon, I hope.

Yours,

Angus

Hoping to slip away unnoticed, I reached the front door with my bags and found my parents in the kitchen doorway, a lit cigarette in my mother's spotted hand.

"Loading up the car," I announced jauntily.

"All righty," said Ma.

Pa kept his own counsel.

They followed me out through the garage. The clearance between their car and the steel shelving was narrow, and I'm happy to say that my suitcase put a long scratch in the clear coat of their Camry. Neither of them seemed to notice.

They watched from the shade of the garage as I hoisted my luggage into the trunk. The cruel, bright morning sun made the dings in my door and bumper perfectly distinct. Perhaps their clouded eyes couldn't see.

Levity seemed the only way to go. "So—it's good-bye," I proclaimed.

"Good luck," said my mother. "Let us know where you are once you get settled."

"Get your car washed," my father said. "It makes a bad impression."

There was no father-son handshake, only a mother-son cheek press. As I backed out, with the windshield framing them, the many and varied emotions included:

• Inexpressible relief

• Pity for them, because they're two of the worst parents I've ever met

• The mischievous impulse to throw the transmission into Drive

• The hope that, when they go, they'll go together, in a crash, so I won't have to visit the one left behind.

Outside the front doors of La Quinta, a smallish, multi-tiered fountain flanked by closely spaced palms suggests stateliness on a tight budget. This was better than I'd hoped for. That the room isn't quite big enough for its furniture—I have to turn sideways to pass between the foot of the bed and the dresser—is entirely forgivable, even symbolically appropriate for this awkward passage in my life.

A month here will cost just a bit more than a month in my apartment. I deeply appreciate the reasonable rates.

How fortunate it is (I thought, as the desk clerk ticked off the amenities) to be a middle-class American citizen, who can survive any setback by whipping out a credit card. There's a limit to the magic, though, a literal end to one's credit, and I have no idea how close to the edge I've stumbled.

That froze my heart, even as I signed my name. If the next bill arrives before my first paycheck, and I can't pay the minimum, or if Bob neglects to forward it, I stand to lose shelter, food, fuel—everything.

Facing the threat of financial ruin, I drove three miles west to the Sports Authority, where I bought goggles and sunscreen. None of their swim trunks fit me; I had to visit a big and tall men's shop in Boca. For the next few hours, I floated in the hotel pool and considered my past and future.

One summer in childhood, I swam every day at our town pool. The first time I passed over the deep end with my diving mask on, my senses misinformed me: for one alarming moment, I felt I was high in the air, looking down, with nothing to support me. On subsequent laps, fear turned into its opposite, and I imagined ecstatically that I was flying, a thousand feet above a blue valley. Though I tried and failed to reproduce that delight today, remembering yielded a pleasure of its own.

My pool time, like Buddha's under the Bodhi tree, was meant to yield enlightenment, a solution to the problem of earning a living. I spent most of it daydreaming, however. Should I call Eka today, or wait until I'm better established? Strong arguments lined up on both sides. The longer I wait, the harder it will be to pry her away; but, if I call before I'm set up, I won't be able to offer acceptable accommodations. Underlying everything is this bind: I need to know she'll join me before I submit to the yoke again . . . but I can't ask her to join me until I put my life in order.

Unable to reach a decision, I gave myself over to the pleasant sensation of bobbing on the breeze-blown ripples. If only I could earn a living this way!

The sun blazed through my thin eyelids, and brought to mind summer days at the shore. My parents rented a house for one week each year, always in a different town because my father hated each of them in turn. They would sit on lawn chairs under the umbrella while Greer and Bob dug in the wet sand and I stayed in the waves up to my neck, rising and falling with the water, quivering with the chill and refusing to come ashore until they ordered me to. What's sweetest about the memory is that it's identical to everyone else's. In this way, I was a normal child.

I might have stayed in the pool till nightfall, except for the two scrawny Hispanic teens standing in the shallow end, one of whom murmured to the other, *"Ballena,"* assuming the gringo wouldn't know the Spanish word for *whale.* They snickered; I rolled onto my belly and dove beneath the surface.

A message from Glen Geduld awaited me. He called my rewrite *passable* and offered me the job—I hadn't understood that I was on probation—but the hours are part-time, and there's no health insurance. Wrapped in thin white towels, dripping on the carpet, I thought: Your turn will come, Glen. A layoff will be your karmic payoff.

His recorded voice went on to give me my next assignment, a single mother named Quantisha Foe, who suffered a traumatic brain injury when she fell from a stepladder while painting her one-story house. (She's had to take a leave of absence from her job as a phlebotomist due to headaches, nausea, dizziness, and fatigue.) Also, I'm to stop by tomorrow and get squared away with Human Resources.

Drip-drip-dripping—melting, it seemed—I faced the future and found myself fatally fucked. I'll need a second income if I'm to support Eka and Davit. Where might I find that? Teaching Zumba classes? And then there's the prospect of profiling one Quantisha Foe after another, forevermore. I must have been a torturer of innocents in my last life, to have earned that.

Someone is showering in the next room and shouting at his wife in French, something about *les fesses plein du sable.* I believe he's complaining about the feeble water pressure and the sand that won't come off his child's *derriere.* They must be from Quebec: no one would cross the Atlantic to stay here.

Find a job you love, and you'll never work a day in your life. I find that oft-quoted advice hilarious. One might as well say, *Find a million dollars up your ass and you'll never lack friends.*

The AC chills me, but the laptop warms my thighs. Mixed with the scent of ten-year-old hotel is a background odor of cigarette smoke, though I insisted on a nonsmoking room—unless that's a residue stuck in my nostrils after two days in the parental ash pit. The king-size bed is just right for me and the woman I wish were here to share it. The TV is big, too—the dark screen so wide that it curves, like the Earth. They painted the walls golden ochre and put in matching carpeting; it reminds me of that Van Gogh wheat field with the black crows circling. Now, at last, I understand: there's something dead down there, unseen amid the golden stalks. A portrait of the artist as a corpse-to-be.

A pattern has emerged. Hope, followed closely by hopelessness. For as long as I can remember, I've done this: found a path, doubted it, abandoned it.

Now that I've recognized the pattern, I should be able to break it. Each time I hear myself say, *It's impossible*, or *It's not worth the effort*, I'll remind myself not to be ruled by my father's teaching.

We'll see how long *that* lasts.

> Tami D, Tami D,
> Oh how happy we could be
> If only I weren't me.

I called her just now. Had to look up all the Driscolls in northern New Jersey, and gambled that her husband was Robert in Verona, not Antwon in Irvington or Yevgeny in Passaic.

Breathless, she'd just come home from a holiday party for the families staying at her church's shelter. No big surprise that she's a churchy type, just a small disappointment.

The plan was to explain my predicament, ask for her advice, and then follow it, on the assumption that any off-the-cuff suggestion of hers would yield better results than following my own rotten instincts. Once the small talk was done, though, I found it humiliating to admit that I called a near-stranger to plead for guidance. Hiding my urgency behind nonchalance, I said, "I need to bounce some ideas off someone. I think very highly of you, and I hope you have a few minutes to spare. Can you talk?"

"Of course," she said. "I'm honored. What's going on?"

What a person! Rather than make me feel like a pitiful lump, she raised my spirits and gave me hope—all in just seven words.

I couldn't bring myself to mention Eka, and so confined myself to the matter of earning a living. She heard me out, and suggested I meet with a career counselor. Her son did it last year. "They can broaden your thinking about what would make you happy. Basically, you list the things you enjoy doing and the things you're good at, and they suggest professions that use your skills and interests. My son ended up working at the Museum of Natural History, building things for their exhibits. He never even knew there *was* such a profession. And he loves it."

Such sensible advice. Suppressing, for now, my certainty that it can't possibly help, I resolved to get myself counseled. (Skills and pleasures, let's see. Glib mockery. Fast typing. Pool floating. Irresponsible drinking. Travel. I should look for work as a gossip columnist!)

I found myself wishing I could keep Tami on the line. Should I confess that I am (or was) the Masked Marauder, and I. Pagliacci, and the Fartful Dodger? It actually seemed possible, so vast was her mercy.

What prevented me was the awful possibility that she would reply, *Yes, I knew that.*

I thanked her for her help, and added, "You're the closest thing I've met to an ideal person."

To which she said, "Well, I don't know about *that.*"

Self-counseling: what might I do to bring in cash and satisfaction?

It should involve water.

I could become a diver, one who searches for lost treasure and missing persons. Not a bad fantasy. I assume the job requires a leaner physique, though.

Captaining a ferry, then. Like Charon, transporting dead souls across the river each morning, and delivering them back again at five. I might look distinguished in an officer's cap. Pouring diesel smoke and engine noise into the crisp harbor air. Drinking Cutty Sark at the bridge—nodding off, slamming into the concrete pier, injuring dozens.

What do I want to do, really? I'll close my eyes; the answer will come.

I'm seeing . . . Japan. A sudden yen to see Mount Fuji.

I could write travel articles, if I could walk more than a hundred paces.

A small boat. Just me in it. Drifting into a fjord. Black peaks rise above me on both sides, streaked with snow. Darkness falls.

I'm Going Home to See My Baby

This may prove a catastrophic mistake, the wrongest of wrong turns. So be it. If I'm delusional, delirious, deranged, at least I have a song in my heart.

Where am I? South Carolina, possibly. Who knows? Who cares! I'm on my way—less than a day stands between me and my love.

By daring to reach for the prize, I hope (for once) to win it.

Hi-yo, Silver. Away!

A quick recap, before sleep overtakes me.

Five days in the Sunshine State sufficed to shoot me out like a rejected organ, back to my home amid the sleepy, rusting factories. For five days, I resumed my role as the chronicler of misfortune. For five days, I ate Texas-size portions of ribs and thought regretfully of Angus and Eka, like Adam and Eve, banished from paradise because of a shared mistake. To sum up, I'm ecstatic to be leaving.

It was Quantisha Foe, most of all, who drove me out. With charming smiles and cunningly displayed cleavage, she bent forward frequently in her scoop-neck dress, stirred Splenda into my coffee, and placed a Ring Ding before me on a gilt-edged plate. Perhaps she saw me as a promising prospect, because we're similarly built. Her story is absurdly sad—especially since she could have prevented her fall by standing on the grass and duct-taping her paint roller to a broomstick—but the queasy confusion engendered by her sugary smile, her ample bosom, and her Christian self-help books (*Blessed, Not Stressed; Heal Your Pain*) helped me see that I'm through with this work.

From the next room, the hammering staccato of machine gun fire and the whine of a diving airplane provided a soundtrack for our interview. When a fearsome headache abruptly drained the life from her face, she left with a murmured excuse and had the older of her boys, a kindergartner, see me out.

In crisis, I pulled into the parking lot of a memorial chapel and searched the Department of Labor's online *Occupational Outlook Handbook*. What might I become? A plastic worker? A surveyor? A member of the armed forces?

A burly gent in a dark suit and yarmulke emerged from the chapel. He eyed me distrustfully as he smoked a cigar in the shade.

Despair and distraction have kept me from updating this document until now. Apart from the career issue, longing for Eka has churned my concentration to slush.

I sent Quantisha's touching profile to Glen Geduld this morning, and dithered away the rest of the day. For dinner, I stopped at a Friday's, although it's Wednesday. The place was packed, and the hostess offered me a seat at the bar. I had a short-lived vision, as she led the way, of telling my troubles to a mustachioed bartender in suspenders as he wiped frothy mugs clean. He would shake his head and perhaps stun me with a brilliant bit of advice, the sensible solution to everything.

The bartender, however, was an efficient Asian blonde in a tank top, with a cute black bow tie around her neck.

A chatty assortment of races and genders sat at the bar. There were a pair of Australian geologists touring the US on vacation; a shy but cordial couple, originally from the Dominican Republic, celebrating their second anniversary; and a group of paralegals, none above thirty, thrilled to be finished with a mammoth real estate closing. After two Jack and Cokes, I turned chatty, too, and announced to the group that I was quitting my job, had no idea what to do for a living, and welcomed suggestions.

That stopped their wagging tongues. What seemed jollity to me touched a nerve of horror in them. I offered an easier question: "What do I *look* like I do for a living?"

Helpful and amiable, they called out: "Lawyer," "School principal," "Talk radio host." No hecklers mocked my size, no comedian called out, *Tennis pro.* For a random bunch, they were surprisingly kind.

The more outgoing of the Australians had a bold proposal. "Have you considered running for president?"

We all enjoyed that. I addressed them sonorously: "My fellow Americans, and esteemed visitors. This is a big country, and it needs a big leader. A man who knows the troubles of the lowly and the annoyances of the rich. A man who, like George Washington, has felt the anguish of dental pain who, like Thomas Jefferson, has declared his independence from marital fidelity—who, like Millard Fillmore . . . but enough. What Americans really want to know is, What's in it for me? I want to know that myself! For now, let me make one thing perfectly clear: I need a job, and you can give it to me, at no cost to yourselves, with a tap of a touchscreen. Ask not what I can do for you, because I can't do much. In conclusion, I bid you a patriotic, all-American *adieu.* So long—farewell—*auf Wiedersehen*—good night."

They gave me cheers, chuckles, and applause. "Hey, how about bringing my boyfriend home from Afghanistan?" the barmaid asked, and I replied, "For you, my dear, anything."

The spotlight shifted to the Australians after that. As they recounted their adventures, I admired the sinuous forms of the half-melted cubes in my glass, and thought of Eka. The longing outgrew my skin, until I burst.

Skipping dinner, I retreated once again to the backseat of my car, and dialed her, cell to cell.

Her voice: anxious, puzzled, Eastern European. "Hello?"

That she didn't perk up when she saw who was calling disappointed me. When she switched to higher-pitched Georgian, I was baffled.

"Eka? It's Angus. Hello?"

More Georgian. Voices bantered on TV behind her. I heard what sounded like footsteps on stairs, and then she whispered, "Sorry—for privacy, I moved."

(She doesn't want me to mess up her arrangement. There is no hope.)

"I see."

"You are at Florida?"

"For now, yes."

"Bob told me you finded a job."

Polite, reserved inquiry.

"Yes, but I think I'll look for a different one."

I expected her to say, *Give a chance to it, not be quitting so soon.* She said nothing.

I couldn't remember why I'd called. What was the message I needed to tell her?

"Eka?"

"Wait—he walks over my head."

While she waited for the doctor's footsteps to pass, I recklessly lobbed my heart at her. "I miss you. Very much."

Her failure to reply stabbed my soul.

"Do you know . . ." (*that I promised myself to win you back, but I'm dying of doubt, please tell me I have a chance*) ". . . the way to San Jose?"

"Excuse me? What do you ask?"

"Nothing. Sorry."

Here she granted me a kibble of hope. "Angus, I worry that you are angry to me. I have terrible fear that you hate me."

"No, it's not true. The opposite, in fact."

A native English speaker would have understood, but I don't think she did.

"I want you know, I don't forget all you helped me. Always I will remember everything."

A woman climbed into the Jeep parked next to me, and sent a nervous glance my way. There was a message in Eka's gratitude. Was it *Come save me, it's not too late,* or *Do not try, it can't be.*

I asked, "How are things going up there for you?"

She turned stoic. "I adjust."

Those two words gave me back my life. *Hold on, my love. I'm coming.*

"I'd better say good-bye now," I told her. "There's something important I have to do."

"Thank you for call me."

"Maybe I'll see you soon."

"Yes? You will visit New Jersey?"

"Could be."

"All right."

More tepid than overjoyed, but that was because she didn't know my secret intention.

"Farewell, then."

"Bye bye. Good luck for everything, Angus."

"The same to you."

And so, here I am, somewhere on I-95, having hoisted myself halfway up the eastern seaboard on a rope of pure faith. I'm staking everything on this. You can't go wrong if you act on your passion, right?

Right thou art, says Romeo's ghost.

Time to sleep now. Good night, unseen Reader. Whoever you are, I wish you happiness and success. Please wish the same for me.

The Moment We've All Been Waiting For

I see myself as I am. No woman would happily choose to marry me. And yet, her fingers swam through the hair on my chest, and she toasted me at our party. Even when she told me about Dr. Oh, she wanted me to stop her from leaving.

I'm not crazy to hope. It's worth the risk.

Ten minutes from now, I'll either have my bride at my side, her loving cheek against my shoulder as swooping swallows trill round our heads; or else I'll be finished, kaput.

A grove of old trees hides Dr. Oh's house from the street. Darkness cloaks the property.

I find that I can't believe in the happy ending. Better not leave the car until I can.

In Delaware, realizing I should get a shave, I cruised the streets of Newark until I found PJ's Barber Salon, where the chairs are still red leather, the steel footrests still say *Theo A. Kochs*, and the combs still lean lazily in a bottle of blue Barbicide.

A visit to the barber is always humbling. For fifteen minutes or so, you confront the face the world judges you by—in my case, a bloated, small-eyed face, not nearly as handsome as the inner me. No wiser than a fop, I wished I were more attractive—though not desperately enough to seek surgical help.

Under friendly questioning, I told the barber I was on my way to propose marriage. "Another one bites the dust," he said.

He was an ex-marine type, with a steel gray flattop. He had hung some WWII-vintage model planes (with decals!) on fishing line above the blue kiddie car that served as the children's chair. Taking his quip more seriously than he'd intended it, I replied, "A bachelor's freedom is overrated."

Like others who depend on tips for a living, he declined to argue.

He let me change into my suit in his back room. When I emerged, carrying the garment bag like a business traveler, he shook my free hand. "Last chance," he said.

"That's exactly right," I answered.

Upon my arrival in Doctor Oh's neighborhood, I gave myself a pep talk. *It's not just your own life you're trying to save. He's a weird little dude; she can't be happy with him. I may be unhealthy and unemployed, but we care about each other. That outweighs everything else. Doesn't it?*

The sun had gone down. Dr. Oh lives on the side of the ridge, amid palaces ten times the size of a normal home— the same place I showed Eka after our visit to Willowbrook. One house had a dozen Christmas trees, all strung with lights, lined up behind a spearhead iron fence. Excitement and terror stewed inside me. I caught myself making a low-pitched zzzzz, like a large flying beetle.

I've been parked here for a while now, across the street from the house, which I can't see except for a dark finial poking up between the trees. I wrote this to calm myself, but it hasn't worked. I should leave the car now, and ring the bell.

As you can see, though, I'm still here.

＊ ＊ ＊

I'm back where I started. No worse off than before Eka appeared at my door. Except for the memories.

Go ahead. Finish what you started.

＊ ＊ ＊

Dr. Oh's house, approached on the cobblestone drive-way, resembles an English college built in 1357. A wide, pointed arch frames the massive door. The stone is rough-hewn. Up above are crenellations. Not what I expected from an unmarried Korean-American toxicologist.

His chimes, grave and regal, reminded me of the many doorbells it's been my lot to ring. This time, though, the grisly drama was my own.

The doctor opened the door himself, complicating mat-ters. (Illogically, I had imagined this scene without him in it.) He seemed to have stepped out of an Eddie Bauer cat-alogue, in his blue button-down shirt and creamy V-neck sweater. I hadn't noticed in our earlier encounters that he has a handsome face. His thick black hair arcs above his forehead and ends alongside his eyebrow, a wave that's always about to break.

Finding me at his front door, he showed neither surprise nor worry, only irritation.

"I need to talk to Eka," I said urgently, half implying that I'd brought a life-or-death message from a loved one.

After looking me over quickly, he said, "I'll get her," and left me at his threshold.

I assume a decorator helped him create his museum-like entrance hall. A baby grand's polished lid reflected one of the two faux-Cezanne paintings that faced each other across the mostly empty space. White-carpeted steps led up the center of the space, then branched left and right. Fresh flow-ers in vases added indigo and violet to the scene. Music—Chopin, I think—filled the room so softly that it seemed an unconscious thought.

Weighed against the solidity of Dr. Oh's stone palace, my dreams were less substantial than air. The following points pressed themselves on me:

- It will be hard for her to live in squalor after this.
- Dr. Oh is closer to her age than I am.
- The wrinkles in my suit don't make a good impression.

She appeared just as the last of my optimism evaporated. She had on a strapless, plum-colored satin dress and silvery arm-bangles. Her lipstick matched the dress; her hair, usually tied back in a bun, hung to her shoulders. Like a husband who comes home early and finds his wife modeling lingerie for the plumber, I felt more or less eviscerated—not because I'd lost a flawless goddess (her bare shoulders were dotted with birthmarks and moles), but because we had been close, and never would be again.

How to escape with a remnant of dignity? That was the question.

"Our reservation is in twenty minutes," Dr. Oh called from a distant doorway.

"We go to dinner," she explained. Constrained emotion appeared on her forehead as sinuous creases, geological strata in cross section, a record of upheaval.

I fell mute. She took up the slack.

"You were at Florida last night. You flied?"

Her voice was higher than usual: taut vocal cords.

"No, I drove."

Dr. Oh called to her again, "I'll be in the den." Apparently he'd concluded that he had nothing to fear from me. I couldn't disagree.

"You look very nice," I said—the only words within reach.

"Thank you."

"I just wanted to see you. I'll go."

She interrupted my departure. "This haircut looks good. And the red burn from sun."

Funny—these small kindnesses opened the door to resentment. What kind of woman walks out on her man because a better provider shows up? There's a name for people like that.

"Angus, what you came to tell me?"

Nothing. There's nothing to say. That seemed the only possible response—but Ellsworth Bardo had a different point of view. *You just drove a thousand miles to tell her you'd do anything for her. If you leave it unsaid, you'll spend the rest of your life wondering, What if? Go ahead, make a fool of yourself. That's what the situation demands.*

Here, then, is my little oration, my self-abasement, as best I remember it:

"I'm sorry, I made a mistake. I thought if I came galloping up here and told you how wrong I was to let you go, I thought you might—but I guess I'm too late. I need to tell you this, though: the reason why I didn't ask you to stay was that I didn't think I had the right, when you could have all this. But once you were gone . . . Oh, the melodrama. Forgive me."

I wonder whether the outcome might have been different if I'd made my plea without hedging. But that's like wondering whether the Axis would have won World War Two if Germany had made use of its Jews instead of killing them—a badly designed thought experiment, an impossible hypothetical—because while I was speaking, her frown kept growing steeper. It seemed that she hated me for saying what I said. On the way up, I'd imagined tenderness, not this. I found it harder and harder to string syllables together.

She didn't attack me, though.

"I can't say to you any bad thing. You did too much good for me. Do you know, I thought you would be my husband? But you didn't tell me, 'Please stay,' you only said, 'Good-bye'—after I showed you I want to stay! This gave to me too much pain. Why you waited for now to tell me? I can't go away with you. I try to make this my life. Lawrence is good, he helps me to study for nurse examen. Soon I begin flute lessons, because always I dreamed of this, but forgot. I can't leave here, this would hurt him terrible. You should say these things to me before, Angus. I wish you did."

This isn't helping.

There's no reason to write another word—except that the story isn't finished.

Hauling my remains away, I twisted an ankle on a round-topped stone. The fear that I would fall in his driveway (and that the Mercedes would run me over) led me to dance a jig, which destroyed my dignity but kept me on my feet.

My view of Eka has only darkened since then. She looks no more angelic to me now than she did when I used to hear her haranguing her mother across the ocean. I can't blame her for choosing prosperity, but she could at least have taken responsibility for the choice. Really: she knew I loved her. She should have known I couldn't ask her to choose me over the healthy, wealthy, and well-groomed Dr. Oh. It was selfless of me to walk out that door. What more does she want?

I'll tell you what she should have done. She should have taken Dr. Oh's proposal as a flattering compliment and never mentioned it. Then, once we were married, whenever I disappointed her, she could have thrown it in my face. *Why I didn't marry this important doctor?*

I thought I was the arch-cynic, but she outdid me. While I, wide-eyed as a Disney princess, dreamed she would leave her castle for love's sake, she was bedecking herself in finery, reducing me to a mere pang.

I see now where misogyny comes from.

Dr. Oh's street winds down a slope. Lacking the will to do otherwise, I let gravity pull me down, past the wide, dark lawns and the school-sized houses.

In the valley, I came to a small shopping plaza and parked in front of Krauszer's. People went in empty-handed and came out with newspapers, lottery tickets, milk. A frail Indian woman behind the register peered out at me frequently. I stayed behind the wheel, limp.

Eventually, two police cars pulled into the lot and parked on either side of me. They weren't there for coffee. Holding a flashlight by his ear and shining it in my face, a young cop gestured to me, a two-fingered bye-bye. I didn't understand at first; then I did. Complying, I turned the engine on so I could lower the window.

"License, registration, and insurance, please."

I was too battered to resent the intrusion. Had he charged me with a moving violation, I would have mumbled, *Yes, sir, whatever you say.*

In the glove compartment, I found sucking candies and a forgotten screwdriver before I located the documents. The cop had to move his free hand away from his holster to accept them. His partner kept an eye on me from the passenger side. While a third cop checked out my record, Officer Fernandez asked, "How long have you been sitting here?"

"I've lost track. A while."

"Is there some reason why you're staying in your car?"

He looked as if he'd graduated from the police academy last week. He spoke politely, and wore a trim leather jacket with a brand-new shoulder patch. For one so young, he projected authority well.

"I just drove up from Florida to ask a woman to marry me, and she turned me down. Now I'm trying to figure out how to keep breathing."

He hesitated only long enough to blink. "I'm sorry about that, sir. But sitting here so long, you've got the store owners worried."

"Ah. Will you give them my apologies?"

"We'll explain."

The third cop mumbled a message in his ear, and Officer Fernandez handed back my papers. Apparently, my record is clear. (That I've never gotten pulled over after drinking is nothing short of a miracle—the only way in which I can be called lucky.) I was ready to back out and go home, but the young officer stayed by my window. "Is there someone we can call for you? A friend or family member?"

The concern in his baby-smooth face—the fear that I might hurt myself, or run down an innocent child—changed my opinion of him. He had reminded me of a boy playing dress-up; now he seemed a good man, uneasily balancing instinctive compassion against his stern new role.

"No, but thanks. I just want to go home."

"Do you think you'd feel better if you talked to someone? We could give you a ride to headquarters, or to Mountainside."

The hospital, that is.

"I appreciate that. But I think I'll just go to bed."

He asked me to wait, and went to confer with his colleagues. Returning, he said, "I'll follow you. Just to make sure you get home safe." He added awkwardly, "My Dad always says, 'No matter how dark it gets, the sun will rise again.'"

His youthful solicitude touched me, but the police escort quickly lost its charm. His headlights assaulted my eyes in the rearview mirror, all the way home. I had to come to a complete stop at all Stop signs—a first—and signal each turn well in advance. Oppression had its benefits, though: with him and his partner watching, I couldn't let myself sink to the ocean floor.

They drove off once I parked in front of Mrs. N's house. The relief was short-lived.

It's painfully cold in the car. The hour is late—almost midnight. It's December 21st, the day that was supposed to be my last. My deadline.

How neat.

Umm . . .

I have many reasons to be done and no reason to go on. But I don't want to kill myself. As turnabouts go, this one is damned inconvenient.

Thirty days ago, I had no fear, or so I thought. Either I didn't know myself or I've changed.

Gray mist outside the kitchen window, no sun. One couldn't ask for a more fitting backdrop—but the actor has forgotten his part.

The apartment was dark when I came in last night. I took the stairs as quietly as I could, so as not to wake Bob and have to tell my tale.

Navigating through the living room by memory, I banged my shin on the coffee table, which had migrated to a new place. He'd rearranged the furniture, I dimly saw, and created a cozy conversation nook where I'd had empty space.

As my eyes adjusted, I made out a basket of pinecones on the table. (Let's hope there are no pests lurking inside.) Three pairs of shoes were lined up neatly on a mat near the foot of the stairs. A salad dressing cruet held dried flowers. My stray newspapers, mugs, and junk mail were gone. He'd even tidied up the bookcase; the newer books, formerly stuffed into the gaps horizontally, had disappeared.

As I took all of this in—*my home is no longer mine*—Bob came out to pee. He let out a startled, fearful, not particularly serene grunt. An instant later, he recognized my shape. "What's going on?" he quietly croaked.

"Not much. What's up with you?"

He said he'd be right out, and asked me not to go in the bedroom. Still preoccupied with Eka (the satin dress, the bare shoulders, her lips saying no), I didn't think to ask why not, but the answer emerged soon enough. She had on a long-sleeved T-shirt that I recognized as his, which covered her behind but not much more. Finding me there, she crossed her arms as if she were naked. "I'm Bob's brother," I explained.

"Hi," she replied, sleepy and subdued. "I'm Deb."

She had long frizzy hair (gray, I think) and more flesh than I'd have guessed my lean brother would like. Neither of us was in a conversational mood.

He introduced us when he came out—she's a reference librarian—and then she took her turn.

"I hope you don't mind," he said.

Did I? Not in the petty landlord way, only in that everybody had somebody except me.

He offered to take Deb back to her apartment so I could have my bed back. I magnanimously refused, and spent the night on the couch.

There was little sleep for me. Like a bad conscience, Eka wouldn't let me rest. I kept seeing her in that dress, and wondered if this was what she'd really wanted all along, to bedeck herself in fripperies.

I yearned to lose consciousness. It took hours.

A spoon clinking against a bowl: Bob at breakfast.

Deb had left for work. There were three tiny cups on the kitchen table, and a blue teapot he must have bought after I left. He was still wearing the sweat suit he sleeps in.

"Shouldn't you be at work?"

"I told them I had a family emergency."

(How much did he know? And how did he know it?)

I pointed out that taking a day off so soon after starting a job was no way to climb the ladder. He shook that off with a toss of the head.

The couch had taken my back to new heights of pain. Sitting up took an absurdly long time. "You should have let me give you the bed," he said.

To put it briefly: though he didn't know about my visit to Dr. Oh's, he sensed that he shouldn't leave me alone. I didn't want him around, and found his concern intrusive and unhelpful.

"If you're depressed," he said, pouring tea for us both (he can't seem to remember that I loathe tea), "you should talk about it."

"I don't want to talk. Just go to work, Bob."

Blowing silently on the surface of his tea, he seemed to be teaching himself to accept that he doesn't have the power to heal me.

In the quiet, I noted that the skin of his neck has turned soft and crinkly—my little brother is decaying—and that his hair has grown enough to need styling. Unlike him, however, I wouldn't dream of telling a brother what to do.

He surprised me with a mild outburst. "Why do you have to be so arrogant?" he asked. "Why won't you let anyone help?"

"I'll think about it. All right? Now please get out of here before they fire you."

He considered that, and finally said, "I should refuse to leave until you talk to me. But you'll never talk to me. So what should I do?"

"Recognize your limitations and go."

After dressing in the bedroom, he told me gravely from the foot of the stairs, "I'll see you later."

The view through the kitchen window is clearer than it's been in years. He must have cleaned the glass on both sides. Another difference between us.

His silly artifacts litter the apartment. A round cushion, diameter of a toilet seat, leaning against the wall. A small tray of sand on the coffee table with an oblong stone resting in the middle. Keys to unlock the Gates of Wisdom, or just Zen décor? I don't know him well enough to say. Never have, never will.

Then there's the copper bowl. The thick little mallet wears soft leather on one end, like a baby's booty. Fern Wengel used to have one of these: a mystical singing bowl that makes a soothing tone when you rub the rim with the mallet. I couldn't make her bowl sing, though. It knew what I was thinking, she said. (With her aromatic oils and her belief in ghosts and such, Fern would have made a good match for Bob. I'll give him her name, in case Deb doesn't work out.)

Well, what do you know—*Bunggggg*, sang the bowl. A very Buddhist sound, ringing then fading to nothing. A plaintive metaphor for a life's diminuendo.

Not sure what I'm going to do. Like a thin balloon, losing gas, I'm buoyed by breezes and dragged down by gravity. I can no longer steer myself.

I should check my e-mail. Maybe I've won a million dollars.

Lena.

She had to wait thirty years. She had to wait until there was nothing left of me.

If she says, *We should meet*, I won't.

Nothing she can say would be enough. I should delete it unread. Repay silence with silence.

Stop this. It's undignified and ridiculous, to fear her after all this time. She can't do anything to me.

Dear Angus,
　　Weeks have passed since your e-mail came.
I am sorry for that. Work, family interruptions
and a small illness distracted me. I needed quiet,
open time, and a certain strength to reach back
to you across the years. Today I will try.

It was a surprise to discover your name on my screen. Often I think of people from the past, and then you appeared to me.

Did you become an investigating journalist? I searched for your name and found only stories of people with problems. Did you marry and make a family?

I didn't. I have accepted that I was not made for that. This solitary life can be painful, but I live with it. In my work I counsel others to help them with depression, but I have not solved the problem of loneliness for myself.

Days of rain have put me in a low spirit. Nevertheless, I believe this is true even on sunny days: in a fundamental way, we are alone. We long for perfect understanding with another, but that is not attainable.

I traveled again in Rome this year. Standing on those old stones, I was there but not there— encased in the bubble of Myself that I can never escape. Often I wish to be a child again, open and delighted with everything new. A poet wrote that one should love one's solitude and sadness, but I think he didn't live as much alone as I do.

As for the facts of my life, I teach one class at the university, see a few patients each week, and supervise graduate students. In the spring, the green hill behind my apartment becomes pale with vitsippa. (I don't know the name for this white flower in English.) I find this to be one of the best moments, a simple beauty that makes a sharp longing.

If you would like to write again, I will be interested to read what you say.

Your old friend,

L.

It was always this way: me gazing at her, her gazing into her own melancholy.

Imagine if, by the force of my will, I'd persuaded her to live with me. Imagine even one evening with her. "Want to go to the movies?" "Why do you wear this mask, pretending to be a frivolous American?"

Yet she was the great love of my life. What an absolute waste.

For thirty years, I've measured women against her, and judged them all inferior, unacceptable. I admired her and yearned for her, because she seemed the purest of spirits, a pursuer of profound truths. And so she may be. But what has that got to do with me?

I could have said yes to Carol, or Diane, or Barbara. None of them was exactly right, but so what? I could have had something like a life.

One doesn't often find so perfect a picture of folly.

There's nothing to salvage from this wreck.

It's time to end the farce.

Sorry, Brother Bob. Don't blame yourself, it's not your fault. You did everything you could. No one on Earth could have solved the problem of me.

Here's my will: keep what you want, offer the rest to Greer. You can donate, recycle or toss what remains, as you see fit.

Your efforts did not go unnoticed, or unappreciated.

With apologies,

Angus

P.S. This is inadequate, I know. I wish I could have left a better note.

(*sheepishly*) Hello again.

So, I couldn't finish the job, despite a sincere intention. I shaved, put on the suit, used the toilet, took five pills

(Compare to the Active Ingredient in Benadryl!) and climbed into the waterless tub, but never put the bag over my head. I wanted to get drowsy first—but kept thinking about cells, how they keep dividing and grow from a single fertilized egg into a breathing, walking creature. What makes them divide? What is the force inside every living cell that drives it to proliferate? The question became a preoccupation. I didn't want to die without knowing. Is it possible that the mechanism evolved on its own, without a shaping hand? That seemed too amazing to believe—almost as incredible as the alternative, an omnipotent Creator in the sky. What does science have to say about this?

I considered climbing out of the tub and searching for an answer, but sleep overtook me.

This too-solid flesh refuses to melt.

And that's lucky for me, because when I awoke, two women were nattering over me in a strange tongue, one of them shaking my shoulder, saying my name, her mascara a blotched mess. It resembled a druggy dream—is there anything I wanted more than for Eka to return and weep over me?—but their continued, incomprehensible conversation proved they were flesh and blood, not phantoms.

Happy as a sick boy who wakes to a room full of Christmas gifts and loving family, I smiled. No matter what the conditions, limitations, and qualifications, I was grateful to see her again.

Nino (such white little teeth, such dark angular eyebrows!) asked, "You are all right?"

I nodded, and hoped I hadn't peed in my pants while unconscious, though even that was only a mild concern.

I hadn't wet myself. I'd only slept for five hours when they unlocked my door.

"How much pills you tooked?" Eka asked. I'd never noticed before how almost-black the irises of her eyes are. "Can you understand? How much pills, and which kind?"

My groggy contentment repelled her urgency. I reassured her: just allergy pills, just four or five, or some other single-digit number.

The antihistamines had dried my throat, and a dust-induced coughing fit interrupted me. She handed me water; I sipped, and asked, "How did you get here?"

"I called cab. Oh, Angus, what you did?"

Nino, sweet girl, smiled indulgently, as if she were our elder and understood all. Deferring to our drama, she excused herself in two languages and left us alone.

So soon after nearly erasing myself, I didn't expect much. "Are you here for a visit?" I asked.

She sat on the edge of the tub and held my hand, shaking her head woefully. "I imagine how it is, to return to you. Not like this."

No, her vision of romantic reunion hadn't included a plastic shower curtain blotched with mold by her hero's head, or old blue towels frayed at the edges, or soap-goo encasing the shower caddy's vinyl rods.

New tears appeared in her eyes. I assumed they referred to my squalor.

She said, "To see you, last night, so hurt—from me!—this crushes my heart. I couldn't stay, thinking of this. And now I come back, and find you like for funeral . . ."

A tear landed on my sleeve—hers, not mine.

"But last night you said . . ."

She shook her head. "Lawrence loves, but he don't listen. Not the same like you. I feel, okay, I can live with this—then, to see you so broke in heart."

Satisfaction warmed and calmed me. I finally did something right.

"Where's Davit?" I asked.

"Upstairs, with our baggages."

She was wearing her old red sweater, I noted: the actual Eka, not the fairy-tale version.

"I'm sorry you had to find me this way."

She picked up my hand and rubbed the knuckles with her thumb. "If I losed you . . ."

Fresh weeping.

"There, there," I said.

Davit just stirred. Now Bob is snoring again. I should finish this and go back to Eka.

In case you're curious, here's what I learned about cell division:

Because cells age and die, they're programmed to divide continuously into daughter cells, beginning at conception, thus ensuring that their DNA will outlive them. A human body goes through about ten thousand trillion cell divisions in its lifetime.

Self-preservation is a force to be reckoned with. Some people underestimate its power. Not me.

A WARM DAY IN MARCH

Where contentment curls comfortably on its couch, trouble finds a tempting target.

Months have passed since I last felt the need to recount the day's damages. I've had nothing to complain about, and thus nothing to say. That changed today.

We visited a garden center after lunch, because she wants to plant dwarf sunflowers in a window box. (When we first realized that the living room of our new apartment faces south, I said, "It'll be brutal in the summer." She said, "We will put flowers!") She has seemed remote and distracted all week, and I haven't asked why, for fear the answer would put an end to my happiness. Specifically, I worried that something I'd said or done had finally opened her eyes to my true character.

Rows of empty steel racks greeted us at the garden center: they won't set the plants outside for another few weeks. It didn't matter, since the seeds, potting soil and window boxes are all kept inside, but the desolate scene didn't help.

She neither spoke nor hummed. Ominous! Like a child hiding under his blanket from a monster, I held my breath and hoped the bad news would go away.

If she moves out, or asks me to (I told myself), then I'm no worse off than before, right? I can go back to living the carefree life of the suicidal bachelor.

No, not really—because the past three months have been spectacularly cozy, better than I had any right to expect.

Despite the stressful bustle of seeking and finding two new jobs, and moving into a new apartment, we've had many idyllic hours together. The day I brought home a walnut curio cabinet—along with a glass butterfly and horse to start her collection—she actually cried. (And no, it wasn't in disappointment at my horrendous taste. "Too lovely," she said. So there.) True, she watches awful television . . . but the pressure of her upper arm leaning against mine fills me to overflowing with contentment. It's the same when we're walking and she slips her warm hand under and around my biceps. The small irritations of living together are insignificant when weighed alongside all this. Yes, she sometimes sounds shrill as a drill on the phone with her mother. Yes, she has coerced me to follow the Weight Watchers program, and to walk with her for painful minutes each night, and to perform arm raises, leg lifts and bends. Yes, she chides me when she catches me with a tub of sherbet and a soupspoon. Yes, she occasionally emits peculiar odors—on certain days of the month, her pee has the same overripe smell my mother sometimes left behind—but imagine the things she could say about me. Her care may feel mildly oppressive at times, but it's still a novelty, more sweet than sour.

Last month, a violent sneeze aggravated my back pain to the point where an overdose of Advil made no difference. She ordered me to see a doctor; the MRI showed a herniated disk pressing on a nerve root, explaining why the pain also seemed to emanate from my heel. Tender but firm, she has enforced every one of the doctor's recommendations: cold compresses, as much rest as possible, and diligent performance of physical therapy exercises. Yesterday, for the first time since the fateful sneeze, I got through the day without ibuprofen. This is good news, because it means I may be able to escape surgery.

I enjoy our routines. I enjoy quizzing her from the NCLEX study guide. Her English is better than I realized: not only can she understand questions like *What effect does stimulating the sympathetic nervous system have on the heart?*, she can answer them correctly and succinctly. (Who knew that nurses had to master these prodigious piles of information? Like those guys who memorize the Koran, they have my awed respect.)

There are times when I gaze at her—absorbed in *Law and Order*, or reading her study guide as she waits for me after work in front of her new employer's house—and wonder how she could have come back to me. I can't see into her heart. The only answer I can find is that, after fifty-five less-than-joyous years, my turn has finally come.

She broke the news on the way home from the garden center. "Angus," she said, "I have fear."

If she had fear, then I had terror. "Mm?"

"I miss my period."

It was an odd sensation, like being doused with scalding and icy water simultaneously: exhilarating relief interpenetrated with horror.

"We can stop at CVS to buy test," she said. "All right?"

"Of course."

Though it's not yet a confirmed pregnancy, she couldn't wait any longer to tell me what she's thinking, which is that having a baby would be calamitous. She named two of her reasons and left the others unspoken. "I love the little babies, but I have studied so much for nurse examen. I don't want to give up this. I worry also over money. I must work. I don't like this way, three months with baby, then all day in child facility."

Her attitude toward abortion: "I don't ever think I would do this. But it would be too hard for us. What you think?"

I think the news overloaded a circuit in my brain. Counter to reason and my own lazy nature, I pushed back against her pragmatism. "It might be strangely interesting to be parents together."

Because she still respects me (miracles!), her jaw didn't drop in disbelief. She said wearily, "To begin all again . . ." and shook her head.

She assumes I wouldn't be much help, that the entire burden would fall on her shoulders. Perhaps she also assumes that I'm not likely to last more than a few years, and then she'll be on her own again, with a second child to put through college.

While she weighed the future and staggered under the load, I found myself levitated, tingling. Sure, any half-wit can father a child—but not I, or so I'd always thought. The weight of reality lifted from me; the heaviness of parenthood hid behind thick drapes. This is how they trap you. This is nature at its most devious.

"I know I've been sloppy about improving my health. But I'm willing to make more of a commitment."

She watched her hands, clasped lifelessly in her lap. I understood.

Sigh.

While I wait for her to take the pregnancy test, there are other changes you may find interesting.

In late January, after I'd exhausted and depressed myself failing to find work, the *Register*'s editor-in-chief called with an offer. As part of a drastic makeover, a last-ditch effort to save the print edition, she wanted to borrow an idea she'd seen other papers try: obituaries for ordinary local folk. "Life stories," she calls them. She tends to speak in keywords, omitting verbs, and she defined her goals this way: "Sympathy. Respect. Telling details. Anecdotes. Exactly what you used to do, minus the pathos." An added perk: since they don't have a desk for me, I can work at home.

And so, at an age when others are researching the exotic destinations they'll tour in retirement, I embarked on a new career. Each night I scan the death notices for possibilities— like the one yesterday that listed two survivors, a sister and an Airedale named Jeter. Four days a week, I visit homes humid with grief and quietly ask questions. Most of the families are eager to tell their stories. After the initial solemnity, I'm free to prod and even laugh with them. I find it comforting to see the *RIP* each death leaves in the fabric of other lives—to see real tears, and to imagine that I, myself, may someday be missed this way, by one person at least.

Yesterday, for example, I sat on a rocking houseboat, the last home of Seymour Tambac, and interviewed his four sons. A gabby cabby, Tambac had had an anecdote for every occasion, drawn from his own experience or that of the famous. He was a particular fan of Winston Churchill's. "He talked fast," one of the sons said, "but he always sounded like he had a mouthful of mashed potatoes." The eldest frowned at that, but the other two nodded in agreement, chuckling.

The point of Seymour Tambac's story is more poignant than amusing, though. He was always the life of the party, the voice you heard in a crowded room. His wife, meanwhile, managed the family with self-effacing grace, and presided over their home with a peaceful smile and few words. When she passed away four years ago, neither counseling nor medication could put Seymour together again. "Like the rabbi said at the funeral," the second son explained, "they were like two trees that grew up side by side. Their branches interwove so much, when one died, the other was left incomplete. Unable to stand. You could see it not as a weakness but a tribute to their marriage."

I'd heard this analogy before, and it always struck me as a sugary consolation for the bereaved, another way of saying, This person had no Self—but at that moment, gently rocked by the wake of a passing tanker, it seemed touching and apt. Not something I'm capable of with Eka, but a feat to marvel at, perhaps to envy.

Sentimentality is eating away at my brain. One more illustration: the *Register*'s archives, still undigitized, are housed in the plant where the paper is printed (a world that features towers of blank newsprint and deafening presses), and when I have to look up old articles on local notables, I'll take the long drive, dig out the yellowed envelopes, and chat with Quintius Zajac. Quint writes about cars; he knows he's been exiled to journalism's Palookaville, but doesn't mind. His favorite topic is his little boy, who's only ten but comes out with clever quotables daily. They were folding laundry last week, for instance, and the kid brandished a pair of Jockey shorts, announcing, "This is an Eyewitness News Brief!" I've never seen a father so delighted by his child. Which raises the question: am I beset with pangs because it's touching, or because I'll never know this joy myself? (Or was it the *khachapuri* Eka served with dinner? A rare but misguided treat.)

Last month we traded Mrs. N's basement for a first-floor garden apartment. (Moving up in the world.) We stayed in Belleville so Davit can play basketball for the high school. It's good to see so much daylight, and Eka has been dressing the place up with houseplants and posters. (A blue butterfly, houses on a Mediterranean hillside, swirling golden galaxies.) We get along well with the upstairs neighbors—Nacho, a Cuban handyman; Argyro, his second wife, who came here from Greece only four years ago; Orlando, his son and partner; and Orlando's daughter, Evelin. If they played their music more quietly, I would like them even better.

(Sports Update: Davit led his team in scoring this season—576 points!—and has already gotten a friendly call from the assistant coach at Rutgers. And I thought his whiteness meant he wouldn't succeed. One more happy outcome refutes my pessimism.)

Speaking of Davit, I like him better than any teenager I've met in years. Watching him dash across the basketball court like a rabbit dazzles me. Nevertheless, he has two faults. One, he leaves things wherever he finishes with them, so that Eka, exhausted after work and often suffering from a backache, must bend to pick up his dirty socks and pulp-flecked orange-juice glasses. Two, by some unerring instinct, he comes home early from nights out with friends *only* when Eka and I lock the bedroom door and seek intimacy. Not that either of us would shriek or whoop otherwise, but we're self-conscious enough without having to finish in silence. (FYI: Despite the barbells clanking in the other room and despite my gut, things have gone better than expected on this front, thanks largely to her surprising skills.)

Until that calamitous sneeze, I'd been walking with Bob every Saturday, under duress—not much farther than I walk with Eka, just enough to provoke moderate joint pain. (Did I mention that I've lost twenty pounds since Christmas, despite my shaky discipline?) The doctor's post-sneeze prohibition of exercise made me ecstatic, but yesterday he said I could begin again, cautiously. Eka, also known as Big Brother's Little Sister, phoned Bob immediately.

We met in the old neighborhood, for novelty and nostalgia, and walked past the sooty factories, as far as the abandoned railroad tracks. I lived on Stephens Street for twenty-three years, and barely noticed any home improvements; in the three months since I moved out, however, the neighbors have installed a new screen door and a brass mailbox. One house is getting all-new taupe vinyl siding. It's as if they were waiting for me to leave.

Bob has been playing mandolin in his girlfriend's band, World on a String. He rhapsodized today on the joy he'd experienced earlier, performing at a farmers' market, when the group magically came together during the bouzouki break on the "Internationale." "We were like the limbs of a single organism, all wired to the same mind. It reminded me of outstanding sex."

Which made me think: Maybe the sex wasn't so out-standing, if playing the mandolin at a farmers' market is just as good. (My abstract fondness for my brother tends to collapse after ten seconds together. His enthusiasms chafe me like coarse wool.)

We exchanged friendly nods with a Hispanic stranger who was mowing the bacon-width strip of grass between his fence and the sidewalk. Bob asked me how things were going with Eka.

I kept the maybe-baby secret. "There's a lot to be said for companionship, but it comes at a price."

He deployed his Yoda smile. "I think you're happier than you've ever been in your life, but can't stand to admit it."

I took up the challenge. "I may have reason to be happy, but that doesn't mean I am. Like the ocean, I'm deep, and don't always respond to the weather at the surface."

"Maybe it's time to start. Why not enjoy what you have?"

"Maybe it's time for you to stop telling me to change."

Though it was the eighty thousandth slap I'd bestowed on his face, he winced.

Itchy-balls dangled like ornamental testicles from the plane tree that shaded my car. Kai's Volvo had taken the space in front of mine. Bob proposed that we stop in to say hello, but I nixed that. I haven't forgotten or forgiven the merciless boot they gave my beloved.

Next door, Don and Denise were maneuvering a cumber-some structure into place in their little yard: an unpainted wooden bench with its own attached arbor above.

"I forgot to mention," Bob said, "Garrett moved into a group home. Cindy moved out, too. She said she wanted to be close to him, but I think it had more to do with start-ing over."

He unlocked his bike and we shook hands. On the way home, I kept thinking about Cindy. Her heartbreak began with me. What do I do with that? There's no way to take back what happened, nothing I can do to help. The best I can do is promise never to recklessly endanger other people's happiness again.

Which may preclude fathering a child.

It's dark outside. Eka is chopping something in the kitchen. If there's a better fragrance than garlic and onion sautéed on a stove, I haven't smelled it.

As Bob pointed out, every day with Eka is better than all the years that came before. The complaints are just patter, a comedy routine. That's why her possible pregnancy has me so distressed. I don't want her to be unhappy; I don't want our felicity upended.

On a lighter note . . .

Yesterday, as the houseboat's hull creaked against the dock (a sound as melancholy as a gull's cry in winter), the sons of Seymour Tambac shared a story I couldn't use, that's too good to waste.

Their father seemed to break free of his depression in his last days. At the hospital, he welcomed his sons enthusiastically, and they hoped he might finally come back to himself at the end. What seemed a recovery, though, was really a severing of some link with reality. This became evident when he made comments none of the sons could understand: about pets they'd never owned, and a colony on the moon. On the day he died, he motioned for his youngest son to come close. Expecting a special intimacy, the son put his ear close to his father's lips. These were the old man's last words:

"Don't let the gas get lower than a quarter of a tank. It's bad for the engine."

As adolescent girls exclaim on television: Oh. My. God.

I was at the kitchen table, trying to decipher the instructions for installing the window box, laughing aloud (between curses) at the idea of me, Angus, drilling holes in bricks, when Eka appeared in the doorway, grim-faced. "Hello, Daddy," she said.

She showed me the test stick, with the blue plus sign in the window. She has decided that she's willing to have the baby—*if we will marry.*

It was a lot to digest at once.

She saw my terror and understood, in part. "I know. You think, Will I be good father? You think, I have unhappy ideas—this is not good way to be father. But I see deep under this, what you don't see. Behind everything, you are good."

I doubt that a year spent weighing the pros and cons would produce a wiser decision than the one I made on the spot. Though I'm old enough to be a grandfather, though I'm likely to prove a wretched parent, though the news made me want to crawl under a blanket and hide, I said, "Will you marry me?" and apologized for failing to kneel.

She came to me and kissed the top of my head. "It will be hard," she said. "Too much waking up in the night."

I tried to see myself struggling to run alongside the youngster as he or she wobbled on a bike, and sank with sorrow. Half the duties of a dad will be beyond me.

She'll take the nursing test as soon as possible, she said, and look for a job, so she'll have something better to return to when she can work again.

"Mm-hm," I said.

She sat across my thigh as if I were Santa. "How you are doing? Happy? Worrying?"

"Yes."

Imagine me with a gurgling infant spitting up in my arms. Imagine me in the playground, pushing a swing, crying out, *Wheee!*

(I can't either.)

Poor kid. Poor defenseless critter.

I know, I know, I'm the one who argued in favor of parenthood. But it's like watching a train bear down on you.

Tied to a chair between the rails, all you can do is watch it get bigger.

Great attitude, Dad.

What sort of child will s/he be? Not like my sister's, I hope.

Note to self: destroy this document before the child's first birthday.

Are we sure we really want this? I had to hold my breath to keep from saying it aloud.

"My sweet prince," she sighed, her fingers nestling in my hair. "First you saved me. Now we make Happy Ever After."

Yes, my beloved.

(What have I done?)

ACKNOWLEDGMENTS

As always, I've depended on the generosity of friends and strangers for help with research.

First and foremost, I want to thank Izolda, who lent me so much of her time and so many of her memories. Nini Bitsadze sweetly contributed almost as much. You are both wonderful.

Though we've never met, Dr. Randy Deskin answered all of my questions and solved the puzzle of the mistaken diagnosis. Thank you, Dr. Deskin.

Other strangers I pestered for information, who generously gave me all I needed, include Reverend Jisho Perry, Jay Levin, Chief David Sabagh, Karen Fuccello, and Patrick Okigbo.

Now we come to the friends, friends of friends, neighbors, and slight acquaintances. It's my pleasure to thank Gary Friedland, Rosa Lantigua, Richard Webster, Steve Schoenwiesner, Tuula Ziccardi, and Phil Read.

I'm also happy to express my long-term gratitude to Bill Lee for his steadfast efforts and his unfailingly supportive words.

Copy editor Barbara Anderson caught many errors no one else had noticed. Thank you, Barbara, for your care, skill, and willingness to compromise (most of the time).

I owe my wife something more than thanks for enabling me to carve out this oddly shaped life. As soon as I figure out a way to repay the debt, you'll be the first to know, Jennifer.

Finally, I want to thank Martin and Judith Shepard for giving this book a home. It means more to me than you can imagine.